Hayner Public Library D...

W9-BXA-915

IMMORTAL
BAD BOYS

RECEIVED

OCT 1 1 2004

BY:
MAIN

HAYNER PUBLIC LIBRARY DISTRICT
ALTON, ILLINOIS

OVERDUES .10 PER DAY MAXIMUM FINE
COST OF BOOKS. LOST OR DAMAGED
BOOKS ADDITIONAL $5.00 SERVICE CHARGE.

IMMORTAL BAD BOYS

Rebecca York
(As written by Ruth Glick)

Rosemary Laurey

Linda Thomas-Sundstrom

BRAVA

KENSINGTON PUBLISHING CORP.
http://www.kensingtonbooks.com

HAYNER PUBLIC LIBRARY DISTRICT
ALTON ILLINOIS

BRAVA BOOKS are published by

Kensington Publishing Corp.
850 Third Avenue
New York, NY 10022

Copyright © 2004 by Kensington Publishing Corp.
"Night Ecstasy" copyright © 2004 by Ruth Glick
"Velvet Night" copyright © 2004 by Rosemary Laurey
"Midnight Court" copyright © 2004 by Linda Thomas-Sundstrom

All rights reserved. No part of this book may be reproduced in any form or by any means without the prior written consent of the Publisher, excepting brief quotes used in reviews.

All Kensington titles, imprints and distributed lines are available at special quantity discounts for bulk purchases for sales promotion, premiums, fund-raising, educational or institutional use.

Special book excerpts or customized printings can also be created to fit specific needs. For details, write or phone the office of the Kensington Special Sales Manager: Kensington Publishing Corp., 850 Third Avenue, New York, NY, 10022. Attn. Special Sales Department. Phone: 1-800-221-2647.

Brava and the B logo Reg. U.S. Pat. & TM Off.

ISBN 0-7582-0621-6

First Kensington Trade Paperback Printing: September 2004
10 9 8 7 6 5 4 3 2 1

Printed in the United States of America

F
Imm

AET-7181

CONTENTS

Night Ecstasy

Rebecca York

Chapter One

Jules DeMario was a creature of the night, in a city where night was king.

From the shadows under a wrought-iron balcony, he watched the boisterous crowd parading up and down Bourbon Street, the pulsing heart of New Orleans.

It was early in the week. Only Tuesday. But every night was party night in the French Quarter, where no annoying laws barred carrying an alcoholic beverage on the street.

And no traffic marred the scene. In the evening, Bourbon Street became a pedestrian playground where music blared from the bars and jazz clubs, mingling with the raunchy conversation of the crowd that flowed like a great, living beast past bars, strip joints and boutiques selling everything from cheap souvenirs and condoms to voodoo hexes.

As on many nights, Jules was drawn to this throbbing mix of humanity, where the crush of warm bodies sent his superhuman senses humming.

Three hundred years ago, in London where he had been born, he would have been dressed in a waistcoat, linen shirt and breeches. But he'd watched social standards reach new lows over the centuries. Tonight he wore well-washed jeans and a dark T-shirt, the perfect outfit for blending into the crowd.

Once his dark hair had been long enough to tie neatly at the back of his neck. Now it scraped his collar and covered the tops of his ears. A little long by modern business standards. But then, he didn't have to report to an office any morning.

Shouts from a few doors down drew his attention. A man on a wrought-iron balcony was tossing newly minted faux "doubloons" and cheap necklaces to the rowdy crowd below, including a woman who had taken off her T-shirt and bra to attract the attention of the guy with the largesse. The sight of her breasts gave Jules an unwanted sexual jolt. Turning quickly away, he headed for the quieter sections of the French Quarter, searching for prey now, his eyes and ears and nose leading him to the perfect victim fifty feet down a narrow alley.

The drunk was sprawled on the pavement, his breath gin-soaked, his jaw slack.

Jules bent over him, cradling the man's head on his arm almost tenderly as he flexed the neck upward and sank sharp white fangs into warm flesh. The man's eyes fluttered, and he put up a feeble fight. Jules quickly quelled the protest with the mind-numbing fog that he cast over his victims like a cloak of amnesia.

He drew perhaps a quarter pint of blood, the alcohol content sending a pleasant buzz to his brain.

He had discovered long ago that there was no need to kill in order to sustain his own existence. He had learned to be judicious. To take what he needed and spare the donor's life.

Standing again, he pulled out a fine linen handkerchief and wiped the traces of red from his mouth. The blood had slaked his hunger. But he craved something else as well—the sexual gratification that only an erotic relationship with a woman could give him. A mutually satisfying relationship where he gave his partner pleasure and in turn fed off that pleasure.

But sexual desire was a two-edged sword. No liaison could last long for him. Unless he wanted to destroy his partner's life, he had to let her go. Knowing the beginning of a love affair was always the prelude to the end had made him strive to postpone the need.

Still, the thought of sexual satisfaction heated the stolen blood flowing through his veins. He sped up his pace, trying to put that craving out of his mind, as he strode toward the comfortable house he had bought at the edge of the Quarter.

It was three stories, the windows on the upper floor sealed against the light so that he could sleep during the day in safety. A block from home, however, he crossed a street where some of the prostitutes in the area liked to hang out. Most of them were either with customers or had gone home for the night.

But one woman was still leaning against the wall of a house. As he came down the block, she straightened her shoulders and stepped toward him. Her heels were high. Her skirt barely covered her hips. Her knit top was low cut and so thin that he could see every detail of her breasts. She was young—barely out of her teens, and he thought of telling her to get off the streets before it was too late. But he knew he'd be wasting his breath.

"Hello, handsome," she purred, giving him what she probably thought was a seductive smile. "Are you in the mood for some fun?"

He wanted to say *no*. But it seemed he had reached the limit of his ability to exist on blood alone.

"I might be," he said, taking a step toward her.

Once he'd shown some interest, she wasn't going to let him get away. On the darkened street, she moved her hand down, pressing it against the fly of his jeans. He knew she would feel no erection. That wasn't the way he functioned. Before the change from man to vampire, his penis had been the center of his sexual satisfaction. But his responses were different now.

He lifted her hand away, then followed her into the narrow passageway between two houses.

"The way I get turned on is to touch you," he murmured, his hands sliding over her breasts, lifting and shaping them.

He stroked his thumbs over the nipples, back and forth, urging a response from her, knowing that she usually kept herself detached from the men she serviced. But he also knew he had the power to drag her into a web of sensuality. His mind reached out to hers, bending her to his will. And as he felt her respond to him, he lowered his head, teasing himself by nipping at the tender place where her neck met her shoulder.

He stoked her response, his own carnal excitement rising to meet hers as he sank his teeth into her flesh. He felt it through his whole body, a blissful tingling that increased when he began to draw blood from her.

One hand slid downward to the juncture of her legs, pressing against her clit through the thin fabric of her skirt and panties, stroking in a way that he knew would bring her to orgasm.

It had been so long since he had done this that he had to fight a wave of dizziness. He wanted to go on and on, drawing the sensuality and the life fluid from her. But when she climaxed, he ruthlessly cut off his own gratification, leaving her panting and limp, her shoulders pressing back against the wall.

"What happened?" she moaned. "What did you do to me, honey?"

"You met a customer who made it as good for you as it was for him," he answered easily, even as he sent her soothing mental commands. "But you will forget what we did. You will forget me. You will only remember that you did very well tonight." Pulling out his wallet, he extracted a hundred-dollar bill and folded it into her hand.

Then he left her and walked rapidly toward home, thinking that he needed more than what a prostitute was able to give him. He needed a lover who could meet him as a mental equal.

Only a few miles away, Taylor Lawson moved restlessly through the little jewel of a Victorian house that she had rented in the Garden District.

It was beautifully furnished. And she'd fallen in love with

it instantly. She'd taken that as a good omen. But that was the only piece of luck she'd encountered since coming to the Crescent City.

With a sigh, she stepped into the artist's studio that she'd set up in one of the bedrooms. As she looked at the partially finished canvas on the easel, she grimaced.

Over the past few months, her work had gone stale. Just like her relationship with her once and former lover, Howard Cumberland.

She'd known for months that he was the wrong man for her, but he'd clung to the dying relationship like a mountain climber scrabbling with his fingernails at the edge of a cliff. The only way she'd been able to cut things off was to move far away—from San Francisco to New Orleans.

She felt a wonderful sense of freedom here. At least in her personal life. But artistically, nothing had changed. She was only plowing old ground. She could still turn out paintings that would sell for thousands of dollars in exclusive galleries. But it wasn't satisfying to *her*. She needed new inspiration. She needed to take her art in an unexplored direction, if she could only figure where to go.

Turning from the easel, she looked at the paintings she'd hung on the walls. They were some of her best work. One was a scene on the beach at Carmel, where she and another lover, Richard Lampton, had gone when they were first in love. They were walking on the beach, naked. Hand in hand, two people totally enthralled with each other.

Next to it was a self-portrait she'd done the night she and Charles Bingham had first met. Her red hair was like fire around her head. Her green eyes were wild with excitement. And her lips had the look of a woman who had just been thoroughly kissed.

So what did these pictures say about her? That she needed a man for inspiration? That she worked best in the first flush of a new relationship? She hated to think that was the case. She wanted to believe that her own inner resources could sustain her interest in her painting. But if that were true, why was she feeling so restless and uncreative?

Leaving the studio, she went back to the bedroom and pulled out the slip of paper that her friend, Evelyn Bromley, had given her when they'd talked about New Orleans. Evelyn had met an extraordinary man down here. Someone she thought Taylor would like. But she wouldn't give out any details. She'd just said to call him.

Taylor might be bold in her artistic subject matter. But like most creative people, she was an introvert. She hated calling strangers. But as she held the paper in her hand, she made a decision. At worst, he'd turn her down. Or they'd meet and wouldn't hit it off. But why be negative? Perhaps he'd be the best thing that had ever happened to her.

Chapter Two

Jules woke the next evening and stretched in his comfortable, four-poster bed. According to legend, a vampire slept in his coffin. But that was just superstitious nonsense, as far as he was concerned.

He'd discovered long ago that any place that was sealed away from the light would do very nicely.

His bedroom was filled with beautifully restored eighteenth-century English antiques. They always gave him a sense of comfort when he woke, because they reminded him of how far he'd come—from the slums of London.

Since then, he had lived all over England—from Kent to Cornwall to Northumberland. And in many countries of the world. But he'd never stayed in one place for very long. Then in the twentieth century, out of curiosity, he'd read some of the books of Anne Rice and decided that New Orleans sounded like a wonderful place for a vampire.

He'd been here ever since. Despite Rice's literary claims, he hadn't run into any others of his kind here. In fact, he'd met very few men like himself—and no women.

His stepfather, John Randolph, the vampire who had saved his life by turning him, had kept his own background hidden. Probably he would have eventually shared his secrets. But he had been killed by a mob almost three hundred years ago, leaving Jules very much alone. With no contacts like himself, the best he could do was read all the books he could find on the subject of the undead. And most of that was hogwash.

Now he climbed out of bed and dragged in a deep breath. Breathing didn't keep him alive, but it did help him think clearly because it oxygenated his brain.

After taking a quick shower and brushing his teeth, he pulled on a fresh T-shirt and jeans before unlocking the tight-fitting door to his room.

Padding barefoot into the kitchen, he leaned over the automatic coffeemaker, drinking in the aroma of a fresh-brewed, rich Cajun blend. Just the smell was wonderful. But over the years he'd trained his body to handle tiny quantities of food, and a little coffee was one of his chief gastronomic pleasures.

Mug in hand, he wandered out to the courtyard at the side of the house and sat in the dim glow from the tiny lights decorating two potted ficus trees. Then he checked his answering service.

The only message was from a woman named Taylor Lawson who cleared her throat before saying:

"I really don't like making calls to strangers. But my friend Evelyn Bromley suggested that I get in touch with you. I'm new in town, and she thought you'd be a good person to show me around."

She followed the observation with a phone number.

He listened again, jotting down the number. The low, throaty voice was very appealing. And he had fond memories of Evelyn. She'd been an intelligent and sensual woman. A good match for him. But his relationship with her had ended like all the others. Usually when a love affair was over, he was able to erase the memory of the liaison from his partner's mind. Evelyn had been too strong-willed for that. He'd only been able to alter her memories slightly.

That was five years ago. And she hadn't sent anyone else to him.

Taylor Lawson must be special. And her voice was a turn-on.

So he called the number.

She picked up on the third ring.

"Hello. This is Jules DeMario."

"Oh yes. I was afraid you weren't going to call," she answered.

"Well, I was away for the day," he lied easily. He'd had centuries to perfect the art of deflecting curiosity about his nocturnal habits.

She cleared her throat. "I was hoping we could get together."

"But you're nervous about meeting a man you don't know," he guessed.

"Yes."

"What did you have in mind?"

"I'm a painter." She hesitated. "And I wanted to do a series on the more shocking aspects of New Orleans nightlife."

"Sounds interesting." *Very interesting.*

"I've been told there are facets of the city that most tourists don't get to experience. And I've also been told that trying to find them on my own might be dangerous."

"That's true."

"Would you be willing to be my guide?"

"That depends. We should get acquainted first."

"Yes. But it's best if we meet in a public place."

Since the suggestion was wise for both of them, he agreed immediately. "How about the old Jax Brewery building? It's been turned into a shopping mall. There's a bar called Ernie's on the top floor."

"The building down by the river?"

"Yes."

"How will I know you?" she asked.

"I'm five-ten. One hundred and forty-five pounds. I have dark hair. Dark eyes. I'll wear a T-shirt that says 'Let the good times roll.'"

"All right."

"And how will I know you?"

"By my flaming red hair. And my look of uncertainty."

"Fair enough. Will ten o'clock work for you?"

"Yes."

Over the years, Jules had learned to adapt to his environment. He spent much of the time between the phone call and their meeting looking up Taylor Lawson on the Internet.

He found that she was a notable artist whose paintings hung in many small galleries on the West Coast.

She'd started selling in her early twenties, ten years ago, and had worked her way up to the rank of respected artist. Her style was representational, with a touch of the hauntingly romantic. Her use of colors was adventurous.

Her publicity photo was just as tantalizing as her work. She stared boldly out at the camera, her red hair a wreath around her head and her green eyes direct and challenging.

Would she be as striking in person? Eager to find out, he arrived at the rooftop bar early, ordered a beer and poured a lot of it into an empty glass that someone had left behind. Then he settled down to wait.

When a striking redhead walked in, he was lounging comfortably at a table near the door. She'd dressed casually, in dark slacks and an emerald green knit top.

As she stood looking around the room, he gave her a little wave.

With a slightly hesitant smile on her face, she crossed to him.

"Taylor?"

"Yes."

"I'm Jules."

"Nice to meet you," she said in that low sexy voice that he liked as much in person as over the phone.

They shook, and he also liked the firm strength of her hand. His own hand was large and warm. One thing he'd been amused about in his reading was the notion that a vampire had to be cold. In reality, he had control of his temperature, just the way he had control over a partner's mind when he was drawing blood. And since he walked through the world of men, he kept his own body at a steady ninety-eight-point-six.

He was aware of her tantalizing woman's scent drifting toward him. And of the way she licked her lips with an endearingly nervous gesture.

He cleared his throat. "What can I get you?"

"Chardonnay."

He ordered from the bartender, then ushered her outside onto the cement deck overlooking the river, just as a tourist paddle wheel boat went by. In the warm night, there were few people outside, and it wasn't difficult to find a corner table.

He crossed his legs at the ankles and stretched them out beside the table, trying to look a lot more casual than he felt. He'd rarely been more attracted to a woman. And he wanted to get to know her better. "So what really brings you to the city?"

She hesitated for a moment before saying, "I needed to get away from a man who wanted to continue a relationship with me—when we both knew it was over."

"That's a pretty direct answer."

"I know. But I hate evasions, and I wanted us to start out on the right foot."

Evasions? Like the guy sitting across from you is a vampire?

He lifted the bottle and covered the opening with his tongue, just letting the beer wet his lips, thinking that if he were totally frank with her, she'd run screaming from the premises.

"I checked out some of your work," he said instead.

"How? I presume you didn't make a quick trip to San Francisco or Monterey?"

"Google."

She laughed. "It's hard to keep secrets these days."

"Some people manage it," he answered. "I like your technique and your subject matter."

"In which paintings?" she challenged.

"All of them. You started off experimenting with forms and colors. And you've matured as an artist."

"I've gotten stale," she answered quickly, her slender fingers clenching the stem of the wineglass. Scraping back her chair, she crossed to the railing and stood staring out at the dark river.

He followed her. "Why do you think so?"

"I need a change of scenery and some new subject matter."

"In the nightclubs of Sin City?"

She raised her chin. "If you put it that way, yes. New experiences often spark my creativity."

He was thinking of a new experience he could give her when she asked, "Can you tell me a little bit about yourself?"

"Like what?"

"You have a British accent. Were you born there?"

"Yes. But I was lucky enough to get away from that cold climate."

"So the sun attracted you to New Orleans?"

"The heat, actually." He tipped his head to one side, watching her. "If we're going slumming, I need to know we're completely comfortable with each other."

"What do you mean?" she asked, the fine edge of nerves audible in her voice.

He knew from her work that she was an assertive woman who had artistic talent, training, and bold ideas about her own work. But now he sensed the vulnerability that she strove to keep hidden.

He lifted the glass from her hand and set it on the table before turning back to her.

Clasping her hand with his, he led her around a corner, to

a small extension of the balcony where they were alone in the humid night with only the sounds and smells of the city drifting up toward them.

It could begin and end here, he thought with a mixture of dread and anticipation. But he'd decided that if this wasn't going to work out the way he wanted, then ending it immediately was best.

Silently, he pulled her close, swamped by so many sensations at once that his brain went from anticipation to overcharged in the space of a heartbeat. He could feel the shape of her slender body. The pressure of her high breasts against his chest. The brush of her red curls on his cheek.

And he was captured by that sweet woman's scent that had tantalized him from the first moment she'd walked into the bar.

She stood quietly in his arms, as though debating whether to take the next step.

He held his breath, and slowly, slowly she raised her face, meeting his questioning gaze.

There was only a brief moment of eye contact—but enough for a silent question and answer. With her permission, he lowered his lips to hers.

He had wanted to know if they would be good together. Good was hardly the right word.

The touch of their lips was like lightning crackling through the night sky in some dark, primeval forest. From the small sound she made, he knew she felt it, too.

The lightning ignited a fire in his belly, the flames flaring white-hot.

It had been two years since he had kissed a woman on the lips. And he knew he had been saving the pleasure for this one. She tasted better than anything he could remember in his life and beyond. Better than fine wine or pure spring water or even blood.

He gathered her in, pressing her breasts against his chest, holding her to his body, swaying slightly as though he had suddenly become unsteady on his feet. He sipped at her lips, nipped with his teeth, then traced a sensuous path with his tongue.

When he'd taken her in his arms, he had thought he was merely testing their compatibility. But now his mind had spun out of control. He wanted her. This instant. He needed to sink his teeth into her tender flesh and draw some of her essence into himself.

It took all the self-control he possessed to break the kiss and lift his head. As he looked down on her with his keen night vision, he could see the unfocused confusion in her eyes.

Lord, what was he doing? Planning to ravage her out here on this balcony overlooking the river? They had some privacy, but not enough for him to do what he wanted with her.

He ached to take her back to his house where they could be alone. Although she had wanted to meet him in a public place, he knew he could change her mind about that now. But he wasn't going to force her. More than her submission to him, he craved her consent. And he knew that waiting for their ultimate joining would make it all the better.

"So, what next?" he asked in a voice that he couldn't quite hold steady.

Chapter Three

Taylor waited a beat before answering. She had impulsively called up a man she didn't know. And now some inner voice warned her to run as fast as she could in the other direction. She had met him less than a half-hour ago, and his kiss had left her head spinning.

He'd said he'd looked her up on the Internet. She should have done the same thing. All she knew about him was that he was handsome as sin. He'd beguiled Evelyn Bromley. He had a trace of a British accent. And he had the power to make her forget where she was and why it was a dumb idea to leap into the arms of a stranger.

Yet at the same time, he had left her aching for more. The question was, could she keep her head long enough to make an informed decision?

Maybe it was the expression on his face and the tone of his voice that swayed her. If he'd looked and sounded smug after that kiss, she would have told him the meeting wasn't working out. But he seemed as overcome by the intimate contact as she. And the look in his dark eyes told her that the answer she gave mattered very much to him.

He hadn't just been playing with her—testing his powers as a lover. He'd been emotionally involved.

She moistened her dry mouth and said, "We were going to go pub crawling or whatever they call it here."

"Where would you like to go?"

"I've heard of a place called the Venus Club," she said boldly.

He raised an eyebrow. "It's not a spot for the timid."

"I think I have the right escort."

He nodded, then held out his hand, ushering her toward the door. "Let's go."

They took the elevator down to the street level, turned right along the busy sidewalk, past the Café du Monde, then across Decatur Street to avoid the dark and shadowed bulk of the French Market. They turned up Ursulines, then onto Dauphine, and she couldn't help feeling a little nervous as they left the crowds and the lights behind.

"Is it safe here?" she whispered, edging closer to Jules. "I mean, we could take a cab."

"It's only another block," he answered.

Her uneasy feeling was confirmed when a man stepped out of a passageway between two houses, a gun in his hand.

The robber hardly had time to demand her purse before Jules turned the tables. In truth, she saw only a blur of motion as he grabbed the assailant by his shirt, spun him around and tossed him back into the passageway, where he landed with a whoosh of breath from his lungs.

She watched, flabbergasted, as Jules kicked the gun away, then waited to see if the man was going to get up. When the robber didn't stir, he calmly pulled out a cell phone and called 911. As soon as he'd finished giving the location, he took her arm and ushered her down the street again.

"Aren't we going to wait for the police?" she asked, trying not to sound dazed.

"I don't want to get involved."

"But can't they trace the source of the call?"

"It's one of those prepaid phones, where you can only call out."

NIGHT ECSTASY / 19

"Oh," she managed to say before asking, "How did you do that? I mean lay him out so fast?"

"Martial arts training," he answered dismissively.

"Oh," she said again, still dazed.

"Let's go, before we miss the show."

"What show?"

"You'll see." He led her up the block and around the corner, where he gestured toward a red brick mansion surrounded by an iron fence. The windows were shuttered, but the sound of loud conversation and music drifted toward them.

"Here we are."

She looked at the building, seeing no sign that said VENUS CLUB. Apparently you had to know what it was.

"A nightclub takes up that whole house?"

"Yes, starting with the bar where people hook up if they don't have a date."

"A date! That's a quaint way to put it."

A grin flickered on his handsome face. "Well, I'm an old-fashioned kind of guy, so this place shocks my sensibilities."

"Oh? What can I expect besides the bar?"

His voice was teasing now as he said, "A cornucopia of delights. If you dare."

She lifted one shoulder. "Of course I dare. How do you know so much about this place if you find it shocking?"

He leaned closer to whisper, "I like to live dangerously."

The way he said it sent a tingle along her nerve endings. Was he just being theatrical? Or was he giving her some kind of warning?

For a moment she debated hopping into one of the cabs lined up at the corner. But she didn't want to leave him yet. So she accompanied him up a short flight of marble steps to a classic portico with white Ionic columns, where he spoke in a quiet voice to a man guarding the door. Although the fellow wore a tuxedo, he looked like a pro wrestler. But after some cash had been exchanged, he nodded pleasantly as she and Jules crossed the threshold, stepping out of the humid night into an even more heated atmosphere.

The front hall was dark, and it took several moments for her eyes to adjust. Then she saw the paintings on the walls and blinked. They were all close-ups of intimate body parts— breasts, vulvas, penises, in black and white.

Leaning closer to one, she decided that the brushwork wasn't particularly well done.

"Not exactly museum quality," Jules murmured, his lips near her ear.

She laughed, knowing that her case of nerves was bringing out the art critic in her.

"Let's explore." Jules took her hand and led her into a room that looked like it could have come out of a sixties movie, complete with a faceted ball spinning on the ceiling, sending floating dots swirling around the room. Couples were slow-dancing, if you could call it that. When she looked more closely, it appeared to be a giant make-out party. Which was kind of sweet, compared to the room across the hall where a porn flick was showing on a big-screen TV.

"Subtle," she muttered.

"Not my choice either. The more interesting stuff is upstairs," he said, steering her to the wide staircase. They climbed to another hallway. "At the back of the house, you can watch amateur strippers."

"No, thanks."

"Well, the ballet room is probably more your taste."

She followed him into a large space where couples and a few single guys stood facing the stage.

A man and a woman dressed in street clothing came out and bowed to the audience.

Jules bent so that his lips were close to her ear. "We're just in time for a performance."

She didn't know what they were going to see, but she let him lead her to one side, where they had a good view of the stage.

Jules stood behind her, his hands on her shoulders as the strains of *Swan Lake* came from hidden speakers.

The dancers began what started as a classic *pas de deux*. But the performance soon became more sexually explicit. When the man lifted his partner up and twirled her above his head, his palm braced itself squarely against her crotch. And when he put her down, his hands cupped her breasts, then went to the buttons at the front of her blouse, which he began to open while she stroked her hand against the fly of his slacks.

It could have been crude. But it was all done with extreme sensuality that made Taylor's blood heat.

The male dancer pulled off his partner's shirt and tossed it away, his hands playing with the cups of her bra, her dark nipples clearly visible through the sheer fabric.

Taylor's response flamed higher, then higher still as Jules pulled her back against himself. Bending his head, he brushed her hair aside, so his lips could nibble at her cheek and then travel to the tender place where her jawline met her neck.

His whole body seemed to vibrate, and he made what was almost a purring sound in his throat as his mouth traveled to her ear and his tongue probed the sensitive channel while his hands traveled up and down her sides, stroking her hips then gliding upward to skim the sides of her breasts.

Her nipples were instantly taut, and she leaned her head back as she arched into the caress.

On the stage, the woman was skinning the man's trousers down his muscular legs. Then he pulled her close, unfastened her bra and tossed it out of the way. She was stripped to her panties now. And he wore only a white dress shirt unbuttoned all the way down the front.

Taylor's gaze remained on the explicit scene, but the show was only a minor part of what she was experiencing now.

Every muscle in her body tightened as Jules's fingers slid inward, inching toward her nipples. But he never quite touched them before he pulled his hands back.

A small sound of protest escaped from her lips.

Onstage, the man pressed on the woman's shoulders so that she went down on her knees in front of him. He sank his fingers into her hair, guiding her face against his crotch.

The edge of his open shirt hid his cock and her face from view, so that it was impossible to tell whether she had really taken him into her mouth. But it seemed that way from the reaction of her partner who threw his head back, his face contorted with pleasure.

Taylor had never seen such an explicit show. Not live and onstage. It might have shocked her if she hadn't been captivated by the sensual currents that Jules awakened in her body with his hands and lips.

He nipped at the side of her neck, pressing his teeth to her pulsing artery as his hands inched downward, stroking over her belly, then her thighs. Again he teased her, trailing his fingers inward, almost touching her throbbing center before moving outward again, leaving her panting for more.

Her neck arched, giving him better access, and his mouth did hot, sexy things to her flesh. In some part of her mind, she was thinking he was a magician who had learned just the right tricks to bring her under his spell.

A sensual fog wafted through her brain. When his finger traced along her lips, she opened to his touch, moving her head restlessly as his hand dipped inside, stroking over sensitive tissue and then along the serrated line of her teeth.

He was swamping her senses. But she had never been a passive lover. With a small sound, she went from submissive to aggressive—trapping his finger between her teeth, nibbling on him, playing with the skin, elated when she heard his breath catch.

Chapter Four

Some time later, Taylor heard people stirring around them. Somewhere along the line she had forgotten where she was and had closed her eyes against the distraction on the lighted stage. Her eyes flew open now, and she saw that the dancers had left the room. She had missed the end of their performance, whatever it had been.

But she had been too wrapped up with Jules to care.

"Do you want to explore some more? Shall we try another club?" he asked.

She wanted to stay with him. She wanted to take him to her house where they could be alone. But some small part of her mind was still warning her that she had just met him.

"Another club," she said, her voice sounding high and a little breathy.

"My pleasure," he murmured, leading her downstairs. This time they got into one of the cabs outside.

"Where are we going?"

"The Warehouse District. To another very eclectic private establishment."

Minutes later, they were getting out in front of what looked like an old factory building. Only some clever person had renamed it THE DEN OF INIQUITY.

This time she insisted on paying the admission fee, then

followed Jules into a space where an elaborate crystal chandelier hung on a thick chain from a high ceiling.

To the right was a room where the designers had gone for an industrial look. Guys sat at metal tables and chairs watching girls twist sensuously around chrome poles or dance inside mesh cages.

"Not my taste," Taylor murmured.

"I think you'll like the garden better."

"Okay."

Jules led her toward the back of the building, where they passed through an arched doorway into what looked like an alfresco setting. But she could tell it was actually a large room, laid out like a romantic garden, with the scent of flowers in the air and pathways wandering through the greenery.

He stopped at a bar and bought two glasses of champagne from a dainty little hostess wearing a low-cut white tunic, then led Taylor down one of the brick paths. As they turned a corner into a walkway lined with violet and orange bougainvillea, he was grinning.

"What's so funny? Are you going to let me in on the joke?"

"Soon."

They strolled down the path, taking small sips of champagne, then turned another corner and came to a small bower displaying a Greek sculpture. On the pedestal were a naked man and a woman, entwined in a very intimate pose. He was sitting, and she straddled his lap so that their genitals were pressed together while his hands covered her breasts.

Taylor stared at the tableau, then made a small sound when she realized that they weren't statues at all. They were living people whose skin had been dusted with white powder to make them look like they had been carved from stone.

"How interesting," she murmured, a little embarrassed and yet turned on.

"Just like the people playing statue on the street down by

Jackson Square," Jules answered with a note of amusement in his voice.

"Not quite!"

"Let's see what other surprises are hidden among the greenery."

He knit his hand with hers, and they soon came to another display area. This time a woman sat on a chair-height Doric column in a very erotic pose. One of her hands was on her breast, the other stroking between her legs, and her face was suffused with a look of ecstasy. Taylor wondered how anyone could hold that pose, until she realized the figure truly was carved out of marble.

"So the trick is to figure out which are real and which are stone," she murmured.

"Or just enjoy the cultural experience," he said.

She laughed, and he grinned back as they came to a section of the room where the bowers were walled off with trellises and covered by roofs, making them into small summer houses. Inside, she glimpsed couples reclining on wide couches.

"Do you want to be more private?" he asked.

"Yes. But not here," she said.

He arched an eyebrow.

"I wanted to meet you in public. But I'm wondering if you'd show me your house now."

"You mean, you've decided I'm not going to . . . do anything you wouldn't approve of?"

Her mouth was dry, but she managed to answer, "I'm finding this place a distraction. And I'd rather not be distracted."

He considered her words, finally giving a little nod. They put down their drinks on a small table before leaving the garden and heading for the front door, where he quickly found another cab. Inside, he leaned forward to give the driver an address, then settled beside her, pulling her close.

"Why do you want to come to my house?" he asked.

"To know you better."

He stroked her shoulder, then trailed his hand down her arm, setting up a buzz in her head. This man was sexier than any show a club could put on.

They got out at a town house in the French Quarter. Stepping under a wrought-iron balcony, he unlocked a carved wooden door. As they stepped into a wide front hall, he turned on a sparkling crystal chandelier.

In the soft light, she looked around with pleasure.

A fine Oriental rug lay on the marble floor. Tall brass candlesticks adorned a French sideboard, and a suit of armor stood in one corner. Wandering farther into the house, she saw Victorian sofas and chairs, beautifully carved cabinet pieces and an exquisite Chippendale dining set. It was an eclectic mix, beautifully arranged.

"This is charming. You love antiques," she murmured.

"Yes. I like keeping in touch with the past. I hate the mass-produced furnishings you see today."

"Your decorator must have loved working with you."

"I did the house myself."

Her eyes widened. "Speaking as an artist, I'd say you have an extraordinary eye."

"I had the time to study the subject and indulge my tastes."

He led her into a small conservatory with wicker furniture and orange trees perfuming the air.

Moving to the side of the room, he slid aside a panel and shuffled through a rack of CDs. When he'd loaded the player, slow dance music came from hidden speakers. After dimming the lighting, he held out his arms to her.

She was usually cautious about new relationships. But she had impulsively asked him to take her to his house. Now she felt a spurt of nerves as she let him gather her against him.

The moment they touched, she was instantly as aroused as she had been in the first club.

Jules nibbled at her ear. To her shock, his next words mirrored her thoughts. "I'm thinking it was a mistake to bring you home."

"Why?" she managed.

"Because we could make love right here." He moved his hand between them, cupping her breast, teasing her pebble-hard nipple. "We both want to."

"Yes," she admitted. Why deny the obvious?

"But we won't. Not tonight."

"Why not?" she asked, half disappointed and half relieved.

"I'm not going to rush you into anything. I want you to be sure before we go any further." He gathered her close again, swaying with her, gliding her body against his, and she found it hard to breathe. When he wrapped her in a tight embrace, it was like being folded into a cloak of sensuality as they danced together in the plant-filled room. While his hands moved over her back, his mouth made small forays over the side of her face, her ear.

When he spoke, his voice was gravelly. "I find it very hard to resist you."

She could have said the same thing about him, but he must know what she was feeling from the way she clung to him.

When he moved her upper body away from his, she made a small sound of protest. He gazed at her with heavy-lidded eyes as he pulled up her knit top, then tugged her bra up and out of the way so that her breasts were bared.

Lowering his head, he stroked his cheeks against her, the stubble of his beard abrading her sensitive flesh.

She moaned as he took one nipple into his mouth, delicately worrying it with his teeth before sucking strongly. When he took its mate between his thumb and finger, pulling and twisting, she moaned again.

Some part of her was standing back, watching in amazement at what she was doing with a man she barely knew.

"If I asked you to stop, would you?" she managed

He lifted his head and looked into her eyes. "Of course. You are in complete control of this situation."

"I don't think so. I think you're too good at what you're doing now."

He laughed softly. "What am I doing?"

"Arousing me beyond the point of no return."

"Am I?"

His hand slid down her body, pressing against her clit, while he lowered his head again and began to suckle on her once more. Helpless to hold back her reaction, she moved frantically against his hand, feeling as if he was anchoring her to the earth and at the same time sending her into the stratosphere.

He built her need, carrying her up and up until orgasm took her. Her whole body shook with the force of her pleasure. And when she called out something incoherent, he covered her mouth with his, swallowing the sound. She had lost the ability to stand on her own, and he gathered her into his arms. Sitting down on a wicker sofa in a nest of pillows, he pulled her clothing back into place, then held her against him, stroking her hair and shoulders and softly kissing the side of her face.

She kept her head against his chest for several moments, embarrassed. She had never behaved quite so wantonly on a first date. Well, not exactly a date.

And there was something more. She had never been a selfish lover.

That thought made her raise her head. "What about you?" she murmured.

"I'm fine."

"You weren't exactly a disinterested participant—and you didn't come, did you?" she asked.

His voice was firm. "No. But I told you we weren't going to make love tonight."

"Then why did you bring me to climax?" she pressed.

"I couldn't resist the temptation. But I think I should take you home."

She knew he was right, because if she stayed any longer, she was going to end up naked in his bed.

He pulled a sleek, low-slung Jaguar out of the garage attached to the house, then asked for her address.

"Will you come in?" she murmured, when he pulled up in front of her door.

"Tomorrow night."

"Are you going to leave without kissing me?" she asked, hearing the wistful sound of her voice.

He gave her a small grin. "We both know that if I do, I'll come inside and ravish you. So I'll come back at nine, tomorrow."

"You're going to make me wait that long?"

"I'm giving you time to think about us. If you change your mind about seeing me again, leave me a message. I won't be available during the day."

Then he was gone, leaving her with a breathless feeling of anticipation.

Chapter Five

It was only a few hours before dawn when Jules reached home. In an agony of need, he prowled the back alleys of the French Quarter looking for his usual prey. Although two drunks slaked his need for blood, his body's demand for sexual gratification threatened to consume him. And he understood that no prostitute would satisfy him now.

Yet he knew he had done the right thing. Taylor must come to him willingly. And he must give her a little time to think about their liaison, even if he knew in his secret heart that he wasn't giving her all the facts.

He had never wanted a woman more. Never been more restless. Once in his light-sealed room, he paced the floor, trying to find the calm center of his being.

But peace eluded him. And even when exhaustion forced him into bed, he lay staring into the darkness.

Usually—pardon the expression—he slept like the dead. Today he didn't doze off until afternoon. And his rest was fitful. The first thing he did when he got up was rush to the phone and check for messages, then thanked God that there was no call from Taylor telling him she had changed her mind. So he was able to relax again—until the craving for her threatened to drive him insane.

He was on her doorstep only seconds after nine. And

when he saw her through the sidelight, he breathed out a sigh of profound relief.

"Come in," she said, in the voice he had been hearing in his head for hours.

"You look lovely," he answered, because it was the truth. Last night she had worn slacks and a casual top. Tonight she was magnificent in a royal blue silk blouse that flowed around her upper body and dark blue silk slacks. Her eyes were bright, and the little bit of makeup she wore enhanced her beauty.

He had to press his hands against his thighs to keep from reaching for her.

"You're renting this house?" he asked as she ushered him into the sitting room. The accoutrements were only a background blur. All he could focus on was Taylor. Above the buzzing in his brain, he heard her speaking.

"Yes, I was lucky to get it furnished."

"What did you do all day?" he heard himself asking.

"First I tried looking you up. You're a very elusive man."

"By choice."

"I found a few references to your charitable donations. And a few references to financial holdings."

"Am I rich?" he asked.

"Very."

He managed a laugh. "That's good to know."

"Why are you so secretive?"

"An old habit. My stepfather got into some trouble back in England. I found it was safer to keep myself as private as possible."

"You were adopted?"

"Yes, but I don't want to talk about myself," he said quickly, hoping that she'd accept his decision. "Did you set up a studio when you came here?"

"Yes. But until last night, I hated the work I was turning out."

"And something changed last night?" he asked, feeling his throat tighten.

"Yes. The studio is upstairs. Come see."

She led him up to a room at the back of the house, and he walked into a room that was full of artwork. Some were her own magnificent paintings. On one wall, she had also taped sketches done with a soft pencil. All of them were scenes from the night before. He saw pictures of a man standing behind a woman, his hands in intimate places. He saw other sketches of a couple dancing, their bodies glued together.

All conveyed a scorching sensuality that robbed him of breath. But they were nothing compared to the unfinished acrylic painting on the easel. She had chosen the scene on the balcony outside the bar where they had first met. A man and woman stood by the railing, looking out over the river at night. She had given herself blond hair. And he was shorter than the man in the picture. But he knew who the people were. They weren't touching, yet the scene was alive with sexual tension.

"You did all that? Since last night."

"Yes," she said simply.

"Did you get any sleep?"

"Not much."

"I didn't either."

"Why not?"

"I couldn't stop thinking about you."

"Do you like the painting?" she asked, her voice not quite steady.

"You know I do. I like the sketches, too. And your other paintings. You're very talented."

"I was beginning to think I'd lost that."

"Never!"

"I was depressed. You brought me back to life, I think."

They both took a step forward. Then she was in his arms, and he was clasping her to him, all the needs he had suppressed the night before welling up.

She made a small sound as her body molded itself to his. When she pressed her face to his shoulder and inhaled deeply, a shiver swept across his skin.

"I was afraid you might not come back," she whispered.

"Why?"

"Last night was so intense. That would scare some men off."

"Not me." He managed a gentle laugh. "The first thing I did when I got up was make sure you hadn't called and told me to forget it."

She raised her head and looked into his eyes. "Not a chance."

Her lips were only inches from his. They trembled slightly and parted. "Jules, do you have me under a spell?"

"No more than you have me."

Neither of them moved. Then, as he had on the balcony, he lowered his head. The first touch of his lips on hers sent a shock wave zinging along every nerve in his body.

Greedily, he angled his head, slanting his lips over hers for the most intimate contact, and she clasped her arms around his neck as she opened for him.

He was good at kissing. But finesse had deserted him. With a frightening lack of control, he devoured her mouth. And he found her greed matched his.

So did his restless drive to explore—to know. He felt like someone had locked him into a seat on a giant roller coaster and cranked up the speed to supersonic. Only the contact of his mouth with hers would keep him from flying into space.

He couldn't catch his breath, even when his lips left hers to trace a damp, scorching trail across her jaw and down the graceful curve of her throat. When he found the wildly beating pulse point at its base, he pressed his teeth there. But somehow he kept himself from piercing her flesh even when he knew that pulse was keeping time with the pounding of his heart.

"Oh, Jules. Oh," she gasped, making him feel as though his brain might explode.

He managed to bring his mouth back to hers as his fingers glided up and down her ribs. He tasted carnal desire and needs that matched his own.

When she sighed out her pleasure, his hands stole inward to cup the weight of her breasts. And when he stroked his thumbs across the crests, he found them hard and tight with arousal. Like his whole body.

She made a tiny, sobbing noise that almost robbed him of sanity. When he swung her up into his arms, she looked at him with dazed eyes.

"Your bedroom?" he managed to say.

"The next room on the right."

He carried her to the wide bed and laid her gently on the satin coverlet. Then he followed her down to the horizontal surface, pressing the length of his body against hers. But her clothing had become an intolerable barrier.

Rolling to his side, he began to work the buttons of her shirt, trying not to rip the delicate fabric.

When he had dispatched the blouse and her bra, he lowered the zipper on her slacks, so he could peel them away, along with her panties.

As she lay naked on the bed, he paused to admire his handiwork. Reverently he touched her delicate collarbone, the enticing curve of her waist, the hollow of her throat.

"Beautiful. So beautiful," he murmured.

"I want you naked, too," she whispered. "I've wanted that since last night."

"Yes," he murmured, exalted and at the same time sad.

He pulled off his shirt and tossed it away. But he left his slacks on because he didn't want her to see that it was impossible for this incredible encounter to give him an erection.

Her legs parted, and she moved restlessly, invitingly.

He gathered her to him, taking long, luxurious strokes

with his fingers through the folds of her sex, then dipping into her, wringing a pleading cry from her.

"Please, now," she gasped.

"Yes, love," he answered.

It was time to take her. But he had never been more reluctant and at the same time, more needy. He wanted her to remember this, to remember everything he had done. But that could not be an option.

So he did what he must. He put her into a light trance, then delicately sank his teeth into the place where her neck joined her shoulder, drawing blood as he continued to stroke her with two stiff fingers that would have to substitute for his cock.

His own pleasure grew as he fed off that sweet blood and the waves of ecstasy coming from her mind and body. Her hips rose and fell, as her arousal built. And when she climaxed, he felt the echoes of her rapture in his own being. It wasn't exactly an orgasm as a man would know it. He dimly remembered that sensation from long ago. This was different but no less satisfying, so satisfying that he had to ruthlessly cut it short so that he didn't take too much blood.

He turned his head, licking the blood from his mouth, tasting her essence on his lips.

Then he bent to her ear, telling her that he had been inside her, that he had made exquisite love to her, and that it had been wonderful for him.

Easing off the bed, he pulled off his slacks and undershorts and tossed them onto the floor where his shirt lay. Then he gathered her into his arms, holding her close as he kissed and stroked her.

She stirred, and her eyes fluttered open.

"Did I fall asleep?" she asked in a puzzled voice.

"You were tired. From being up so late. And all that feverish work today."

"Yes." She focused on his face. "That was incredible."

"Yes," he answered, because that much was true. "Sleep some more," he whispered. "So I can hold you in my arms."

She nodded against his shoulder, and he helped her sleep again, then allowed himself the incredible delight of simply holding her, while he absorbed the wonderful woman scent of her body, stroked her silken skin, and listened to the sound of her breathing. He had missed this human contact. This contentment. If he could have kept her in his arms for the next hundred years, he would have done it.

But his pleasure must come in measured increments, governed by the sunrise.

Finally, when he had spent all the time with her he dared, he brought her back to wakefulness. "I have to go."

"But you just got here," she murmured.

"No. It's very late."

Easing away from her, he began picking up clothing from the floor.

She watched him, and he knew that her thoughts were still foggy. "What about tomorrow?" she asked, her words slightly slurred.

"Tomorrow night. We can go down to Jackson Square if you want. Or to one of the other clubs."

"I'd rather be alone with you," she said. "Making love."

He nodded and kissed her one last time. "I don't want you to tire of me too quickly."

"There's no danger of that."

"We'll keep the relationship interesting." He squeezed her hand. "I can let myself out. And I'll be back tomorrow night. At the same time."

"Promise," she whispered.

"I promise."

Chapter Six

Taylor lay in bed, feeling relaxed and sated. She remembered Jules coming here. She remembered him kissing and caressing her. She remembered him carrying her to bed and undressing her. And she remembered the part afterwards when she lay naked in his arms. In between, she could remember the ecstasy of orgasm. He was a wonderful lover. And he had brought her rare pleasure. But she couldn't remember exactly what they had done. She tried to recall the weight of his body pressing down on hers. She tried to remember the feel of his penis moving in and out of her. That part was vague. He must have aroused her so thoroughly that she hadn't paid attention to the details, only the feelings.

But that was enough, she told herself. More than enough. Climbing out of bed, she stretched muscles that felt a little bit sore from the exertion of lovemaking

There was a kink in her neck. Well, not exactly her neck. More like the place where her neck and shoulder met. It felt a little sore, and she rubbed it as she walked into the bathroom, then peered at the spot in the mirror, seeing a little set of red marks. Like insect bites.

She went very still, feeling a small shiver steal up her spine. She had the odd feeling there was something she should remember. Something vitally important. But as soon as the thought surfaced, it skittered away.

She stood for another moment in front of the mirror, then shrugged and turned on the shower.

While she was under the pounding water, she began thinking about what she wanted to work on. Quickly she dried off and threw on some clothing. Then she rushed down the hall to the studio and began sketching.

Two hours later, she had a good start on an acrylic painting of a man and a woman lying in an ornate brass bed, basking in the afterglow of making love. She stopped briefly to run down to the kitchen and grab some cheese and crackers. But she didn't stop for long. When the doorbell rang at nine, she realized she'd been working all day, without thinking about how she looked.

And now Jules was here. Padding barefoot downstairs, she spoke to the closed door. "I've been working all day. I'm a mess."

"Do you think I care?" he answered from the other side of the door. "Or are you making excuses to send me away?"

"I never make excuses." As she spoke, she turned the lock.

He came into the front hall, his gaze searching hers. And in that moment, she saw his vulnerability.

"Did you think I'd changed my mind about us?" she asked softly.

"You could be having second thoughts."

"Never."

"Then let me see what kept you busy all day."

Torn, she finally ushered him upstairs, then held her breath as he stood in front of the canvas she'd started. It wasn't finished. But the lovers were clearly visible, their bodies partially covered by a sheet, their sated expressions proclaiming their recent pleasure.

He didn't speak for a long time, and she took her lower lip between her teeth. She'd thought the painting was good. But now she was showing it to the man who had inspired the burst of creative energy.

"Well?" she finally asked in a small voice.

He turned back to her, and the look of awe on his face made her heart skip a beat. "This is fantastic. I knew you were good. I didn't know how good."

"It's not too . . . revealing?" she pressed.

"It's perfect. Very erotic and very intimate."

"You inspired me. Well, not just you. Us."

"I'm glad."

"I could use some more inspiration."

His laugh was low and sexy. "Oh, could you?"

"Let me get cleaned up. You're lucky I work with acrylics and not oils."

"Why?"

"Because I'm not going to have to use turpentine to get the paint off my hands."

She left him in the studio, hurried to her bedroom and then into the bathroom.

After washing her hands, she decided that a shower might be a good idea.

When the water temperature was adjusted to hot, she stepped under the spray, thinking that she could probably keep her hair dry if she showered carefully.

But in the next moment, the sliding door opened, and a hard male body came up behind her. A naked body.

"Jules. What are you doing?"

"Helping you get nice and clean."

She started to turn. But he clasped her shoulders, holding her against his length, a muffled sound rising in his throat as he bent his head and nuzzled her hair.

Now it wasn't simply the heat of the water that enveloped her. It was the heat of the man who held her in his arms.

He touched his fingers to the place on her shoulder that she'd looked at earlier.

"What happened here?" he asked, tension in his voice.

She responded to his obvious worry. "It's nothing. I mean, I'm not sure. An insect bite, I guess."

"Okay."

She felt him relax as he bent his head, nibbling at her earlobe, then tracing the interior whorl with his tongue, before stiffening it and probing deeply. The sensation was so erotic that she couldn't hold back a small gasp.

"You're so sensitive. So responsive," he murmured.

"With you."

She felt him smile against her cheek. Then he reached for the bar of lavender-scented soap. His hands were in front of her, strong, masculine hands.

As she watched, he lathered them.

"This smells good," he said.

"Yes."

She had been working hard all day. Yet she had also been thinking of him, because he had been her inspiration. "Jules, I never met anyone like you," she whispered.

"I can say the same thing. You are a rare treasure."

Some men might have said that casually. She sensed that Jules never would, and the words touched her at some deep level that she barely understood.

Although she had known him only a few days, it seemed as if she belonged to him. But she was afraid that if she let him know the intensity of what she was feeling, she would scare him away.

Wanting to see his face, she tried to turn toward him. But he held her where she was.

His soap-slick hand stroked over her shoulder, then downward to her breast. The sensual touch made her nerves dance and tingle. Heat shot through her, heat that had been building all day while she worked. Heat that his hand on her body released.

She threw her head back so that her lips could find the side of his face. But she wanted more.

"Let me turn around," she begged.

"I want you like this," he answered in a husky voice. "Just like this. For your pleasure. And mine."

"Why?"

"It's very arousing to me—having access to your naked body. Having you in my power."

"Oh," she gasped as his soap-slick hands played over her wet skin with a total lack of resistance that was like fire lapping at her nerve endings.

"Oh Lord," she breathed, when he lifted and shaped her breasts, then circled the nipples.

"You like that?" he purred.

"You know I do."

Just with his knowing touch on her breasts, he brought her close to the edge. Then he rinsed one hand under the shower spray so that he could grasp her nipple, squeezing and pulling and sending the flames licking higher. The hand slid down her body, found the slick, swollen folds of her sex and began to caress her there.

"Jules." She tried to reach behind her to find his cock. But he clamped her hand to her side.

"Let me give you as much pleasure as you're giving me," she begged.

"You are, love. Believe me, you are," he answered and the strangled sound of his voice told her how much he liked what he was doing.

He moved her so that the water beat down on her breasts while he teased her with his fingers, one hand on her sex and the other in the crack of her ass, his touch so sensitive that he brought her to the brink of climax, then moved the front hand away so that she gasped and wiggled and tried to force him to give her satisfaction.

"Please," she begged. "Please. I have to come. Now."

Her plea must have swayed him, because he brought his hand back to her clit, stroking and pressing, making her tremble as the power of her need built.

"Yes, that's right, love," he murmured. "Show me how much you can feel."

She reached one shattering orgasm, that had her screaming with pleasure. But that was only the beginning. He barely let the aftershocks subside before he was pushing her to new heights. And as spasms of pleasure took her, she felt his kiss on her shoulder.

She could barely stand, barely move. Only the support of his arms and his body held her up as he brought her to a third shuddering orgasm.

He turned off the water, opened the door of the shower, and reached for a fluffy towel. Wrapping her like a child fresh from the bath, he cradled her in his arms while he dried her hair and her body before carrying her out of the bathroom and laying her on the bed.

Exhausted, she dozed. And when she blinked her eyes open, he was dressed again and sitting on the side of the bed.

"You are so sexy," he murmured.

"So are you," she answered lazily.

"I promised to show you some more of the French Quarter."

She would have snuggled in the bed, but he got her up, and helped her dress. Then he took her out to a tempting little sweets shop where he bought them both huge waffle-wrapped ice cream cones. Rocky road and strawberry for her. Banana and chocolate for him.

She didn't see him eat much. Maybe she was having too much fun window shopping in the antique stores along Royal Street.

But his ice cream disappeared. And he threw away the cone, saying he had never liked that part.

"I was brought up to eat every bite," she said, finishing the nub of her own cone.

"You were poor?"

"Middle class. But my mom used to remind us about the starving children in India."

"I was one of the starving children in London."

She shot him a surprised look. He'd hardly talked about himself, but apparently she'd gotten him in the mood to reveal something about his past. "But you've done very well since then," she said carefully.

"My stepfather rescued me. Well, he wasn't really my stepfather. But he took me to his country estate. And saved my life."

"Why?"

"I think he wanted a son. So he picked me."

"He must be proud of the way you turned out."

"He died," Jules said, his voice full of loss.

"He was old?"

"No. He had . . . an accident." He tightened his grip on her hand. "But I don't want to talk about me or John Randolph."

"You didn't keep his name?"

"He never officially adopted me. But enough about me. I want to know about you. Your family. They must be thrilled with your work."

She laughed. "They hate my work. They are narrow-minded, uptight people who live in the middle of Kansas."

"Well, that explains it!"

She laughed. "Maybe. My mother wanted me to be a teacher. She and Dad were willing to send me to the university to get a teaching degree. But they recoiled in horror at the idea of art school. So I ran away to San Francisco."

"How did you manage?"

"I had a little money saved up. My aunt insisted on giving me a little more. And I worked—sometimes as an artist's model."

"Naked?"

"Does that shock you?"

"Of course not! You must have been quite a distraction for the males in the class."

"I did my best to look frumpy."

He laughed. "Resourceful. But you couldn't hide your lovely figure."

"I slumped."

He laughed again.

She was enjoying herself so much that she didn't realize how late it was until there was almost no one else left on the street.

"I should take you home," he said.

"I don't want tonight to end."

"But you need your beauty sleep. Because you're going to work all day tomorrow."

"I think that's right," she admitted.

When they reached her door, she said, "Stay here with me."

"I want to. But I can't."

"Why not?"

"I need to be alone sometimes."

Alarm leaped inside her. "You're not trying to back out of the relationship, are you?"

"No!"

"Jules . . ."

He pressed his fingers against her lips. "You are the most exciting woman I have ever met. I want to be with you as much as I can. But I need solitude."

"Why?"

"Maybe I'm writing a book, and I need to work."

"And maybe you're not."

He reached for her and hugged her tight, and then he turned and hurried back to his car, leaving her feeling afraid and a little disoriented.

Chapter Seven

Over the next few weeks, Taylor's days were filled with feverish work, the best paintings she had done in her life. And her nights were filled with Jules DeMario.

"You should contact some gallery owners," he said one evening as they looked through the collection of paintings she'd turned out.

"Which ones?"

"Montpelier. St. Laurent."

"Oh sure. Those galleries are the best in the city."

"And you should be in them. They'll want you. All you have to do is show them your work."

Although she knew she was good, she wasn't sure she could join those rarefied ranks. But she figured the worst thing that could happen was that the gallery owners would turn her down.

She contacted Martin St. Laurent first. He'd heard of her by reputation, and he came over the same day she called.

Five minutes into the viewing, he asked for an exclusive deal, with terms that made her eyes bug out.

She accepted—giving him ten paintings to start. In the first twenty-four hours, she sold three, at higher prices than she had ever asked in San Francisco.

St. Laurent wanted replacements, which she gladly agreed to supply.

That night, Jules was late, and she waited impatiently for him to arrive so she could tell him the great news. Then she saw the twinkle in his eye.

"You didn't by any chance buy them all?" she asked.

"No. I only bought one, love. The one I wanted so badly—your picture of the couple lying in bed looking so happy and relaxed."

"Jules, I would have given that painting to you, if you'd asked."

"And taken away the pleasure of walking into the gallery and buying it? No! I'm so proud of what you're doing. So proud that I have a small part of it."

"You have a big part. I've never been more creative."

"I'm glad."

She stepped toward him and felt suddenly dizzy. When he caught her in his arms, he looked alarmed.

"It's all right. I just felt a little light-headed."

"How long has this been going on?" he demanded, cradling her in his arms as he sat down on the couch.

"I'm not sure. About a week."

"Have you been to the doctor?" he asked, worry and perhaps guilt clearly visible on his features.

She rushed to reassure him. "I'm just run-down. I mean, I've been working all day—and staying up late with you."

"I know that," he murmured. "You need to slow down."

"It's hard to do that when I wake up every morning with ideas for paintings."

"Then maybe you need to get some sleep at night."

Alarm twisted through her. "What do you mean?"

"I've been putting off a business trip," he said slowly. "Maybe I should take it now."

She wanted to protest. But she could hardly hold him in the city if he had things to take care of elsewhere. Still, she heard herself asking, "What kind of trip?"

"To take care of things I've let go," he answered evasively.

She bent her neck, resting her forehead against his shoulder. "Are you using that as an excuse to break off with me?"

His grip tightened on her shoulders. "No! But I think I'm not good for you."

"Why?"

"Between me and your work, you're burning yourself out."

She raised her face to him. "I could stop painting."

"No," he said again. "But you need to get some sleep. I'd guess you're not eating properly. And maybe you need . . . to build your blood up. You could be anemic."

"I guess that's right."

"If I brought you a voodoo potion, would you drink it?"

"What kind of potion?"

"A health tonic."

"You believe in that kind of thing?"

"Yes."

She was skeptical, but the look in his eyes told her that her agreement was important.

"All right," she said softly, thinking that if it was too unpleasant, she could always pour it down the drain.

"Then let me go get you something now."

"I can come with you."

"I want you to rest." He stood, laying her gently on the sofa, then covering her with a throw that was draped over one arm.

She allowed him to fuss over her, because it was easier to let him take charge at the moment.

"I'll let myself out. And I'll be back soon."

Outside, Jules climbed into his car and drove to the French Quarter, his thoughts in an agony of despair. Selfish disregard for Taylor's health had driven him to take too much blood from her. Slowly but surely, he was killing her, and the best thing he could do was disappear from her life. He wasn't good for her in so many ways.

She had told him about her early life. Her father had been a mail carrier. Her mother had been a teacher's aide. She had gone to church and Girl Scouts. And he was thankful that she had broken out of the narrow small-town environment where she had grown up. But deep down she still had a core of conventionality.

He knew she wanted him to make a commitment to her. And he longed to offer her a stable future. Their lives were suddenly twined together so intimately. He felt more for her than he had felt for any other woman in hundreds of years. Yet he only shared with her what was safe to share. And that left a glaring hole in their relationship.

For her own good, he should disappear from her life. But when he thought of walking away from the best thing that had ever happened in his miserable life, blind selfish need made his throat clog. He couldn't give her up. Not yet.

So he drove to a little shop on a side street where the desperate could buy secret potions.

The old woman behind the counter looked at him appraisingly. He had been here fifteen years ago, and he knew that he hadn't changed in that time. Neither had she, really, except that she was a bit more stooped.

"And what brings you to me after all these years?" she asked in a quavery voice.

So she remembered. He acknowledged the comment with a slight inclination of his head. "I need to . . . strengthen a woman's constitution."

"As you did before?"

"Yes," he admitted.

"Is your lover sick?"

"She needs to build up her blood."

"Ah," the crone answered, giving him another long look, and he couldn't help thinking that she knew what he was.

Were there others of his kind in this city? Vampires he hadn't met? And how would they greet him, if they knew he walked among them in the night?

But he didn't ask any questions. And he was profoundly grateful when the woman told him to wait while she prepared something. She went into the back and was gone for about ten minutes. When she returned, she was carrying a small, ornate glass bottle, closed with a cork stopper.

"She should take a few drops of this in a glass of wine, twice a day."

"Thank you."

"Be careful of her."

"I want to."

"Don't make assumptions about the relationship."

"What is that supposed to mean?" he asked sharply.

But she only gave a shake of her head. "You must find out for yourself."

He left, glad to be away from the woman's probing gaze. Taking care not to break the speed limit and get stopped by a cop, he drove to a liquor store on St. Charles and bought several bottles of good wine, then hurried back to Taylor's house and let himself in.

She was dozing on the sofa, and he hated to wake her. But her eyes snapped open when he approached.

"Jules?"

He knelt beside her. "I've brought you something to drink."

"I won't drink it if it tastes nasty."

He laughed. "You take a few drops twice a day in a glass of wine. I've bought you a couple of very nice Merlots to go with it."

In the kitchen he had uncorked the bottle, added a few drops of the potion, and sipped the results. Even with his acute sense of taste, there was nothing objectionable about it.

So he brought the glass to Taylor, sitting beside her while she took a cautious sniff, then a little swallow.

He couldn't bear the idea of being separated from her. Yet he knew that he must—at least for a few days. So he gathered her close again.

"I was thinking I don't know much about you," she said as she sipped the wine.

"What do you want to know?"

"About your boyhood."

"It was rough and unpleasant. My parents weren't married. My mother tried to do the best she could raising me. But she was sick. And I scrounged dinner from garbage cans. Or stole food from a street vendor. And I was a fairly good pickpocket, too," he added, wondering how she would react to his early history. Perhaps she'd push him away, and that would solve both their problems.

Instead, she took his hand. "That sounds . . . hard."

"It wasn't much fun."

"How did you meet your stepfather?"

"He sometimes came down to the bad part of town."

"Why?"

"I think he got something out of feeding the poor," Jules answered, and silently added, *and it was a safe place for him to find blood.* "I guess he saw something in me, because he asked if I wanted to come live with him in the country. Of course I did. And that changed my life."

"I'm glad."

"He sent me to a local prep school. And he taught me a lot at home. He knew so much about the world. About science. And sociology. And agriculture. I was damn lucky. I still miss him."

"I'm sorry. But I understand. I miss my aunt. She'd been a dancer on the Broadway stage. She understood me better than my parents ever did. She was the one who suggested I go to a big city on one of the coasts."

"She wasn't afraid you'd get into trouble?"

"Probably. But she knew I needed my independence."

He loved hearing about her life. But he wasn't going to keep her talking tonight.

As he cradled her against himself, he stroked her temples, sending her into a light trance. When she was under his spell, he gave her orders. "You need to sleep. You need to take care of yourself while I'm gone. Drink your medicine. Get to bed early. And don't work too much."

"Um."

"What did I tell you?"

Dutifully, she repeated his instructions.

"Good." He bent to brush his lips against her temple. "I'll call you as soon as I get back."

Before he could change his mind, he got up and let himself out of the house, fighting the mixture of sadness and dread that threatened to envelop him.

Chapter Eight

Jules spent the next week in the depths of depression. Mostly he sat inside his house or in his garden, brooding. And every other night, he went out and drew sustenance from the drunks and homeless people who were easy marks for a hungry vampire.

Then he would drive to the vicinity of Taylor's house and watch her through the windows.

It heartened him to see that she drank the potion. And in a strange way, it cheered him to see her wandering around the house looking lost. Sometimes she went into her studio. And he saw that she was trying to work. But the spark had gone out of her paintings. And as often as not, she would slash her pallet knife over what she had done.

He wanted to knock on the door. He knew she would rush into his arms. And he ached to hold her close once again. But he knew that he would make love with her. And he knew that would be dangerous to her health. So he walked quietly away. Sometimes he went back to his empty house. And sometimes he visited shops in the French Quarter and bought her exquisite presents, things he would give her when they got back together again. Tokens of the love he could not express in words.

Six evenings after he had told her he was going out of

town, he walked out into his garden and found a lonely figure sitting in one of the wrought-iron chairs.

Despite all his good intentions, his heart leaped inside his
chest when he saw it was Taylor.

"What are you doing here?" he asked in a thick voice.

"I couldn't stay away from you. Just the way you couldn't
stay away from me."

"What do you mean?"

"You were out there in the dark, watching me, weren't
you?"

"How do you know?"

"I felt you. Suffering the way I was suffering." She stood
and went to him. And he was helpless to do anything but
clasp her in his arms and hold her tight.

Heat leaped between them. Sensuality that would not be
denied clamored for release.

He knew then what he was going to do.

"Come inside."

"I was hoping you weren't going to send me away," she
breathed.

He led her up the stairs—not to his bedroom, but to a
guest room he had never used.

Then, as he had six nights ago, he touched her temples,
putting her into a light trance. "I'll be back in just a few minutes," he murmured. "Wait for me here."

She smiled and closed her eyes. And he charged out of the
house and toward the French Market, knowing he would encounter plenty of victims there.

Recklessly, he drank from one man. Then another. And
another, filling himself with blood.

John had told him he could make love as a man. Not
often, but once every few years if he wanted. He had never
felt the need before. But he felt it now.

And when he came back to Taylor, he was engorged with
the life fluid from a dozen men.

He touched her temple, waking her, and she blinked. "Where were you?"

"Just getting something for you to wear." He handed her a box, barely breathing as he waited to see her reaction.

She opened the package and lifted up a delicate silk gown.

"It's beautiful," she breathed.

"I kept picturing you in it. Would you put it on for me? Just that. Nothing else."

She nodded wordlessly, then took the box into the bathroom.

While she was gone, he hurried down the hall to his own room. He knew he was good at the ways he had learned to please women. Now he was venturing into barely remembered territory. As a man, long ago, he had made love with a few women. But he probably hadn't been very good at it. Now he could turn out to be a miserable failure.

Wanting to set the scene as perfectly as possible, he changed the sheets. Then he got out a pair of the silk pajamas he sometimes wore when he wanted to lounge around the house.

When he came out of the bathroom, he found Taylor standing by his bed, looking as lovely as he had imagined in the green silk.

"This is your room?" she asked in a voice that told him she was as nervous as he was himself.

"Yes."

"I love it. You're not afraid to admit you like elegant furnishings."

"Yes," he managed to say around the lump in his throat.

He saw her slick her palms against her sides, saw her flush and loved the effect of the rosy hue. "It may sound strange, but I feel like this could be our wedding night," she whispered.

"Yes. This is a special night for us," he answered, thinking again that he felt like an inexperienced bridegroom.

His stomach muscles clenched. He didn't even know if what he had planned was going to work.

Praying he could please her the way a normal man would, he reached for her and gathered her close. To his delight and relief, his penis instantly filled with blood.

"Oh!" he heard himself exclaim. The sensation was extraordinary. He had experienced a normal male erection so long ago that he hardly remembered the wonderfully full sensation, the centering of his arousal in that one part of his body.

He didn't know how long it would last. But he wanted to enjoy it while he could. Not just for himself, but for the generous and beautiful woman in his arms.

His hands stroked up and down her back, trailing over the silky fabric of the gown. Hungry for her taste, he angled his head, bringing his lips to hers, gratified by her instant response. She breathed his name, then opened for him, meeting his tongue with darting strokes that made him light-headed.

"I want this night to last forever," he said into her mouth, raising his hands and cupping her breasts, loving the exquisite feel of her hard nipples through the thin fabric.

"That's so good," she whispered into his mouth as her hands slid downward, pulling his hips against her body.

He was so unprepared for the sensation that the feel of his engorged cock pressed tightly to her middle made him gasp.

Then her hand slid between them, cupping around his penis through the silk pajama bottoms, and he thought he might explode in her fingers.

He must have made some kind of exclamation because she nodded against his chest. "Lord, you feel so good." She dragged in a breath and let it out. "You never let me do this, do you?" she asked in a slightly puzzled voice.

"Because it's so intense," he managed to dredge up an answer to her question, as he took her hand away from his erection, then dragged the gown over her head before laying her on the bed. Stretching out beside her, he let his gaze caress her as though this were their first time together. The tight points of her nipples seemed to beg for his attention, and he circled them delicately, then took them between his thumbs and fingers, smiling as she arched toward him.

She returned the favor, removing his pajama top, then stroking her hands over his chest, playing with the thick hair, then finding his nipples and circling them with her fingers, making them throb with sensation.

But they weren't the only part of him that throbbed. He could feel the blood beating in his penis. And as she undid the snap at the top of his pajama bottoms and pushed the front open, he looked down at himself in a kind of daze.

His penis was standing up from his body, hard and stiff, the sight fascinating and thrilling.

When she slid her hand down his chest and then his abdomen, stroking his ribs and stomach, he heard himself make a pleading sound.

He had told her that grasping his cock was too intense. But he wanted it. Wanted it badly.

And she obviously knew it. This time her touch was dainty as her fingers delicately circled the head, then stroked up and down the shaft. All his senses went dim. He could barely see. Barely hear. There was only the magnificent pleasure of her fingers teasing him, before she suddenly took him in her fist and slid her hand firmly up and down his length.

As if from far away, he heard himself moan.

"You are velvet-covered steel," she whispered.

His voice turned low and urgent. "I feel like I'm going to explode. I don't want it to happen like this. I want to be deep in you when I climax." As he spoke, he marveled that he could manage coherent sentences.

"God, yes." She lay back against the sheet and held out her arms to him.

He was still worried about his performance. But need was greater than fear of failure. With a sense of wonder, he moved over her, the tip of his penis poised at the feminine entrance he had only explored with his fingers. Slowly, savoring the sensation, he pressed into her, hardly able to believe the feel of her tight sheath closing around him.

Exalted and awed, he looked down at her, stunned that he was joined to this woman.

"Taylor," he murmured.

"Yes, love."

He kissed her lips as he began to move, focused on her and the wonderfully erotic sensation of his shaft moving in and out of her.

He wanted to hold back. But the feelings were too intense and too unfamiliar.

His penis jerked inside her. And as he climaxed, he felt her inner muscles contract around him.

She cried out her pleasure, following him over the edge into a free fall of rapture that was so unique for him and so unexpected that he could only gasp out a wordless sob.

Chapter Nine

Sunlight filtered in around the edges of the curtains when Taylor woke in her own bed. After their glorious lovemaking, she had wanted to spend the whole night with Jules, but he had taken her home just before dawn, then left.

Closing her eyes, she lay in bed, smiling as she savored every detail of the night before. They'd had intercourse three times. And she could recall every glorious, sexually fulfilling moment with him. Making love last night had been magical. But as she thought about the night of lovemaking, a feeling of uneasiness began to steal over her.

She could remember last night in vivid color, like a movie in her mind. The way an idea for a painting came to her.

No other night with Jules came to her with that kind of clarity. Not in detail. Every other time, she could picture him stimulating her. She remembered the glorious climaxes, the sense of fulfillment. But she couldn't recall any of the actual things they'd done when she'd been most aroused.

A shiver went over her skin. Except for last night, the details of their lovemaking were a blank. If she was honest with herself, last night was the only time she could be sure she'd actually had intercourse with him.

And there was so much she didn't know about him. He'd hardly talked about his background. She didn't know any of his friends or the people he did business with—whoever they were. She'd only met him at night. And she'd never spent the whole night with him because he'd locked himself in his own house before dawn.

Throwing back the covers, she stood and found her legs were shaky. Stiffening her knees, she marched into the bathroom. Not wanting to look, yet feeling compelled, she studied the place on her neck where she'd thought the insects had bitten her. The place was bruised and the wounds were healing. But she found similar places on her body. One on the other shoulder. Another on her inner thigh. And a third at the top of her right breast.

She stared at the spots. Maybe there were some kind of insects living in her bed, biting her while she slept. But why did the marks always come in twos?

She didn't want to think about the answer. But she knew that she'd been drifting along for too long in a sensual fog–created by Jules DeMario. She'd let him run her life.

No, that wasn't fair, she corrected herself. But she'd certainly fit herself into his strange schedule.

He'd met her for drinks that first time at the bar in the Jax Brewery building. But they'd never gone there for lunch when the view from the balcony would have been spectacular.

A shiver went through her. Back in her room, she pulled on a robe, then went into the small bedroom where she'd set up her computer.

She sat for a long time staring at the screen, feeling her heart pound. Finally she booted it up, connected to the Web and brought up a search engine.

Again she hesitated before typing "vampire" into the find box.

With one exception, her nights with Jules had been a blur. The night after her computer search was the worst of all, because she was so nervous and scared that she could barely function normally.

But she couldn't condemn Jules on the basis of her own wild speculations. So she greeted him enthusiastically and tried to say the right things to him, tried to act like she was eager to make love with him again after the joy of the night before. And it must have worked. Because they did make love again. This time in her bed.

And when she woke the next morning, it was the way it had always been in their relationship. She could remember him turning her on. She could remember vibrating to the orgasm he gave her. But she couldn't remember the details.

Of course, now she didn't have to.

Getting out of bed on shaky legs, she went to the ornate basket she'd set on her dresser and took out the small, very expensive video camera that she'd hidden there.

With hands that she couldn't keep steady, she rewound the tape, then brought it down to the den, where she put it into the VCR.

"Do you really want to see this?" she asked herself.

The answer was *no*.

But she knew that she had to see what had transpired between herself and her lover the night before.

So she sat rigidly in an easy chair with her pulse pounding in her ears as she fast-forwarded to the moment when they'd walked into the bedroom.

Everything started off normally, and she breathed out a little sigh as she watched them kiss, watched herself slowly unbutton his shirt, take it off and stroke his chest the way she had the night before.

She remembered that. She remembered him slowly, tenderly undressing her as they stood beside the bed. But when she had tried to clasp his penis, he'd grabbed her wrist and pulled her hand away.

Her heart began to drum so hard in her chest that she

thought she might have a heart attack. But she kept watching.

She didn't recall him grabbing her hand. She didn't remember him laying her on the bed naked and coming down beside her, still wearing his slacks.

She watched him kiss and caress her, murmuring soft endearments, watched his knowing fingers slip into her vagina, stroke her clit.

Then he spoke again, and the words made her blood run cold. "Forgive me, love. Forgive me, but I can't get enough of you."

As she watched, he bent his head to her shoulder, pressing his mouth against her flesh.

Thank God she couldn't see much of what he was doing because his face was pressed against her. But she saw his fingers stroke her sex, saw her own hips rise and fall as she strove to reach climax. And as the shuddering spasms took her, she saw his body vibrate with hers as he shared her ecstasy.

When he lifted his head, his mouth was bloody, and she gasped. She saw him lick his lips, then lick the blood from her shoulder while she lay on the bed with her eyes closed, unmoving.

Then he got up and took off his clothing, climbed into bed and gathered her close as though they'd both been naked the whole time. She could see his penis now. It was flaccid. Probably it had been flaccid the whole time, because that wasn't the way he usually got his sexual gratification.

"So now you know," a voice said from behind her.

She screamed and jerked around. Jules was standing in the doorway, his arms folded across his middle, as though he had a terrible pain in his stomach.

"How . . . how?" she gasped out.

"I usually sleep during the day. As you may know, sunshine is poisonous to my skin. But the sunblock they make these days is amazing. If I put it on carefully, it protects me for short periods of time. Of course, it's an effort to stay awake in the daylight. But I did it today."

"Why?"

"Because you were acting nervous last night. You weren't yourself. And when I thought about it, I remembered the basket on your dresser. It hadn't been there before."

"Then why did you go ahead with what you were doing?"

"At the time, I wanted you too badly to think straight."

"And now what?" she asked in a quivery voice.

He gave a small shrug. "That's up to you."

"Are you going to kill me?"

He didn't move from the doorway. "You mean, murder you because you've found out my secret?"

"Yes, that," she said, feeling frightened and at the same time strangely detached.

"If I want, I could make you forget anything disturbing about me. You know, like your friend Evelyn."

"Yes. She wouldn't tell me any details of your relationship. At the time, I thought she was being coy. Now I know why." She raised her chin. "You broke it off with her."

"I always do," he said, his voice low and edged with pain.

She knit her hands together and squeezed hard, fighting to ignore her emotions. She didn't want to feel sorry for him. She didn't want to feel anything. Coldly she asked, "If you kept taking blood from me the way you've been doing, would that kill me?"

"Yes."

"Well, that's refreshingly honest. Do you usually kill your victims?"

He winced. "I never kill my . . . victims. Well, three hundred years ago after John Randolph saved my life by turning me, I killed a few people. It was my inexperience. I had to learn how to control what I do. I only take enough blood to live."

"Except with your lovers," she said, pressing him because he was finally telling her the truth about himself.

"I need blood to survive. But I need sexual gratification too. I try to go without that. But eventually the need becomes too great for me to ignore. You came along at the end of a long, dry spell."

"What a flattering way to put it!"

"That might be why it started. It changed pretty quickly. You are the most extraordinary woman I have ever met. I . . ." He stopped, and she saw his Adam's apple bob. "I couldn't give you up. I tried."

"How did you manage to have intercourse with me—that one time?"

"I left you at my house and went out. I took blood from a dozen men. I was in a hurry to get back to you, and I was reckless."

She winced. He was silent for several moments, then went on. "But our relationship has sorted itself out, hasn't it."

"Yes."

"I'm sorry I took advantage of you. I won't bother you again," he said stiffly. "You should go back to San Francisco."

"Don't you dare tell me what to do. If I want to stay here, I will."

He gave a tight nod. "Of course. I shouldn't presume to tell you what to do."

The look of sadness on his face tore at her. She had cared about this man on some deep, hidden level, but she turned her head away. "I think there's no point in continuing this conversation," she said.

"As you wish," he answered stiffly.

She listened as he walked down the hall and out the door.

Would the sun hurt him? Had he taken sufficient precautions? Why should she care? As he said, he had used her. In the worst possible way. He had taken blood from her. He had risked her life. And now she was safe.

She should feel angry. She should feel relieved. But all she could feel was sad.

Chapter Ten

He should be angry. She had made that video recording without his permission. But all he could feel was sad and lost. He was the one who had lied to her from the beginning. She had only been trying to protect herself. And he couldn't blame her for that.

He had told her to go back to San Francisco because he couldn't stand the idea of knowing she was just a few miles away.

Maybe he should be the one to leave. He had spent eighteen years making himself comfortable in his house. But he could sell it. He could move back to England. Or he could pick some other location entirely.

He had made elaborate arrangements in the past. But doing any of that now seemed like too much trouble. He was tired. Maybe it was time to end his own life. All he'd have to do is drive out into the countryside where there was no shelter and wait for the sunrise. But he couldn't even work up the energy to do that.

He was so weary that he slept long hours, then went out briefly when hunger drove him to take enough blood to sustain his miserable existence.

Sometimes he wasn't even sure why he was doing that.

Other times he knew that he was living to watch Taylor work as he lingered outside her windows.

She was still in the house she had rented. And she was painting late into the night. Her work wasn't joyful. It was dark and disturbing. Now she painted lovers surrounded by shadows. And the man in the pictures was often pale and almost transparent, like a ghost.

He saw sadness and anger. And a new maturity that made him so proud of her.

He hadn't destroyed her ability to work—just her trust. He hated that. But he knew he would never let his own selfish needs rule him again.

He dragged himself out of bed one evening and went through the motions of getting dressed in jeans and a T-shirt. He hadn't bothered with coffee in weeks. It no longer gave him pleasure to take a few sips. But he was still drawn to the garden.

After switching on the small lights, he wandered onto the patio. As soon as he set foot on the old bricks, he knew that the aroma of the flowers was mingled with another familiar scent.

His gaze darted to the wrought-iron patio set. Taylor was sitting rigidly in one of the chairs, her gaze fixed in his direction.

His mind stopped working. Without thinking about what he was doing, he surged across the patio, dragged her out of the chair and into his arms, holding tight, stroking his hands up and down her back and across her shoulders, his lips pressing into her hair as he said her name.

It took several moments for him to realize that she was standing rigid and unmoving in his embrace.

"I'm sorry." Carefully he turned her loose and took a step back. His heart was pounding, but he managed to say, "Why did you come here?"

He watched her take her lower lip between her teeth. "I had trouble staying away."

He could only nod.

He ached to reach for her again. Instead, he pressed his palms against his thighs, watching the play of emotions on her face.

She clenched and unclenched her hands. "I came back to see how I'd feel if I saw you again."

"And how is that?" he managed to ask.

She sucked in a breath and let it out. "I feel guilty."

"About what?" he asked, hardly able to believe what she'd said.

"I was angry about your using me. But you're not the only one. I called you up because I had come to a point in my artistic life where I couldn't work. And I felt like I needed new experiences. You provided them. I used you to spark my creativity. And it was a success. It still is, actually."

"I know," he whispered. "The paintings you're doing now take my breath away."

"You've been outside my house at night, haven't you?"

"Yes. I keep coming back, because I can't help myself. If you want to stay in the city, I'll move away."

Her hands clenched and unclenched. "That's not what I want," she said in a barely audible voice.

He managed to ask, "Then what?"

"I want . . ." She stopped and cleared her throat. "I want us to try again."

"How?" he asked, hardly daring to believe that he'd heard her correctly.

He saw her swallow convulsively. "We have to be totally honest with each other. I mean we have to make the sexual relationship honest." She paused again and dragged in a breath, before letting it out. "I want to make love with you. But I have to know I can handle what you're really doing. So you have to promise that you won't put me into a trance. I have to know what's going on."

She had handed him hope. Now she snatched it away. "You think you can deal with that?" he asked in a low voice.

She raised her chin. "I don't know. Can you?" she challenged.

He knew then that his greatest enemy might be his own fear. A cold chill came over him when he tried to imagine what it would be like taking blood from her while she watched him do it.

Could he? He didn't know.

Hearing the thickness in his own voice, he asked, "When would you want to try that?"

"Now."

Not now, a terrified voice inside him screamed. *Not yet.* But he refused to play the coward.

Instead, he closed the distance between them, folding her close. When she trembled in his arms, he couldn't stop himself from thinking this might be his one last time with her. Her words had been bold. But did she really know what she was asking?

Still, he was helpless to deny himself what she had so recklessly offered. His eyes closed as he stroked his lips against hers, entranced by the sensation. It was remarkable how such a light touch could start up a buzzing in his brain. But he had always known this woman's power over him was beyond anything else in his experience.

He savored every nuance of the kiss, starting with that light touch, then gradually deepening the contact. Her tongue met his, and he was intoxicated all over again by the taste of her and the feel of her in his arms.

Yet some part of him couldn't quite relax into the pleasure of being with her again. Trying to ignore his doubts, he slid his lips against her cheek, then nibbled at her ear.

Her fingers winnowed through his hair. As though she knew what he was feeling, she whispered against his jaw, "It's all right. Don't hold anything back. See what you're doing to me. Right from the first I knew we would be wonderful together."

She took his hand and carried it to her breast, and he felt the hard pebble of her nipple pressing into his palm.

Raising her face toward his, she murmured, "We're not going to do anything I haven't asked for."

"Yes," he answered above the roaring in his ears, because he still couldn't imagine the crucial moment. The moment when she felt him sink his teeth into her tender flesh and begin to draw her blood.

She strung kisses over his cheeks, his chin, his nose, and those sweet tokens made him bold. Captive to the heady pleasure of the moment, he knit her hand with his and led her inside.

When hesitation caught up with him again, he found she wasn't going to allow his second thoughts. Taking charge, she led him to the comfortable den off the living room. Yet when she began to open the buttons down the front of her blouse, he saw her hand tremble. Gravely, he reached to help her, their fingers getting tangled up together as they opened the placket. She raised her face to his as she pulled the blouse off and reached to open the catch at the back of her bra.

Then she was standing naked to the waist in front of him.

With a sound deep in his throat, he traced the sweet shape of her breasts. They were soft and quivering, the tips wonderfully hard, stabbing into his palms.

Bending, he swirled his tongue around one pebbled crest, then sucked it into his mouth.

"Oh, Jules," she gasped, clasping her hands around the back of his head, holding him to her for a long moment, before stepping back and skimming her slacks and panties down her legs.

She was gloriously naked, so totally vulnerable that she made his heart ache. She was silently proclaiming her trust in him. And he knew he must give her the same trust. So he pulled off his T-shirt, then reached for the snap at the top of his jeans.

He didn't want to stand naked in front of her and have her see that he wasn't aroused in the way a normal man would be. But he took off his jeans and shorts, because living a lie with her was no longer an option.

For better or worse, he must reveal his true self.

"Jules, you have a wonderful body," she murmured.

"I wish it responded like any other man's would."

She moved closer, combing her fingers through the hair on his chest, then lowering her head to circle one taut nipple with her tongue.

When he sucked in a sharp breath, she raised questioning eyes to his. "Does that feel good?"

"Yes."

"I'm glad. Glad of everything we have together."

She took his hand, tugging him down to the soft rug, then snuggling beside him. Reaching for his cock, she stroked her fingers over the head, then circled him with her fist.

He didn't have an erection, but her touch was like sweet fire traveling over his penis.

"That's good," he breathed. "So good. With you."

She kept her gaze on him. "You've never felt this way . . . with another woman?"

"No. I never let another woman see my naked body or touch me like that."

"I'm glad. Glad I'm the first. And now I want you to love me."

"We can't have intercourse," he said quickly, because he didn't want to give her any false ideas.

"I know," she answered just as quickly. "Love me the way you have before. Well, not exactly like before. I want to enjoy every moment of it."

He was helpless to deny her. To deny himself what he had been craving all these long weeks of separation. Still, his movements were slow and deliberate as he stroked the inner curve of one breast, then the other, gratified when he heard her breath catch and then quicken for him.

He bent to her and sucked one distended nipple into his mouth while he tugged and squeezed the other, wringing a small sob from her.

Every fiber of his concentration was tuned to her, to the tiny sounds she made and the ripples of sensation that flowed across her body as he stroked downward toward her sex. When he reached his goal, his fingers played with her, easing her velvet folds apart for his attention.

She was hot and wet for him, her color deep. Her clit was standing up, begging for his touch, and relief flooded through him as he drank in her response. She was with him every step of the way—so far.

He dipped two fingers into her vagina, then withdrew to the sensitive rim, pleasuring her there before stroking upward toward her clit, giving her the amount of pressure he had learned that she liked.

She lay in his arms with her eyes closed, but she kept her hand on his penis, gently stroking and squeezing him, and he realized that he liked the contact and that he had hardened somewhat in her hand.

He felt her tension gathering. Then her eyes blinked open and focused on his face.

"Don't make me wait any longer. I need to come," she gasped out. "And I need you to take your pleasure."

He had never wanted a woman more urgently, more violently. Yet this was the moment he had dreaded. He could make her come and forget about his own pleasure.

But then she would get up and walk away from him, and he would never see her again. That might happen anyway.

He felt poised on a knife edge of dread. He wanted to plead for understanding. Instead, he lowered his mouth to her shoulder. Tenderly, he kissed her ivory flesh. Then he pierced her skin with his special teeth.

Taylor made a small sound, and he felt as though barbed wire was twisting in his gut. He needed to ask if he had hurt her—was still hurting her. But he couldn't lift his mouth now.

He started to do what he always did. He started to invade her mind and turn her thoughts into a rosy glow. But she gripped his arm.

"Don't," she gasped out. "Don't mess with my head. Not this time."

It was difficult for him to obey her command because hiding his true nature was so ingrained. But he did it, because it meant the difference between keeping her with him or losing her.

And he couldn't deal with the loss. So he drew his mental powers back into his own mind, even as he drank her sweet blood while he stroked her sex. When he felt the first contractions of climax take her, he stoked her pleasure, staying with her, drinking her life fluid and the passion she gave him.

She cried out, her inner muscles clenching and unclenching around his fingers, her hand squeezing his cock. And he felt a shudder go through his whole body as his own pleasure reached its ultimate peak.

She gasped his name, then went still in his arms. He lifted his head, wiping his mouth on the back of his hand as he cradled her close, his anxious gaze on her face.

Tension stiffened his whole body. He had done something dark and forbidden to her. She had asked him to do it. But the request had nothing to do with how she was feeling now—about him, about them.

"Taylor?" he managed to ask.

"Thank you," she breathed. "Thank you for sharing your secret self with me."

He was too overwhelmed to answer. All he could do was gather her to himself, feeling a wave of relief like a warm wind blowing through the room.

She moved her head comfortingly against his shoulder and reached for his hand, knitting her fingers with his, holding tight to him.

"Taylor, oh God, Taylor," he murmured, touching the place

on her shoulder where he had drawn from her, where he had marred her white, almost translucent skin. "Did I hurt you?"

"Just a little."

"I'm sorry."

"Don't be. That little pain added to my pleasure."

His gaze searched her face. "You wouldn't lie to me?"

"Never."

He nodded, reading the truth in her eyes, and impassioned words tumbled from his lips. "I've never felt for any other woman what I feel for you."

She kissed his collarbone, his neck, his cheek.

"Thank you for trusting me," she murmured. "I know it was hard for you."

"Yes. But I had to. I wanted you too badly to back out— once we started."

"I was counting on that." She stroked her thumb over his lips. "I think I've fallen in love with you. That's the real reason why I came back."

He felt his chest tighten. Sitting up, he propped his back against the bottom of the sofa and looked down at her.

"You can love a man who has to go out at night and drink the blood of innocent victims to live?"

"That's a pretty stark way to put it." She sat up, too, then reached for the shirt she'd discarded on the floor. When she started gathering the rest of her clothing, he reached for his, too.

Dressed again, she sat down on the sofa, and he joined her.

"I want you to understand what you're getting into," he said.

She found his hand again. "When I stopped being upset, I started thinking a lot about my feelings. And reading about . . . vampires."

She had said the word, and it hung in the air between them.

"A lot of what you read is garbage," he said tightly.

"Well, I'm hoping you'll set me straight. I'm hoping you can let me into your life."

"It's not pretty."

"It's what it must be."

He marveled at the understanding she was willing to give him. He had never dared ask for such understanding. Perhaps no other woman could have given it to him. But he knew from her work that her ability to share her emotions was extraordinary.

"You are very brave to know what I am and want to be with me."

"I'm not brave. I'm selfish."

"No."

"Let's not waste time arguing." Changing the subject abruptly, she said, "I've seen you eat food. So that's possible for you."

"Just a little."

"Good—because I'm not much of a cook."

He laughed. "I guess there's some advantage to getting hooked up with me."

She nodded, then asked softly, "Will you tell me about John Randolph?"

He had kept his secrets for so long. Now it was a strange experience to let down his guard.

"John Randolph was a lonely man. I think my kind are all lonely. And he felt guilty because he had killed people before he learned how to take only a small amount of blood. I think he went down to the London slums looking for victims. But he was also looking for a way to atone for the deaths he had caused. He took me back to his estate and raised me like a son. And by the time I found out what he was, I loved him. I don't mean sexual love. He was like the father I never had."

"Why did he make you like him?"

"Because I had what you'd call TB today. I was slowly dying, and that was the only way to save me." He raised up on his elbow and looked down at her. "He told me that making a vampire isn't easy or safe. He told me that he'd tried it before and no one had ever lived through the transformation. I didn't have much to lose at that point. Just a few weeks of pain and coughing."

She tightened her grip on him.

"Maybe I trusted him enough for it to work. After the change, he taught me what he knew. He taught me how to feed without killing. Then a new vicar came to the little church in our village, and he started preaching about godless creatures of the night. A mob came after us. John led them away from the house. That's how I escaped."

"He saved you."

"Yes. I was able to take some of the gold and jewels he had hidden in the house. His fortune gave me a good start."

"But you've been alone all this time."

"For close to three hundred years. Except for the times when I linked up with a woman. And that was never for very long." He dragged in a breath and let it out in a rush. "And I don't know what to do about us. When I'm with you, I want to make love with you. But it's clear that I can't keep taking blood from you."

"When we make love, your pleasure comes from drawing my blood?" she asked softly.

"Yes. And from my feeling your climax."

"And when we had intercourse? That night was good for you?"

"God, yes."

"And a little while ago, it felt good when I stroked your penis?"

"Yes," he answered, marveling that they were having this conversation.

"So if we could have intercourse some of the time instead of what we just did—that would work for you?"

He wanted to look away, but he kept his gaze steady. "Yes, but I don't think it's possible very often."

She reached in the pocket of her slacks and brought out a flat packet. Inside were elongated blue pills.

"What are those?" he asked.

"Viagra. You've heard of it?"

"It's something that men take—to make them get an erection."

"Exactly." She cleared her throat. "Would you consider trying them?"

He got up and walked to the window, staring out at the garden, seeing the flowers shimmering in his night vision. Because there was no alternative, he had accepted his life away from the sun—and along with that many other things about himself. But what if long-established habits had blinded him to new alternatives?

He had been desperate to make love with Taylor the way a man made love. And he had done it the only way he thought was possible. Now she was telling him there might be another way. An easier way. Would it work? Or would his hopes be crushed?

He turned back to her and saw the unguarded look of wanting on her face. "For you," he said. "Anything for you."

"You don't want it?" she asked.

"Yes, I do. It's just a little difficult to rearrange three hundred years of thinking."

"But you're very adaptable. They didn't have cell phones three hundred years ago, did they? Or the Internet."

"Right." He took the packet from her and looked down at the directions.

"I think you take one. With some water."

"Then what?"

"You have to wait for a half hour—or an hour."

"Would you wait for me in the garden?" he asked.

"Yes."

Taylor didn't know if she'd done the right thing. What if the Viagra had no effect on his system? Well, they'd be no worse off than before. Jules DeMario was the most extraordinary man she had ever met. She wanted to be with him, and it was clear he wanted to be with her. When she'd given him an ultimatum, he'd broken rules he'd laid down hundreds of years ago.

He wanted this to work—and so did she. That might be the crucial factor.

Still, her nerves were strung taut as she stood in the garden staring at a bank of vivid yellow flowers. When she heard footsteps crossing the patio, she stiffened. It had to be Jules. Yet he said nothing. And she was sure the experiment had been a failure.

He came up close behind her, the way he had at the nightclub. And later in the shower. Only this time was different. This time she felt an unmistakable hard shaft pressed to her bottom.

"Jules," she breathed.

His hands came around her as he bent to nibble his lips against her neck, her ear.

When he had done this before, he had kept her facing away from him, and she understood the reason why. This time, he turned her in his arms, and she saw the look of wonder and gratitude on his face.

"It appears that magic blue pill was a good idea," she murmured.

"Very good."

He gazed down at her for a long moment, looking so powerful and yet so vulnerable that she wanted to weep.

When he lowered his head toward hers, she raised up on tiptoes, meeting him halfway. The mouth-to-mouth contact was like a bolt of white-hot fire, sizzling along her nerve endings.

But that was only the beginning. He used his lips, his tongue, his teeth, and she did the same, while they touched each other, hands stroking over backs and shoulders, gliding over ribs, drifting down to hips.

A groan welled in his throat when he angled his mouth, first one way and then the other, as though this were their first kiss, and he was just beginning to explore the magic between them.

When he lifted his head, he took her by the shoulders, creating a small space between them so that he could meet her gaze, his eyes burning into her.

"I didn't know how lucky I was when you called me on the phone," he said in a husky voice.

"Both of us were lucky." She gripped his muscular forearms. "Jules, whatever happens now, however this comes out, I want you any way I can have you."

"When I put you in a trance, I didn't give you a choice," he said in a thick voice, and she knew he still couldn't believe that she would come to him of her own free will.

She stroked her finger over his lips, then inserted it into his mouth, touching the teeth that he had used to pierce her flesh.

"I had a choice when we made love a little while ago. I have a choice now," she said in a strong, clear voice. "And I choose to be with you."

"Oh Lord, Taylor."

He swept her into his powerful arms, lifting her up. As though she had no more weight than flower petals, he carried her down the hall and up the stairs to his bedroom. No ordinary man could have done it so easily. He showed no signs of exertion as he set her on the floor beside his bed.

She looked around in wonder. The only illumination came from the glow of candles flickering around the room, and she saw how he had used the time since he'd taken the pill. The room was like a warm, secret cave, complete with a sensuous velvet spread on the bed.

"This is beautiful."

"Like you."

Between kisses, he began removing her clothing and his.

And she helped him, trying not to tremble. When they were both naked, standing side by side on the rich carpet, she reached to touch him.

Except for that one time, he had made love to her only with his hands and lips. But he was hard now, his penis standing out proud and firm from his body. And she caressed him gently, gratified that her idea had worked.

"This is so new for me," he said in a husky voice.

"For me, too. Now that we're communicating in a way we never did before."

"Yes."

"So can I ask you—how often have you done this?"

"Had intercourse?"

She nodded.

"The only time since I changed was with you. I never felt the need for it with any other woman. Only you."

She kissed his shoulder, his jaw. "And how many times before that?"

"Only with two women. One was a servant in John Randolph's house. The other was the nurse who took care of me when I was sick. I think she felt sorry for the dying young man."

She thought about what those encounters might have been like, and about his later experiences. Certainly in this sexually explicit culture, he'd seen lots of things that weren't even whispered about when he'd been young. Maybe he'd even watched porn movies. But there was a big difference between watching and participating.

Perhaps he was following her train of thought because he said in a gruff voice, "And you have more experience."

"Does that upset you?"

"It makes me worry about pleasing you."

"Put that worry out of your mind. What would please me now is to have my wicked way with you."

"What did you have in mind?"

"That's for me to know, and you to find out," she answered, striving to sound bold when her insides were quivering.

She wanted to please him. She wanted to show him there was more to a sexual encounter than he could imagine. And she hoped she had the skill to do it.

"Lie down," she murmured.

When he had stretched out on the velvet coverlet, she knelt on the bed beside him.

As she expected, he reached for her, but she lifted his hand to her lips and kissed it before putting it back on the bed.

"Let me enjoy myself with you," she said. "Let me have control of our lovemaking this time."

"All right," he whispered.

Giving them both time to adjust to her dominant role, she stroked her fingers over his shoulders, then combed through the hair on his chest, enjoying the feel of the springy strands before finding his nipples, circling and teasing them.

When he sucked in a sharp breath, she smiled down at him, then trailed one hand lower, over his ribs, his abdomen. His muscles jumped under her fingers.

Probably he thought she would go right for his cock. It was standing up tall and firm, begging for her attention. With a little pang of guilt, she bypassed that hard shaft and stroked her hand over first one thigh and then the other.

"Are you trying to drive me insane?" he asked in a strangled voice.

"Haven't you ever seen that TV ad—for anticipation?" she asked, then leaned over his body, to give him a long, lingering kiss on the lips while she brushed her breasts against his chest.

When she lifted her head away, he looked up pleadingly.

"Maybe it's time to get specific," she said as she reached down with a hand he couldn't see and took his cock in her fist, giving him a few sensuous strokes that wrung a throaty exclamation from him. Before he could get too far into that, she switched to a lighter touch, using her fingers to stroke his hard shaft and then circle round and round the head.

He gasped out his pleasure, his hands digging into the sheets. Then he gasped again as she leaned down, dragging her tongue along the length of his erection before taking as much of it as she could manage into her mouth. He cried out when she began to suck on him as though someone had just given her a delicious lollipop.

His hips bucked off the bed, and his cry of pleasure ended in a strangled groan.

She pulled back, nibbling her lips against the head of his shaft as she spoke. "You like that?"

"I . . . didn't know anything could feel that good."

She smiled at him, lifting his balls into her hands, gently playing with them as she slid his penis into her mouth again, moving up and down his length as she sucked and licked, devoting herself to what she knew would give him pleasure.

He was making deep, strangled sounds now, his hips straining as she felt tremors gathering in his body.

One of her hands reached to link with his as she quickened the pace of her attentions to him. He cried out, orgasm rocketing through him.

Swallowing had never been her favorite part of going down on a man. But she remembered from the previous experience that his body produced only a small amount of ejaculate.

So she continued to pleasure him until she felt his hand on her chin.

"Taylor. Taylor." Her name rumbled in his chest, and she looked up at him, seeing the satisfaction—and the wonder—in his eyes.

He reached for her, and she came down beside him.

"I . . . didn't know . . . that would be . . . so intense," he whispered.

"I thought you might not. My guess is that your partners were pretty conservative."

He stroked her hair, then raised up on one elbow so that he could look down at her.

"That was beyond anything I could imagine. And I want to return the favor."

"I was hoping you would."

"But I've never done that to a woman. My mouth was always busy doing something else."

"Well, you're a wonderful lover. I have every confidence in you."

When he lowered his head to her breast, she remembered he had plenty of experience using his mouth to give pleasure.

"That's so good," she whispered.

He gave her a wicked grin, then trailed his tongue down her body, pausing to play with her navel before finding the hot, swollen folds of her sex.

He was a quick learner. Or more accurately, he was adapting techniques he had already learned. He had made himself into an expert at arousing a woman and bringing her to the peak of sensation, and now he pressed two fingers into her, stroking in and out while he used his mouth and tongue on her labia, then her clit.

But he didn't finish it quickly. Maybe he was acting on the concept that turnabout was fair play, because he brought her close to orgasm, then backed off, until she was writhing on the bed, raising her hips.

"Jules, for God's sake, Jules," she pleaded, grabbing frantically at his hair, and he went back to her clit with his mouth and tongue while he thrust deep into her vagina with his fingers.

She made a high, frantic sound as her inner muscles clamped around those fingers, and she went up in flames. He kept stimulating her until the aftershocks subsided. Then he moved up beside her and gathered her in his arms.

"Thank you," she whispered.

"The pleasure was mine. All of it."

He held her, stroked her, rained small kisses on her face

and neck. And when she felt his cock pressing stiffly against her thigh, she raised her eyebrows. "Are you telling me you're ready for another round?"

The smug expression on his face was priceless. "Maybe this time we can try what I think is called 'the missionary position.'"

"Just so you're willing to try something more adventurous after that."

They spent the night making love. The Viagra combined with his iron constitution was mind-blowing. When it was close to dawn, she raised her head and looked down at him. "I'm exhausted. Do I have to go home for the day?"

His expression turned uncertain. "I'm going to sleep like the dead. Especially after that workout you gave me."

"Do you mind my staying?"

"A little."

She knit her fingers with his. "I'll go if it makes you feel . . . safer."

"No. I have to keep reminding myself that I can trust you completely."

She squeezed his hand tighter. "You can. The way I know I can trust you."

"Yes."

He folded the comforter at the end of the bed, then slipped under the covers, and she settled down beside him.

"If you go downstairs, close the door behind you."

"I will."

After he had fallen asleep, she sat up, stroking back the dark hair from his forehead.

It was still hard for her to grasp that she was in a relationship with a man who was so much more than he had first seemed to be. And it was still hard to come to grips with their future.

They had agreed to be together—for now. But there were things they hadn't talked about in detail. He'd told her that making her like him was dangerous. Was she willing to take the risk? Not yet. Not now. But when she got old, would she change her mind? She didn't know.

All she knew was that, for the present, she and Jules DeMario had something together that she had never imagined. Something good. Was it going too far to call him her soul mate?

She couldn't answer that yet, either.

But she thanked God that she had the time to explore their relationship. She slept for a few hours. When she woke up, she turned to kiss him on the cheek.

He stirred, and his eyes blinked open. For a moment, he looked shocked and confused. Then he focused on her, and he smiled. "I never wake until the next night," he murmured.

"A lot has changed," she said.

"Yes."

"Maybe we'll have you out waterskiing on the gulf."

He managed a sleepy smile. "I doubt it. But we've already done things I never imagined."

"And there's more to come." She pressed her face against his shoulder, loving the feel of his strong arm around her. No couple had a guarantee, but what she saw for herself and Jules was bright with all kinds of possibilities. And maybe forty years from now, they'd have to reevaluate where they were going.

Velvet Night

Rosemary Laurey

Chapter One

Vickie Anderson propped her feet on the porch railings, flaking off old paint in the process, sipped her ice tea, and leaned back in her rocking chair. It had been a long, hot drive from DC, but worth every mile. She hadn't realized how much she needed to get away. Up here she could forget crime, job stresses, and regulations. As the first firefly flickered in the warm June night, Vickie let out a long sigh and tension seeped out of her aching body.

This old house, deep in the Blue Ridge Mountains, was the perfect haven from the pressures of being a cop in the nation's capital. She had the warm night, honeysuckle in the woods, crickets in the long grass, two owls calling to each other in the trees, and the sound of an engine racing up the road.

Who on earth was it? This was the only house this far up the mountain—not counting the old fishing cabin on the lake.

The noise grew louder. Not a car or truck. It was tinnier and shriller, and getting louder by the minute, until a red motorcycle raced around the bend, bringing with it an aura of power and speed, the smell of fuel, and a cloud of dust on the dry road.

Who in the name of sanity was that? The southwest Virginia

representative of Hell's Angels? Whoever it was, they slowed, turned around, and were coming back. Vickie grabbed her empty glass but unbreakable plastic wasn't much use for self-defense. Pity she hadn't brought her gun with her. Was Gramp's shotgun still in the closet beside the fireplace? Did she have time to find it?

As the motorcycle came to a halt, Vickie stood, ready to run for the gun. The rider looked up at her, waving a leather-gauntleted hand as he set the bike on the kickstand. He was tall, covered in black leather like a second skin, his eyes hidden behind the dark visor of the red helmet. If she had any sense, she'd run and pray the spare shotgun shells were still in the Mason jar on top of the fridge.

Instead, she stared like a snared rabbit as he lifted a long leg over the saddle of the bike and turned to face her. "You must be the Andersons' granddaughter," he said, as he unsnapped his chin strap.

Vickie was all ready to say that yes, she was, and armed (fingers crossed) and had four brawny brothers out back. But before the lies of self-defense came to her lips, she looked up at his face, and without quite knowing why, walked over to the porch railing. He came closer, helmet under his arm, a dark mass of curls framing his face.

He paused, just a yard or so away, and from the height of the porch, she looked down at the most compelling pair of dark eyes she'd ever seen. "Hi!" was all she managed to get out. The steamy night was making her breathless.

"Hello!" He smiled. "I'm Pete Falcon. Mrs. Burrows mentioned I'd be having a neighbor for the next few days."

Mrs. Burrows, at the general store and gas, gossiped too much! "I'm Vickie Anderson, just up here for a few days of utter solitude." As heavy a hint as she could drop without actually saying, 'bugger off!'

She should have gone for 'bugger off!' Or should she?

As Pete stepped forward, placing one leather-booted foot on the first step, he moved into the full circle of the light.

Dear heaven! She had the distinct impression she had seen him before—in a "hunk of the month" calendar. He was beautiful: dark eyes glinting in the night, and a wide, full mouth smiling up at her. And tall. Heavens, yes! With broad shoulders that filled his leather jacket. And she was gawking at him! Her tongue was as good as fused to the roof of her mouth—until it flapped loose. "Would you like a glass of tea? Have a seat on the porch." What a stupid thing to say! Especially as he took the rest of the steps two at a time, his leather-clad thighs gleaming in the glare of the porch light.

"Sure. Thanks! It's been a long, dry ride up from Boones Mill."

"Have a seat! I'll get it!"

The screen door crashed behind her as she darted into the house. She all but ran through the living room into the kitchen, grabbing a clean glass from the cabinet, and yanking open the fridge before she made herself calm down. The cool of the freezer soothed her flushed face as she reached in and grabbed a handful of ice. She hadn't asked if he wanted lemon. What the heck, he was getting it!

By the time she squeezed two wedges of lemon into the glass, the panic attack—or whatever it was—had eased. She still wasn't sure exactly why she'd invited a total stranger onto her porch and offered him refreshment. He could be the local rapist for all she knew. Nonsense! He was merely a hot and thirsty biker just ridden up the mountain.

Hot being the operative word.

Vickie had to stop herself from ogling him as she walked back with his tea. He stood at her approach and opened the screen door, closing it carefully so the spring didn't bang, and giving her the perfect chance to ogle his luxuriant blue-black ponytail. He turned back to her and smiled, and her throat went dry. He was close. Too close. And covered in black leather from his boots to his shoulders. His jacket was unzipped at the neck, revealing a vee of male skin and a fine sprinkling of dark hair. As if that wasn't already far too much for comfort, two other zips hung open: one on either side of his chest. For ventilation in the heat, she imagined, but right now, his thin, white undershirt shone against the leather like the moon overhead against the night sky. If she looked a little closer, she was certain she'd see the outline of two dark nipples under the soft, washed cotton.

She was not looking closer! "Here's your tea."

His hand closed over the cool glass, his fingers just missing hers by a hair's breadth. "Thanks."

He stepped away and sat down on the glider. She walked back to her rocker, angling it slightly so he was completely in her line of vision.

He took a long, slow drink, uttered an appreciative "Mmm," and licked his lips. She almost echoed the movement, but remembered, just in time, to take a deep, relaxing breath instead.

A few moments later, he broke the companionable silence. "You're very trusting. You ought to be more careful who you invite into your house."

He was telling *her!* "Should I turf you off my porch then?"

His smile had to be a trick of the light. No one in creation could look that sexy with just a smile—and okay, a glint in his impressive, dark eyes. "Nah. I'm safe enough but there are some roughnecks and reprehensibles around these parts."

He was so dead-on serious, she had to chuckle. "Oh. The Adamses are still around, are they?"

He looked. Just looked. His face stiller than she could have imagined. "You know them?"

"Everyone from here to Roanoke does! If they're lucky, only by reputation. When I was a kid, I was convinced the TV Addams family were named after them, and had no difficulty deciding scary, old Forrest Adams was a vampire."

Her visitor looked almost offended. Another trick of the light. "Yes," he said, "but there's not too many Adamses around anymore."

"All in the county jail again?"

His face relaxed. "A couple of them. There's even a few gone respectable. Just one or two reprobates left."

Quite enough! Vickie shuddered, remembering Sonny Adams rubbing poison ivy on her face, while his brother Micha sat on her. That Micha had also broken out all over had been scant consolation. "You live up this way?" Who wanted to talk about the George County Adams Family?

"Yup. In the house up the end of the road."

"The fishing cabin?"

He nodded. "Yes. I look out on the most magnificent view of the lake from the back porch."

"My grandfather used to take me fishing there. We spent hours on that jetty, with lines and bent nails baited with red worms."

"The dock has been rebuilt. You must come and see it sometime."

If he'd been eighty, she might have accepted, but as it was ... "Thanks." No way! She'd come here for peace of mind, and just these few minutes with Pete whatever-his-name-was, was rapidly disturbing it. "You work down in Boones Mill?"

He shook his head. "In Roanoke. For an environmental group. I cover this part of the state."

That told her nothing, not that she was the least bit interested. She'd just wanted to change the subject from "come and see my jetty." But she couldn't help watching as he tilted the glass and drained the last of his tea. She had to be imagining the way his throat muscles undulated as he swallowed. No way in this light could she see that clearly.

"Thanks for the tea, it hit the spot." Pete set the glass down, smiled again—just to quicken her heartbeat probably—and stood. "I'd better be off."

Yes, he should!

"Ride carefully. The woods are dark." Why was she worried about him? This was a man who could definitely take care of himself.

"I see well in the dark." And his teeth flashed well in the dark, too. "Thanks for the drink."

"You're welcome." She smiled. How could she not, when he took her hand in his, his fingers long and strong but surprisingly cool? So cool, his touch sent goose bumps skittering down her spine. Had to be because he'd been holding his glass.

His eyes gleamed down at her. "Take care, Miz Anderson, and remember what I said: there are some odd types wandering around these days. Just because you're miles from the main road, is no reason not to lock your doors and latch your windows."

And having a sexy hunk in black leather up the mountain was an even better one. "See you!"

She had no idea why she stood on the porch, watching long after his taillight disappeared up the road.

He was an unmitigated idiot! As a new-blooded vampire, he'd been warned often enough that he lacked the control of a mature vamp, but no one warned him he'd be as impulsive as a hormone-crazed teenager. Or even more stupid! He'd all but barged onto Vickie's front porch, just because he'd caught a whiff of human blood and a glimpse of her short, silky hair in the moonlight.

John, his mentor, had warned him to stay away from women for a few years, until he got his impulses under control. Damn good advice it had been too! But Pete Falcon had had to make a lunge for the first woman he glimpsed. Okay, not a lunge precisely. He'd restrained himself that much, and she wasn't the first. He'd seen several in the past few weeks, but Mrs. Burrows down at the shop and gas hardly counted. Neither did any of the other women living hereabouts. But Vickie Anderson! He could feel his fangs descending as he thought about her smile, the silvery, silky sheen of her short, blond hair, and the luscious scent of her body in the moonlight.

The woman sent every single one of his vampire senses into overdrive. And not only his senses. He'd just discovered how uncomfortable a vamp erection was under leathers. Hell, he'd been half-afraid she'd notice it even in the dark.

He slowed the bike as he approached his cabin. This had been one ride where the engine hadn't felt good between his legs.

He needed to be alone and get himself under control before he ventured out again. He had to call John to report in, and needed to feed.

"Nothing so far," Pete said into his cell phone, "and I've covered hundreds of acres. All I've found is that one stand of pot I mentioned last week, and that was so small I think it was for home consumption."

"There has to be something, somewhere," John insisted. "Forget pot for now! We've got crystal meth flooding the area, and we're next thing to certain it's not coming in from outside."

"I'll keep looking. Remember that old road I said might have had tracks that the storm obliterated a few days back? I'll go back there."

"Great! Keep going, Pete. It's there. We just have to find it."

Easier said than done—even a vampire couldn't work miracles, and thinking about that . . ."I need advice." Pete gave a strictly censored account of his new neighbor.

"If you're that interested, I'd say you might be ready for human feeding. Be sure you throw a glamour on her first. You don't want her waking up and screaming in horror. Very upsetting for both of you." Something about John's attitude teed Pete off. "Mind you, once you get the hang of it, it's much easier. Human skin's thinner than the deer and horses you've been using. All it takes is a little nip. Veins are easier to find too."

Pete almost snapped at John. Comparing Vickie Anderson to a horse!

"Be careful, and enjoy yourself!" John gave a totally un- necessary laugh. "It can be fun with mortals! You could call it the ultimate one-night stand."

It took all Pete's self-control not to snap his cell phone shut there and then. Unfortunately he had to listen to a string of suggestions of where to look next, and totally superfluous advice about being careful as they were dealing with desper- ate and ruthless people. Pete had learned, while still a mortal, about desperate and ruthless people.

He snapped his phone shut after agreeing to meet John in Roanoke the night after next.

Outside was warm and soft as dark velvet. As a mortal he'd never fully appreciated the beauty of the night. Pete rev- eled in the calm warmth around him, as much as he did the snap of frost on a crisp winter evening, or the night breeze at the beach. Night was different every time and every place, and wonderful when a fascinating woman slept five miles down the dirt road.

He left his bike and ran towards Vickie's, loping at an easy pace. The moon had risen and cast dappled shadows through the woods on either side. He passed the old logging trail. Later. Right now, he had better things to do.

Vickie's house came into sight. All lights out, even the porch light that had drawn him like a moth to flame when he'd first glimpsed her silver hair and pale face in the night. If his heart still beat, it would be racing. Damn good thing he didn't sweat, or his hands would be clammy and his shirt sticking to his back. His mouth ached as his fangs primed to bite.

Could he do this right? What if he hurt her? Took too much? Suppose he mucked up throwing the glamour and she woke? He paused in the middle of the dry dirt track, and ran his hands over his hair, shaking his head so his ponytail brushed his shoul- ders. Hell, this was too much, too hard. John had not given him enough instruction. It could not be "just" like a deer or horse. Damn! He never got a hard-on over whitetails!

For the first time in nine months, he sorely missed being able to take a deep, calming breath. At least he didn't have an anxious pulse throbbing in his ears. Just a cold weight in the pit of his stomach, and the boner of the century.

Should he go back home and calm down? Prowl the woods a bit until his mind settled? Hell, no! He wanted Vickie Anderson. Needed to feel her warm skin and taste her rich blood. And he'd do it right. As a mortal he'd always made sure his partners received as much pleasure as he did; it wasn't going to be any different now that he was dead.

He'd hold her lovely body in his arms, stroke her short, silky hair with his fingertips, brush her eyelashes with his lips, and ease her smooth skin with kisses before he bit, and he'd make damn sure he left her smiling in her sleep.

He hadn't felt nervous when he walked up her porch steps before. Why this ache in his gut now? Must be his pants, suddenly two sizes too small. Hell, he was hurting. He needed her!

He had to get himself together, or he'd mess this all up. He was vampire. This was part of his nature, how he'd lived. He'd follow his instincts and give her the loving of her life.

He crossed the porch, his footsteps silent in the night. Using his mind, he unlatched the screen door on the inside. Too easy! Even a mortal could have done that. The front-door lock was old and took little effort to open. She needed better protection than that with drug runners lurking in the woods and hollows. Pete grasped the doorknob and turned it slowly. The door opened.

He looked into a neat living room, with old-fashioned furniture, and a braided rug in the middle of the plank floor. An open doorway led through to what looked like a kitchen. To the right a floor fan hummed in the entrance of a darkened room. Behind the noise of the fan, he heard a heartbeat and gentle breathing.

Vickie was so close, he could taste her in his mind. Her skin would be sweet, her blood warm, rich, and heady. Her body soft and supple in his arms. He couldn't wait. Silently, he stepped forward.

And slammed against the metaphysical barrier that barred vampires from mortal homes.

Chapter Two

It took all his control not to wail aloud in frustration. To come this close and hit an unsurmountable and impenetrable obstacle. Why? How? Hadn't she invited him into her house? He slammed his body against the invisible block, clawing at the air with his nails, but nothing shifted. She might just as well be in Antarctica for all the chance he had. Hell, he should be the one in Antarctica. He needed cooling down. Fast.

He stepped back, growling in his mind. It made no sense. She'd asked him in, damn it! Or had she? As he looked around the dark porch and the unmoving glider, he remembered her words, in her light, welcoming voice: "Have a seat on the porch."

That was as far as her invitation went. And as far as he could go.

In his pent-up frustration, he leapt down the steps and ran at full pelt down the road and into the woods, racing as fast as his vampire speed could carry him. Dodging trees and jumping undergrowth, scaring every nocturnal animal for miles around. Clever move, that! Now there wasn't a deer within a couple of miles. He might find a slow-moving possum. The prospect did not appeal.

He leaned against a tree, threw his head back and howled long and loud. It felt better and eased his raging erection, but now even the possums and field mice had fled. He leaned his head back against the rough bark and shut his eyes. He wasn't going to feed tonight unless he was very, very lucky. There was old Mrs. Burrows down at the grocery and gas. He let out a weak chuckle. Plump, chain smoking, and great source of local gossip, Mrs. Burrows and her sagging neck held no appeal.

Hell, he didn't want to feed, except from Vickie. And come to think about it, he wanted more than feeding. Whoa there, boy! Better actually get invited into her house first before he let his horny thoughts get him hard again.

Might as well spend what was left of the night doing what they paid him for.

He was not far from a cleared hollow, so he went in that direction. A nice stand of tobacco in the lower fields, and knee-high meadow grass on the hillsides. Nothing illegal there. Shame. He'd have been delighted to uproot a couple of acres of thriving pot.

He stepped back into the woods, climbed the first sturdy tree he found and peered around. The countryside could be amazingly boring at times. He descended, jumping the last few feet just for the hell of it. Gauging his position by the stars, he started back, coming out of the woods a couple of hundred yards up the old logging road he'd agreed to check. He stood in the shadow of the trees and looked around. There were unmistakable tire tracks in the dirt. Who, in the name of creation, went driving up a disused road that led nowhere?

Definitely worth investigating. A bit of tracking might take his mind off his only slightly abated physical condition. Keeping to the trees, he followed the road half a mile or so, and reluctantly turned back. Dawn came too damn early in summer. But yes, without a doubt, tracks in both directions showed someone was going up and down the road. Regularly.

So, the night hadn't been entirely useless. He'd only failed in the most important part.

Once home, he settled in his day haven. As the sun rose over the mountains, he thought of Vickie, and the way her full lips smiled in the moonlight. In seconds, he was dead to the morning.

Vickie was on her second cup of coffee, looking out across her grandfather's now-overgrown garden, and listening to a woodpecker tapping the walnut tree. The steady rhythm of the bird searching for insects took her back years. She remembered her grandmother sitting beside her, shelling peas or snapping beans, and her grandfather hoeing between the rows and singing to himself. She was so glad they'd decided not to sell when they retired to Hilton Head. The house needed a bit of work, yes, but that she could afford. She'd rather spend money here than on overpriced real estate in the District. Invest a few thousand, and she'd have a retreat waiting whenever she needed one. And given the stress of her job, she needed a bolt hole.

Sitting in the morning warmth, sipping coffee, lost in the quiet of the countryside was the closest to calm she'd known in months. She took another sip of the fragrant coffee, wondering if a week was really going to be long enough. A shot rang across the woods and with a flash of green, the woodpecker fell to earth among the neglected grass.

Vickie was out of her seat before she stopped to think, and saw two men come though the woods from the left.

They were laughing together and didn't even notice her until they were a few yards away.

"Well, hello, little lady," the younger one said.

The sight of his oily smirk brought back nasty memories. "Good morning, Sonny. Mr. Adams," she added, nodding at the older man. Sonny was glaring and Lucas Adams just gaped, revealing tobacco-stained teeth. "Are you in the habit of shooting on my land? If so, I'm going to ask you to stop."

Lucas Adams's weasly eyes narrowed. "It were a wood-pecker," he said, as if that explained everything.

"So I noticed."

"Lookee here," Sonny said. "You just can't let them birds take over. Next thing you know, they start on the house, and before you know it, the place collapses round your ears." He paused. "And I remember you, you're the Andersons' grand-daughter, the one what went off to some preppy school."

Seemed pointless to point out that the house had aluminum siding. "If anything needs shooting, I'll take care of it."

Sonny closed his mouth before asking, "You shoot?"

She crossed over to the tree and looked down at the corpse and the few stray feathers the bird had shed as it fell. "Yes," she replied, fighting back tears at the sight of such destroyed beauty. "And I'm the only one who shoots on my land." Now she would have to dig out her grandfather's shotgun. And by the way the pair of them scowled at her, might as well be prepared to use it.

They walked away, taking the longest way through the grass. Vickie hoped it was full of chiggers.

She buried the woodpecker at the end of an abandoned row of blueberry bushes. Something inside her snapped while throwing the red earth on the still-warm body. What sense-less killing! And what the hell were the Adamses doing shoot-ing on her land?

The bird suitably interred, she strode back into the house, leaving her coffee cooling outside and hauled the gun from the closet. It hadn't been used in yonks. She could take care of that. She could get gun oil and shotgun shells at the gro-cery and gas. It wouldn't hurt to have the word spread around that she was armed and ready. Just in case the Adamses weren't the only ones shooting up the wildlife.

The front door stopped her in her tracks. She knew she'd locked it last night and latched the screen too, but now the front door was open a chink. Must be the old locks no longer held. She'd fix that. A couple of sturdy bolts would do the trick. For those she'd have to drive into Roanoke.

She stopped at the grocery and gas, certain Mrs. Burrows would let the entire county know the Andersons' grand-daughter up from DC was buying up gun oil and shells. Locking the bag in the trunk, Vickie headed down the moun-tain, noticing more than she had yesterday, how things had changed in the past few years: new subdevelopments, a shop-ping center, even an all-night gas and convenience store on 220.

In a large hardware store on the outskirts of Roanoke, she found what she needed: heavy bolts, for the front and back doors, and latches for the screens. While she was here, she might as well take care of the windows, so added a dozen window locks, and for good measure a new screwdriver, to save scouring the house for Gramp's toolbox. That done, she headed for the checkout and turning the corner, all but bumped buggies with Sonny Adams.

"Why if it isn't Vickie Anderson, again!" His grin gave her an unwelcome closeup of two broken teeth. He looked as if he was economizing with razor blades too. On models in *Vogue*, stubble looked sexy—on Sonny it looked scuzzy. "No hard feelings about this morning?" he asked, a greasy lock falling over his forehead.

Vickie looked him over from his straggly hair, to the bro-ken nails and calluses on his hands. He had a buggy loaded with lighter fuel and packets of lye. What on earth was he doing with enough fuel to set fire to half the Blue Ridge? Did she really want to know? If this were back in DC, she'd sus-pect . . . "Okay then?" he asked, taking her hesitation as agreement.

"Sonny," she replied, her voice calm and cold. "If you, your father, or any one of your brothers, cousins, or uncles, step on my land again, you'll leave with buckshot in your hide. Remember that!" Her anger soared as she thought of the beautiful bird now dead under the dirt. Shoving her buggy around Sonny's, she made a beeline for the nearest checkout.

She was still fuming as she drove out of the parking lot. Why was she so upset?

Accumulated stress, no doubt. And, she had to admit to herself, a touch of fear. The Adamses were bad, and now she'd pissed them off. What the hell! She was armed, and by the time she went to bed tonight, she'd have the house locked up like a fortress.

So much for coming here to forget about felons and crime for a few days.

Cup of coffee at her elbow, Vickie dismantled and cleaned the shotgun. For old times' sake, she filled a Mason jar with shells, putting the rest in the drawer in the kitchen table. The cleaned gun she propped behind the pantry door. She'd sleep with it beside her bed.

She was armed. Now to fortify her house.

A screwdriver was woefully inadequate against age-hardened wood. She spent over an hour searching for her grandfather's toolbox, running it to earth in the basement.

The old electric drill still worked, and made the job much easier. The light was failing. She'd better get a move on. She had a new bolt on the screen door and was fixing the first one on the front door, when she heard Pete's motorcycle. When he stopped in front of the house, she smiled. Seconds later, she asked herself why that pleased her. A minute later she knew exactly why. Pete had a killer smile, gleaming dark eyes, long, silky lashes that gave new meaning to "bedroom eyes," and an aura of power that made her feel safe.

Nutty really, but there it was.

"Come in," she said, stepping back from the already open door.

He looked as if she'd given him the moon, the stars, and a couple of universes.

"Thanks, are you busy?" He glanced at the drill in her hand.

"Just fitting new locks."

He stopped almost in mid-stride. "Something happened?"

"I noticed this old lock doesn't hold. So I'm taking care of it. If you can wait a couple of minutes, I'll get you something to drink." Her grandmother's notions of courtesy dictated she leave this and sit with him on the porch, but darn it, she wanted the job done.

He lay his cool hand over hers. "Why not let me do them? Just this one bolt, right?"

"Two here and another couple on the back door. Won't take me long."

"I'll be faster." His hand closed over hers with cool strength. "Let me do them for you."

It was a temptation to accept his offer. She was perfectly capable of doing it herself, but . . . "Thanks." She released her hold on the drill. "Sure you don't mind?"

His night-dark eyelashes flickered as his wide mouth curled at the corners. "Certain. Won't take me more than a couple of minutes."

She couldn't hold back the grin at his macho exaggeration. "Need any help?" She resisted the urge to smooth back the dark curl that fell over his brow as he shook his head.

"I'll manage. A few screws are a piece of cake. Won't even need the drill."

Playing big strong he-man, was he? The role fit him perfectly. "Okay. Want something to drink?"

"Got some of that sweet tea?"

"Would lemonade do instead?"

His eyes creased at the corners when he smiled. "Sure." He reached for a screw from the open packet on the floor. "You get the drinks. I'll take care of the hardware."

She forced herself to walk away as he unzipped his leather jacket. She was not going to stand there and ogle him—no matter how tempted.

The lemonade wasn't exactly fresh squeezed, but not bad considering it came out of a can. She filled two glasses with ice and added a slice of lemon to each before reaching for the pitcher. Picking up both misted glasses, she made her way back into the living room.

Pete had just finished. The man worked fast! "That didn't take you long," she said, holding out the glass.

His forehead creased as he looked up at her. "I don't mess around," he replied. "If it needs doing," he paused, reaching for the glass, "I get it done." He took a long drink and handed the glass back. His lips left a little semicircle in the condensation. "Why not have a seat on the porch and put your feet up and I'll take care of the back door."

She was in the rocker with her feet up before she realized she'd been bulldozed out of her own house. So what? If he was out to steal, he'd be disappointed. She trusted her cop's instincts here. Vickie leaned back as the rocker tilted with her weight, and closed her eyes.

"Vickie?" Pete filled the doorway, propping the screen open with one hand and holding up a window lock in the other. "Want me to fix these too? Won't take me long. You were smart to get them, your window latches are flimsy in the extreme."

Might as well. It was why she'd bought them, after all. "Thanks. Sure it's not asking too much?" The man had come by for company, not manual labor. Who was she kidding? The look in his eyes suggested he wanted way more than lemonade and conversation.

"No prob," he replied, with a smile that convinced her that last thought had been spot-on. "Won't take me long. Seems crazy to leave them in the package when you need them."

Why argue with a man who knew his own mind? Why be so easily persuaded? She wanted those darn locks on. Knew she'd feel safer with them, but hell, now she owed him. Okay, she'd bake him a batch of cookies or fix dinner one evening.

Or . . . her mind went off on a tangent at other repayment possibilities.

Heaven on Sunday, what was she thinking? She was not about to offer sex for services rendered. Shame, really! Being raised respectable was a downright nuisance at times. She'd not say "no" to Pete Falcon's arms around her, her head on his shoulder while he eased his cool hand under her shirt and over her bra. She bet he'd snap it open with one flick of his long fingers. No fumbling and getting hung up over the hooks and eyes for him. And when he brushed his fingertips over her breasts . . .

Pete twisted a brass-headed screw home with his finger. Holding the bolt up with his left hand and setting in the screws with his fingernail was much faster than mucking about with the drill. Faster! It was the difference between snail space and running. Smart woman to get the window locks, too. Trouble was, just being in her bedroom gave him a hard-on. Something about the carved wooden bedhead and the creamy, crocheted spread sent his animal urges rearing.

And verging on the bestial they were too! He pictured Vickie naked under that crocheted spread, sheets drawn up, and one smooth white shoulder showing just enough sweet flesh to tease and stoke his desire. He imagined running his hands over her breasts, and stroking her neck until she dropped her head back, giving him complete access to her perfect vein.

His fangs tingled. Damn! He was hard as a rock again. His own fault this time for letting his imagination run riot. Better get screwing. Wrong verb, that! Pete shifted his hips to ease himself within his pants. Better fix the widow latch.

If only she had air-conditioning and could leave the windows sealed. At least the lower sashes were screwed tight, only the top half opened. Just to be sure, he took a handful of nails from the open toolbox she'd left in the sitting room, and nailed the screen tight to the window frame. No one was taking that out anytime soon.

"You're fast," Vickie said as he walked out onto the porch and reached for the lemonade. Not quite as rich as blood, but in the circumstances, perfectly adequate. "You've done them all?"

"Every last one. Every door and window can be locked up tight." Darn, he should have twiddled his thumbs another twenty minutes, to make it believable. He'd learn—eventually.

"Thanks." Her smile made the misjudgment worthwhile. "I'd have been still doing them at midnight."

"Anytime. Anything else need doing?" Other than herself! Abel, that would have to wait.

"Not right now. I'll only be here a few days." Damn. "I wouldn't have bothered with the locks, but after this morning . . ."

"What happened?" Interrupting her, but . . . "Trouble?"

She brushed off his concern with a shake of her head, biting her lip as if to draw back her words. "Not really. Just the Adamses shooting on my land."

"Shooting? Shooting who? You?" He grabbed her by the shoulders, only just stopping himself from pulling her close to keep her safe. "What were they shooting?"

She gave a quirky little smile as if to apologize. "A woodpecker."

He stared, noticing the glistening in her eyes. Whatever was stressing her was more than a dead bird. He ran his hand up the side of her face to wipe away a tear. To his delight, she let him. She pressed her hands against his chest, before leaning in and resting her face against his shirt. "I hadn't seen one in years. It was so beautiful and they shot it dead!" She gave a little sob, sniffed it back and stepped away. "I'm getting wound up over it, I know, but it was so utterly gorgeous, tapping away on the black walnut tree, and they killed it. I know, I shouldn't be surprised. They are a pair of no-goods if ever there was one. I'd just forgotten how nasty they were."

"Nasty" seemed woefully inadequate, but the last thing he

wanted to do right now was disagree with her. "Did they threaten you?" If they had, he'd yank their balls off.

She shook her head. "No, just did their oily, sleazy, 'we're just being neighborly' act. I told them I'd be the one shooting if I saw them on my land again."

Seemed the backwoods were as dangerous as the projects. "Better be careful. They're not worth manslaughter charges."

Dear heavens. She had a lovely laugh, like wind in the pines, or a summer breeze over long grass. "I don't think buckshot is likely to kill them. All I've got is an old shotgun—not an uzi!"

"You know how to shoot?" Bad move, that. Her eyebrows lifted and an unamused smile twitched the corners of her mouth.

"Yes, I do."

The set of her head and the edge in her voice convinced him she knew how to handle a gun. He just hoped she was on the side of the good guys. Odd that she'd appeared here, right now, when things were coming to a head.

Even odder that he could think that, while his body clearly indicated definite interest. How could it not? She was the closest thing to beautiful he'd ever seen: her skin pale in the night, her fair hair framing her face, and straight shoulders and firm chin clearly indicating she'd still not quite forgiven the slur on her marksmanship.

He wanted to sit down and talk to her. Find out who she was and what she really was doing here. He also wanted to take her to bed and make wild, passionate love all night. And no doubt scare the willies out of her when she saw his fangs. All he could do was visit her in the night. Later. Let her get to sleep first. "Better be going. Let me know if there's anything else you need."

She gave an odd little smile—almost wistful, which didn't seem in character. "Thanks for fixing the locks and bolts."

"My pleasure."

The smile widened. "See you later."

He took it as a promise, almost skipping back to his bike. He had his invitation. He could come and go as he pleased.

He pleased.

He'd be back.

He turned to wave, but she had gone. Locking and bolting the doors, he hoped.

What were those felonious yobs doing on her land? He wasn't having rednecks bothering his woman! He almost laughed. She wasn't his anything—*yet*.

Chapter Three

Just as well Pete had dropped by, or she'd still be wielding a screwdriver, but even better he'd gone. Pete Falcon was too much of a temptation. The last thing she needed was amorous entanglements. She came up here for peace and quiet, not wild and wonderful sex.

Talk about jumping the gun. The man fixes a few bolts and latches as a neighborly gesture, and she's having sex with him in her mind.

Hell, why not? Wasn't it the ultimate in safe sex? And the man was splendid. Just the sort to take a starring role in a few night fantasies.

She gathered up the glasses and put them in a pan of soapy water, along with her supper dishes, and took a long shower to cool off. Locking her window half open, Vickie settled down between the cool sheets.

She was asleep in minutes.

Pete waited two hours after Vickie's bedroom light went out. Now to enter her dreams.

The front door opened to his mind and he stepped into her house. Nothing blocked his way and never would again. She had given him entry, would give him sustenance, and in return he'd fill her dreams with ecstasy.

The crocheted cover was a snowy heap at the foot of her

bed. The pale curtains shifted in the night breeze, and the soft brush of her breath whispered in the silent room. She turned her head to one side, as if offering her neck. One arm she draped across the pillow, the other rested on the sheets pulled down to her waist.

She wore shell-pink satin pajamas. How could she have known he loved the touch of satin against warm skin? He hadn't until this minute.

He was hard, just watching her.

She seemed so frail. So vulnerable. So mortal.

So sexy.

With each gentle breath, her breasts rose and fell under the satin that covered but did nothing to conceal. The soft nubs of her nipples pressed against the pale fabric, her breasts making soft mounds under the satin.

Certain she was asleep, Pete sat on the edge of the bed, watching. He'd thought her beautiful the very first time he set eyes on her, but now, sleeping in the moonlight, she was exquisite. Soft, warm, and relaxed. Her rich, mortal blood, coursing through her veins.

Fixing a few bolts and latches seemed grossly inadequate payment for all that he was about to take. But he could, would, do more. Watch out for her, and keep the Adamses at bay.

Pete's fists clenched at the thought of that lot troubling her. Not much he could do about it while he was dead to everything during daylight, but if they tried anything during his waking hours, he might just ignore John's repeated warnings about harming mortals. He wasn't sure the Adamses counted as human, anyway.

Why blight these moments with Vickie with thoughts of felons and lawbreakers? He had her all to himself and he yearned to feast.

He rested his hand over her left breast to feel the pulse of her mortal heart. Sensation throbbed through every vampire nerve, and rushed straight to his cock. She was magnificent. Naked, she'd be wondrous.

His hand slid over the pink satin, until his fingertips rested on the pulse at the base of her neck. He yearned to bite and feed. Later. He wanted to savor the sleeping woman he lusted after.

It was lust. Blood lust. But lust pure and simple? No. He wanted Vickie skin to skin, ached for her living body curled against his. Dare he strip and climb under the covers? Not this time. He had a night's work ahead of him.

Leaning over, he poised his lips above hers, feeling the sweet brush of her breath, and sensing the life within.

He kissed her. Just brushing lips as he shut his eyes, to better sense her sweet warmth, before pressing her lips until they parted. He resisted the urge to delve deep and caress her tongue with his. Later. For now, he contented himself with lips on lips, as his hand cupped her luscious breast, stroking the living flesh under the satin, and sliding over the lustrous fabric to caress her other breast.

Vickie sighed with pleasure as he kissed harder. Now touching tongue to tongue before lifting his mouth. She let out a little whimper. Disappointed? She wouldn't be.

He cupped both breasts, easing his hands down her torso and pushing aside the sheets as he stroked her belly. Her legs shifted, as if to part for him. He had to fight back the urge to rip apart the satin and enter her sweet warmth hard and deep.

Vampire he was. Animal he was not. He would not take her sleeping. Pleasure her, yes. Feed he must, but no more.

A heavy ache twisted deep inside. If only he could make love with Vickie, hold her in his arms as she consciously gave herself to him.

Yeah, right! Would be nice to fly like vampires in movies too. This was reality. He was not going to fuck her, no matter how strong the desire.

He brushed her warm belly with the flat of his hand, resting a moment on the softness between her hips. He was so tempted to move lower, to cup the heat between her legs.

Better restrain himself. He caught the scent of her arousal. Sweet Vickie. She was almost ready for his bite.

He allowed himself to slide his hands under her pajama top, his sensitive fingers glorying in her warm flesh in his hands, sensing the life under her skin, the blood coursing through her veins.

Soon . . .

Slowly, to prove to himself he was disciplined as much as to relish the anticipation, he popped the tiny pearl buttons one by one, and spread the satin open.

He brushed her already-hard nipples, easing over her breasts, up to the base of her neck. Her pulse was steady, the blood flow strong. His gums itched in anticipation.

He was ready. But was she?

With the pad of his finger, he traced a line up her ear. She arched her neck in readiness. He couldn't hold back his smile. Soon. Very soon. With the back of his hand he caressed the side of her face and stroked her chin. Slowly, he ran his hand over her short, fair hair. She seemed so vulnerable in the night. So fragile. So mortal.

The very substance of the life he lacked and the source of the sustenance he craved.

He kissed her, right at the base of her throat, before covering her neck with gentle kisses: soft and light like the fluttering of a butterfly's wings. Under his caress, she sighed and moaned, turning her head as if to make her neck more available. Pleasure rippled through her. The scent of her arousal filled the quiet room.

His mouth fastened on the base of her neck, on the soft skin that covered her pulse, his lips moving with her heartbeat, his fangs readying, and his mind attuned to her every breath and the rise and fall of her breasts in the dark.

Her heartbeat quickened as her unconscious need matched his rising desire. He pressed closer to the firm pulse under her skin. His fangs descended. Between heartbeats, he bit, piercing the skin with a clean, fast nip, latching tight.

It was as if he were drowning in her essence, floating on her mind and burrowing deep in her soul. He felt her joy and her burgeoning desire. He caught glimpses of anxiety and worry, but felt them slip away in the tide of pleasure that swamped them both. He let his mind drift until it seemed it was touching hers. The taste of her skin, the richness of her blood, and the scent of ready woman, overwhelmed him. He was one with her joy, her arousal, her need. Sensation peaked between them. Aware he was close to the rim of desire, Pete eased his mouth off her neck, and gently licked the wound to seal it.

Her chest rose and fell as fast as if she'd been running. Her head lolled to one side, exposing the small red marks of his fangs. The wounds would heal fast. He hoped the satisfied smile would remain a long, long time.

He wouldn't forget in a hurry.

He was loath to leave her. It stung deep knowing he had to go the way he came. Unseen, unknown, and unremembered. Damn, John hadn't told him the half. Hadn't even mentioned the incredible bond forged between vampire and provider.

Pete looked down at his sleeping love, knowing deep in his soul, he'd established a connection between Vickie and himself for as long as she lived. Worry surfaced like a sear in his heart. Would she ever know? Could he ever tell?

He rebuttoned her pajamas, drew the sheets up to cover her chest, and left the house silently. Leaving a chunk of his heart behind.

Nothing like a good night-prowl to clear the mind. Tonight it didn't work. Maybe he didn't want to clear his mind of Vickie Anderson. Maybe he'd rather dwell on her warm body and rich blood. Maybe thoughts of her smile, her laughing eyes, and the sweet scent of her arousal were more engrossing than searching for a meth lab in the woods.

There was no "maybe" about it!

He was smitten.

New at this vampire life he might be, but he'd been long enough a mortal to recognize the signs. He had it bad. He didn't just have her blood in his veins. Vickie was deep in his mind and heart. Too bad he had a job to do and a report to make tomorrow. He could hardly tell John he'd spent the entire night writing odes to Vickie's breasts! Come to that, no way was he discussing Vickie's breasts, or any other part of her for that matter, with his mentor.

The old logging road needed closer investigation. Might as well start there. He had more than enough energy. He'd never imagined the rush of power that now coursed through him. He almost felt he could fly, like vampires of legend.

He settled for a good, fast run.

He'd seen tracks, but as far as he knew, the road led nowhere. Just petered out in the woods. He kept to the edge, to avoid leaving footprints. His mind was still half on Vickie, and what, if anything, would come of their relationship. What relationship? He almost laughed. What chance was there? Hadn't she mentioned leaving soon? Back to her life, whatever and wherever it was. A life that didn't include a vampire.

Maybe this preoccupation with Vickie made him careless. Perhaps it was truly well hidden. But the first time he noticed the bear trap was as the metal teeth closed around his right ankle, and he fell, face first, into the undergrowth.

Chapter Four

A night sound awakened her: perhaps an owl sighting prey, or a deer too close to the house, maybe a raccoon in the trash. But as Vickie lay, eyes only half-open, her sleep-fuddled mind still trying to recapture her disturbed erotic dream, she heard nothing more. No clink of garbage dragged along the ground, no rustle in the grass.

Maybe thirst woke her. Her mouth felt abnormally dry, her tongue stiff and itchy. She was parched. Vickie rolled over and sat up, swinging her legs to the floor. Not bothering with slippers, she padded into the kitchen and downed two long glasses of ice water. Better. Much better.

Back in bed, she settled to sleep, but couldn't. She was tense, tight and wound up. Who was she kidding? She was horny! Whatever awakened her, disturbed one of the best erotic dreams she'd enjoyed in weeks. Years maybe. Quite possibly ever.

She leaned back on the pillow, looked up at the ceiling, and wondered what it said about her if her subconscious had that sort of thoughts about a nice, gentlemanly neighbor. Sheesh! Let the man stop to give her a hand, and she took his entire body. Damn luscious body it was too! She shut her eyes, trying to remember exactly how she'd dreamed of Pete Falcon without his leathers, without anything except his skin and dark black hair sprinkled over his chest and belly, and thick and curly around his cock. No wonder she was dry-mouthed. She was turning into a sex maniac.

She was soaking wet between her legs. She had trouble even thinking about anything except Pete's lips, hands and glorious body. She was in dire need. Her breasts felt hot and heavy and she ached between her legs.

Rolling onto her face and rubbing herself against the sheets wasn't enough. If anything it made things worse. She turned onto her back, and slipped down her pajama bottoms. Spreading her legs, she gently brushed her bush. Yes! Her body responded at once. She went deeper, parting her vulva to slide her finger over her damp flesh. She pressed two fingers inside, working in and out as she imagined Pete's cock inside her.

Beyond inhibition, she was a wild woman flying on need and desire. Letting her fingers fill her, Vickie rubbed her nub with her other thumb. A jolt of sensation met each touch. Wanting to make it last, she eased the pressure, circling her nub as waves of pleasure thrummed out from her core to all but engulf her mind. She was soaring on a raging tempest of emotion and pleasure. As her arousal built, she worked her thumb faster and harder, magnifying her pleasure, until all she knew was her body's wild need and desire. She was climbing great breakers of joy, vast billows of physical sensation, until she reached the crest. Her mind flew. Her being took off on a wild climax that left her body throbbing as she lay in a sweaty heap. Her heart raced as the last ripples of delight fanned out across her mind and body.

She was so loose as to feel boneless, so satiated as to think she'd never experience such intensity again. Vickie pulled the sheet over her still-heated body and closed her eyes. She'd sleep like a babe after a release like that.

An hour later, she gave up.

Sleep utterly eluded her.

It wasn't tension. She was still relaxed, her body loose, and her mind pretty close to the same condition. She was just unable to settle. Stupid as it seemed, she wanted to walk in the woods and feel the night around her.

And no doubt encounter the Adamses poaching or dynamiting fish.

She'd stay away from the lake. She just needed to stretch her legs. A good brisk walk and she'd no doubt sleep like a log.

Vickie pulled on jeans and T-shirt, and walking boots over her socks. Grabbing a flashlight, and making sure the doors were locked behind her, she set off down the track. She was going in Pete's direction, she admitted that much to herself. She just wouldn't walk that far. The old cabin was a good five miles up the road.

It wasn't even a mile to the old logging road. She hadn't been up here in years. Wasn't sure why she went now. An odd nagging drew her. A sense that something was wrong. Right! Most likely Sonny Adams hunting deer out of season. She ought to go home and read to cure her insomnia. Or clean out the attic, as she'd promised her grandmother. Vickie walked on, the flashlight on full beam now. If Sonny was out here, she'd be sure to scare off the wildlife to thwart him.

She rounded a bend as the road narrowed where the woods encroached on the verges and paused. A dark shape lay huddled to the side of the road. A fallen tree? Wrong shape. Wavering between flight and investigation, Vickie shone her flashlight in that direction, ready to snap it off and freeze if it turned out to be a bear or mountain lion.

She took a step closer as she heard a weak voice call, "Help!"

"Pete?" It was his voice, but sounding wrong. She ran towards him, the beam dancing wildly.

She knelt, as he tried to sit up. "What happened?" Being careful not to dazzle him, she directed the flashlight beam down his body until she saw his foot. She couldn't hold back her gasp. His right foot was tight in the teeth of a bear trap. She'd never actually seen one before—but she'd heard tell of them. This was big enough to take down a bear, let alone a man. The wavering beam of her flashlight revealed mangled and torn skin, blood, and the white glint of bone. No way could she release this with her bare hands. If it was bear-proof it was definitely woman-proof.

"Have you been trapped long?"

"Too damn long," he replied, "but I'm happier than hell to see you here. Often stroll through the woods at night like this?"

If he was trying to lighten things, it wasn't working. "Seldom. You're darn lucky I had insomnia tonight. These things are illegal!"

"You don't say! Can you get me out?" He sounded desperate, his voice tight and sharp.

She stood up. "I hate to leave you. You keep the flashlight. I'm going back to get something to force that trap open."

"Take the flashlight. You need it more."

She wasn't sure about that. Trapped and immobile in the dark, that was the stuff of nightmares. "Keep it, Pete. If only to scare off animals, and it will help me find you when I get back. I'm going to cut across the woods. It's shorter that way."

Shorter, yes. She wasn't sure about faster. In spite of the moon, it was damn dark. Branches and twigs scratched her arms and legs, and a couple swiped her face. She hoped to hell it wasn't poison ivy. She'd worry about that later. As the woods thinned, she ran faster, crossing the road and racing towards her house.

It took forever, rummaging through Gramp's toolbox until she found a crowbar, and stopping to grab bottled water and a first-aid kit. She doubted Band-Aids and Neosporin were adequate, but it was all she had, until she got Pete to the hospital. She grabbed her backpack, shoved it all in and added a blanket and a towel—he was no doubt suffering from shock—and hoisted the lot on her back, gasping at the weight, and set off.

Running.

She went back via the woods. A mistake. The moon had disappeared behind the clouds. Every twig, branch and root seemed intent on tripping or hitting her, and the backpack got heavier by the minute. But by the time she decided the road would have been far quicker, she'd gone too far to turn back. In the distance, she glimpsed the faint beam from her flashlight—she'd been right to insist he keep it. Without that to guide her she'd be stumbling round the woods and breaking something herself. Maybe tripping off another damn trap. That thought slowed her a bit, but a faint "Vickie!" from the direction of the light spurred her on.

"Coming!"

He sounded weak. Heart pounding and blood rushing in her ears, she raced the last few yards, ignoring branches slashing against her face and legs. He was hurt badly—and what if a bear or something came prowling while he was helpless?

The flashlight was lying on the ground, just inches from his limp hand. He'd either fainted or . . ."Pete?" He opened his eyes as she grabbed the flashlight. "I'm back, and I have something to get you out of there."

"You're a saint, an angel, and an answer to prayer," he said, his voice tight and strained. "The metal is biting so hard, I'm helpless."

He must have hit his head. He sounded concussed, as if slipping in and out of consciousness.

"Don't worry, Pete. I'll get you out of this and fetch my car." Not bringing it had been a mistake. No time to dwell on that now. She draped the blanket around his shoulders as he dragged himself to sitting. By the look of the ground, he'd tried to drag himself and the trap, but a chain anchored it to a nearby tree.

Pulling out the crowbar, she set to work.

Releasing the trap was easier said than done. Pete held the flashlight, but the beam wavered as his wrist shook, and the damn trap was rusted together. Gritting her teeth until her arms and shoulders hurt from the effort, Vickie finally pried the teeth apart, being rewarded with a loud metallic scrape as the trap snapped open.

Pete pulled back his injured leg as if the metal were burning, shutting his eyes as he let out a long gasp of relief.

"You are a saint," he repeated. "Vickie, I love you. You saved my life!"

Nice thought, but didn't men always make wild declarations at moments of high stress and relief?

"Not sure I'd go that far, and if I don't get you to a hospital, you might still die of tetanus. When did you last have a shot?"

"Don't worry about that. Let's just make sure this contraption never snares anyone else." He pulled the chain and brought the trap closer. "No wonder they're illegal."

Whoever set it was not likely to let that concern them. And right now her concern was Pete. Even by flashlight, the damage to his leg was clear enough. He'd bled freely. His wounds had to be dirty. The trap was encrusted with rust.

Neosporin was not going to be anywhere near enough.

She pulled out the bottle of water. "Thirsty?" she asked. "You can have some of it, but I need to clean your wounds. I'll bandage them as best I can, and get you to the hospital."

"Don't bother, Vickie. Go home and I'll take care of myself."

Her snort echoed in the night. She hadn't meant to, but macho wasn't in it. "Pete, it's broken. You can't walk on it."

Ignoring him, she twisted the bottle top loose and pulled up his damp and sticky pants leg. "This will be cold, I'm afraid, but it will clean off the worst, and might stem the bleeding." She poured it as gently as she could over the worst of his injuries. The bleeding seemed to have stopped. In the dim light, the gashes didn't seem as bad as she'd first thought. Maybe his blue jeans had protected him. Maybe the light was so bad she couldn't tell.

His leg might not look as bad as she feared, but he did. Haggard wasn't the word. "I don't care what you say, you're going to the hospital. You've lost buckets of blood, and . . ."

"I'm not going to any hospital, Vickie, and that's that!"

Might be more convincing if his voice hadn't wavered at the end. "We'll talk about that later." Once she had him in her car and headed down the mountain. "Want a drink?"

"Thanks." He croaked it out. His eyes were half-shut and sunken in the sockets, and his breathing so shallow as to be unnoticeable. And he didn't want to go to the hospital. Men.

"Here." She moved closer, intending to tilt the bottle as he drank.

He stared at the bottle a few seconds, as if uncertain what to do, before he reached out and grabbed her wrist. He wasn't that weak after all. He jerked her close, a frantic look on his face. The water bottle fell to the ground. Before she could retrieve it, he yanked her arm closer, staring at a long, bleeding scratch.

"Blood!" he said, his voice tight but oddly gentle.

"It's nothing, just a scratch from a . . ." She broke off, horrified, as he licked up the line of the scratch. His tongue was cool and smooth, and in very, very different circumstances, it might have even seemed sexy. Especially as fired up as she'd been earlier, but right now . . .

She stared as he licked up a smaller scratch, pausing to look at her. His eyes gleamed in the night. Hell, they glittered with an odd light. His face took on a strange cast of excitement, anticipation and . . .

She yelped as he bit her wrist.

Cripes! Weird beyond imagining. She tried to move but he held her arm with both hands, his grip not the least like that of a man who'd been semiconscious five minutes earlier.

"Stop it!" she yelled, pulling away. She might as well be trying to move a parked car with her toe. Pete had her in a viselike grip and was sucking her blood.

Dear saints in heaven! What was he doing? Some weird moonlight rite? Kinky, twisted . . .

Warm, soothing, gentle . . .

Vickie sighed as her resistance faded, and she relaxed beside him. Whatever Pete was doing—and way out there it most definitely was—it was . . . incredible.

She shut her eyes and leaned into him, resting her head on his shoulder, and letting her free arm curve around his waist.

Each movement of his lips rushed a thrill of sheer, unadulterated pleasure deep down to her core. Slumped against his chest, she let out little whimpers of delight, as every nerve ending in her body sang to the pressure of his lips. The first pain of his bite was long-forgotten. Wafts of sensation clouded her brain, as her body sank into a great pool of pleasure. She was floating, her mind lost in a great mass of sexual delight.

Unbidden, her hips rocked against his thigh as her sighs became groans of arousal, as the thrill that started between her legs spiraled tighter and higher, her mind lost in a wild haze. She was dimly aware that she was building to a climax, but too fogged in her mind to do anything but rock against him and whimper.

Until he lifted his mouth off her wrist.

From drunken ecstasy, she jerked into stunned awareness.

She was in the middle of the woods, and rolling in the dirt with a strange man.

A *very* strange man.

Still holding her wrist, he looked up. She felt herself impaled by his intent eyes. "Thanks," he said. "I'm sorry it had to be like this."

Like what? This was nuts. Impossible! As she fumbled for words, he ran his tongue over her arm, cleaning off the last drops of blood.

"What the hell were you doing?" she managed at last.

"I was in dire need. I had to feed. The metal of that trap sapped my strength." He paused, licking his lips clean.

"Sorry to presume without asking, but the scent of your blood . . ."

"What are you?"

He was silent a good thirty seconds, the quiet of the woods hovering around them. "Vickie, I'm a vampire."

Chapter Five

Now she did pull her arm away, jumping up and moving to put distance between them. She'd read about types like him. Freaks who fed off blood and called themselves vampires. She just never thought she'd meet one up here. Mind you, given that the Adamses were an example of the locals, she shouldn't be too surprised at a resident bloodsucker.

"I know what you're thinking," Pete said.

"I doubt it."

"You think I'm either weird, crazy or perverted."

Pretty close but if he were any of those, she'd better humor him. She could run faster than him, if push came to shove, but felt no menace from him. Only a lingering joy from his embrace—if that wasn't kinky, what was? She'd worry about her reaction to that later. Right now . . . "I'll get my car and take you to the hospital. You have to need treatment—a tetanus shot if nothing else."

He shook his head. The moon emerged from behind a cloud, and cast dapples of light and shadow, so his skin looked almost transparent in the dark. He did look healthier, less wan, and his eyes had their usual, almost feral, gleam.

That alone was hardly destined to allay her worries. Sexy on her own front porch—where she could lock the door on him—was one thing, but out here in the middle of the woods, when she was feeling hot, aroused and light-headed?

He smiled.

It didn't help one little bit.

"Vickie, I'm not going anywhere near a hospital or a doctor. I know you don't believe me and that's understandable. But I don't need medical attention."

"That's utter nonsense. Are you doctor-phobic or something? Your ankle was mangled by that trap."

"It was broken," he agreed. "*Was*," he repeated. "Look at it now." He stood up.

Her throat clenched. She swallowed, or at least tried to, as a weight seemed to drop in her stomach. It had to be some incredible trick of the moonlight, but when he pulled up his jeans leg, all that was visible was a jagged, raised line of proud flesh, like a newly healed scar.

If it weren't for his blue jeans dark with blood, she'd think she'd imagined it. Maybe she had. Was she hallucinating? She shook her head to clear the buzzing in her ears. It was going dark . . . As if from a distance, Pete said, "Vickie. I didn't mean to scare you."

She was falling, but never hit the ground. "Are you okay?" he asked as she felt her body rise in the air. Before she could answer, everything went black and silent.

When she came to, she was bouncing in his arms, lying slap-hard against his chest as he ran down the road. "Pete?" she said, trying to ease out of his grasp. Might as well try to shift her house off the foundations. He had her in a tight hold. She tried pushing away, feeling constrained by his strength, and close to overwhelmed by his male scent.

"Stop it, Vickie," he muttered. "You came close to causing the first vamp heart failure in history. Keep still, will you? I'm taking you home."

Vickie turned her head to the wind. What speed was he running at? Fast enough to need to hold tight, despite her misgivings. Feeling his strong chest under her fingers rekindled the wild arousal she'd thought satisfied. And as for leaning her head against his shoulder as he ran through the night . . . She was not dwelling on the possibilities.

As they neared the house, Pete slowed to something approaching Olympic runner speed, taking the porch steps two at a time and coming to a halt inches from her front door. She readied herself to be set on her feet. Instead, he shifted her to one arm as he opened the door.

The door she had most certainly locked.

As Pete released his hold, she hoped she could stand on her own two feet. She could. That was something. "I think I'm entitled to a few answers," she said. None too sure where to start her questions.

He nodded. "Later. Right now you need to rest. You also need to replenish your body with fluids. I took a good deal of blood back there."

She was not having this conversation! She was not discussing body fluids with a vampire. She had to be dreaming. She was hallucinating. The Chinese food she'd eaten for dinner had some tainted Oriental spice.

"Get back in bed, Vickie, I'll bring you something to drink."

"No way. I'm making myself a cup of tea."

Pete watched her march into the kitchen, confusion and uncertainty in every step. She was angry and upset, and most likely wished he'd just disappear.

He wasn't going to.

He owed her something. What would have happened to him come sunrise if Vickie hadn't chanced by? She had rescued him. Saved his vampire hide. The trap had had him tight. The iron was fast draining his strength. A few more hours and he'd have been unable to lift his head. He owed his continued existence to Vickie. Who was he kidding? He wanted her. Bad. The taste of her blood in the woods had only rekindled his earlier desire. Hell! It was because he was fixating on the taste and scent of Vickie Anderson, rather than his surroundings, that he'd not noticed the damn bear trap in the first place.

He shouldn't blame her. He was the vampire. The strong, the powerful. She was mere mortal, incredible, sexy, desirable. Ha! Vickie wasn't "mere" anything. She'd saved his frigging life. How many mortals had ever done that? And how many vamps would put themselves in that situation? Heck, he'd even admitted what he was. Not that he could have concealed it. Having a ripped-up leg heal itself was not exactly easy to hide.

What was happening between them? He didn't need to ask that one. Vickie was attracted to him. Her reaction when she bent over him in the woods, hadn't just been neighborly concern.

So, it was mutual lust. He grinned. Nothing quite like it as far as he was concerned. The need that had simmered since he'd fed just after sunset, roared in his mind and stirred his body something wonderful.

Wonderful! Yes, he'd make it wonderful. He'd caress her slowly, taking his time, savoring the softness of her skin, her wondrous curves, and her beautiful breasts. He'd kiss her pink nipples until they hardened under his lips. He wanted to taste her, all of her: the soft roundness of her belly, the smooth insides of the thighs, the sweetness of her core. He couldn't wait until . . .

She banged the kettle on the stove as he stepped into the kitchen. She'd turned the lights on and got the first clear sight of him. He followed her horrified gaze. His right jeans leg was ripped and soaked with blood up to his thigh. As they both stared, a hopeful fly landed on the still-drying blood.

"Pete," she said, her voice not completely steady. "You might be immune to all the normal microbes that attack humans, but do you really want to sit around like that?"

She was right. She was also accepting he'd stay around awhile. And yes, he did look a fright. "Mind if I take a shower?" He was pushing his luck, but . . .

"Give me a minute."

She left him standing in the kitchen, watching the kettle on the flame, but was back in moments. "I put out fresh towels for you. I don't have any clean clothes that will fit but I did find a pair of overalls that belonged to my gramp. They stink of mothballs, but are clean. If you like, I'll fling your clothes in the wash."

"No, thanks." He smiled to take away the sting of his refusal. "Give me a plastic trash bag and I'll take them home with me." He couldn't let her find the camera he carried, or the sealed bags for samples, and especially not the small, but efficient, tranquilizer gun he'd never had occasion to use—yet.

He wrapped them carefully in his undershirt and rolled them up inside his clothes as he stripped off and prepared to step in the shower. Hot first, to get rid of the blood and dirt, followed by a good, cold dousing.

Vickie went into the kitchen. She could not stay in the living room. Listening to Pete Falcon in the shower was way too much at the end of a very long night. Between events in the woods, her wild dreams earlier, Pete's incredible statement that he was a vampire, and the impossibility of a mangled ankle healing miraculously, she was feeling more than a little frazzled. She reached for two mugs. She had no idea if Pete liked mint tea, but she needed soothing.

Or did she?

Maybe a wild night with Pete Falcon was exactly what she needed. Might at least get the man out of her system. He was hot, sexy, and his whole bearing suggested he'd be darn good in bed. He was a kook. He thought he was a vampire. She was nuts to even have him in the house. He'd carried her home in his arms after she fainted, after he'd had an injured ankle that healed before her eyes.

The entire evening had to be a wild stress-induced dream.

Noticing the kettle boiling, she dropped two tea bags in the mugs, poured water from the now-boiling kettle, and reached for the honey.

The object of her lust stood not a yard away. Smiling.

Gramps had never looked this sexy in those overalls. Not in her lifetime at least.

She smiled back at Pete, as she set the cups on the old scrubbed table and sat down. "I made us some tea."

"Thanks." He pulled out another chair. "You need to drink a good bit, Vickie. I took far too much from you, but I was in dire need."

They were back here again, right where she wasn't sure she wanted to go, but . . . "You really did suck my blood, didn't you?"

He nodded. "Yes, out there in the woods, and . . ." He stopped and shook his head, frowning and looking down at his mug before looking up to fix her with his dark eyes. "Your blood healed me and saved my life. I'll owe you forever for that."

"If you are a vampire . . ." Something she still doubted and put down to—she wasn't sure what. "How could you have been dying?"

"Iron can harm us, and the teeth of that trap cut through my flesh to the bone."

She'd seen the injuries—and the incredible healing but even so . . . "I thought it was wooden stakes that did vampires in."

His full lips curled. "You've watched too many 'B' movies. Wood hurts, that's all. Metal hurts too, but saps strength. If I'd still been there at dawn . . ."

"So the sunlight bit is true?" She couldn't believe she was having this conversation.

He nodded. "For those of us who are newly made."

"And you are . . . ?"

He paused, as if deciding how to answer. "I was killed not quite a year ago. My transformation happened only a few hours later."

"Oh!" Woefully inadequate, but the best she could manage. What else could she say? He'd been killed. Should she offer condolences? Or congratulations on joining the undead? Under the circumstances, "Oh!" covered things about as well as anything else.

To fill the silence that seemed to stretch between them, Vickie offered him a spoon and the jar of honey and fished out her own tea bag.

"You believe me," he said as he brushed aside her offer of honey. "I half-expected you to call for men in nice, clean, white jackets."

"Yeah, I believe you," she replied as she stirred honey into her tea. She took a sip to test the heat, hoping perhaps the act of swallowing might remove the sensation of utter amazement that threatened to suffocate her. "I wouldn't have if I hadn't seen your leg heal. But I did." She set the mug down on the table with a clunk, aware she was about to spill it, and watched her hands shake as if palsied.

"I've scared the living daylights out of you, haven't I?" He reached across the table, gathering her hands in his. "I never meant to. I shouldn't have told you but you saved me. I couldn't lie."

"You'd have been hard pressed to come up with a convincing lie after what I saw!" Her giggle was halfway to panic. She was totally confused and getting hot and horny for a vampire. The next giggle came out higher pitched. She had to get herself together . . .

"It's okay," Pete said, raising her hand to his mouth. "I've thrown too much at you. Far too much. I'm sorry."

She looked across the table at Pete Falcon. Took in his now-drying hair, the broad shoulders, covered only by narrow strips of well-washed denim, and the strong hands that held her still-shaking fingers.

She wanted to say something, but had no idea what, and more than words, she wanted . . . He lifted her hand to his mouth and gently kissed her fingertips. Her mouth went dry. Her throat tightened until she could barely swallow, her heart raced, and as for the rest of her body . . . Ridiculous after such a gentle kiss. Until he brushed his lips over her knuckles and she whimpered.

"You want it too, don't you?" he asked.

Vickie nodded.

Pete was up out of his seat in a flash. For the second time that night, he swept her up in his arms. Only this time, it wasn't a stride through the moonlit woods, but a few short steps to her bedroom.

"Sure about this?" he asked again as he slid her down his body and set her on her feet.

She grinned and reached up. Running her hands over the back of his head, she pulled off the band that held his ponytail, and let his still-damp hair spill over his shoulders. "Yes," she replied. "I'm sure."

She might still be dreaming, but never in her wildest moments had she imagined lips like his. Cool. Ardent. Hot. Demanding. Sweeping her along in the strength and desire behind the soft, insistent movements against her mouth. A wild longing stirred deep within her. She kissed him back. As her hands locked behind his head, he wrapped his arms around her and lifted her off the ground, pressing his lips harder against hers. Another muffled whimper, and her mind zapped. Thinking was too much effort and a major distraction. All she knew, all she wanted to know, was the caress of his mouth on hers, and the sweet, cool pressure of his tongue as her lips parted and he came in deep. She responded with a wild, almost animal need.

Long pent-up desire flooded her mind and body. Her tongue returned his caress, until she was taking the lead, demanding more, needing more, wanting everything. Pete took back control, urging and asking as much as she could give. Offering more and more as her hungry desires rose to meet his demands. She was still off the ground. She barely missed it. Pete's power and strength held her, surrounded her, supported her. She eased her hips into his, rubbing her soft belly against the strength of his erection.

This was utter lunacy. Perhaps she'd been sane for far too long.

"Oh, Vickie," Peter muttered as he set her on her feet and looked down at her lust-darkened eyes.

She eased her hands over his near-naked shoulders, caressing his cool skin, before slipping her hand inside the bib of the overall. Right handy garments for what she had in mind.

He chuckled and lifted his mouth off hers. "Out to strip the clothes off me, are you?"

Why not? What she'd already seen suggested the rest would be worth her while. "Yup," she replied, snapping open one buckle. The bib fell and she got a glimpse of his smooth, broad chest, a fine sprinkling of dark hair, and one dark nipple, that was every bit as beautiful as she imagined that first evening. Brushing aside the bib to get a better view of Pete's definitely splendid chest, she leaned forward and gently licked his nipple. In seconds, it was hard and proud. Sure proof that his desire equaled hers. "I'm quite sure," she said, and released the second buckle.

The too-large overalls were around his ankles.

She stared and gasped.

She'd wanted to feel more skin, but such total, utter and exquisite nudity was . . .

All her wildest dreams come true.

Beautiful was woefully inadequate.

Incredible was a pathetic attempt to describe the sight before her eyes: blue-black hair spilled over his broad shoulders, lying dark against pale skin in the night. She rested her hand on his wide, strong chest, brushing the scattering of dark hair that narrowed and thickened to a dark cloud of curls at his groin. Curls that drew all her attention to his rampant cock.

She licked her lips as blood pounded in her ears and the wild fluttering in her belly spread, until her entire body thrummed with desire.

"Pete," she whispered, her voice low and tight.

"Like what you see?"

Vickie grinned at the mix of male arrogance and suppressed anxiety that tinged his question. "You betcha, fella!"

She brushed her finger over his proud nipple, slowly tracing a line down his chest, over his navel and . . .

He grabbed her hand. "Something's wrong here. I'm naked and you're still clothed. Can't have that!"

"Do something about it then."

His "something" was to gather her in his arms, and dump her on the crocheted spread. She purred in anticipation as Pete ran his hands up her legs, and brushed gentle circles on her belly.

Her breasts rose and fell with her hastened breathing. "I want you, Pete," she whispered, meeting dark eyes that gleamed with the same fire that burned deep inside her.

Pete kissed her. Softly. Just brushing lips. "You've got me, Vickie." He eased his hands under her T-shirt and gently cupped her firm breasts. She responded immediately, her nipples hardening under his touch. The sweet scent of her arousal filled the quiet room. She wanted him. His heart swelled till it seemed to fill his chest. She was never going to forget this night. Ever.

He'd do anything and everything he knew to make it incredible for her. He eased up her T-shirt, sliding one hand up her back, setting the flat of his hand between her shoulder blades, as he raised her up, slipping off her shirt with his other hand. It took seconds to snap open her bra and drop it on the floor.

She was utterly beautiful. He'd been attracted the first time he saw her. Smitten earlier this evening. Now he was lost. Totally.

He kissed each breast, fluttering his tongue over each firm nipple, drawing the warm flesh into his mouth until she sighed. "Vickie, you are incredible," he whispered. He kissed over her breasts, down to her warm belly. He couldn't hold back his grin. His touch aroused her, and he wasn't stopping until she was totally fulfilled.

He cupped both breasts with his hands. "Your breasts are lovely. Perfect size, too." He eased a hand down and inside the waistband of her jeans. "While I sit here admiring your breasts, you're still not naked."

"Do something about it then, buster."

Who'd refuse that offer? He had her jeans unsnapped faster than she could follow with mortal eyes, and peeled the worn denim down her legs. While he was at it, he whisked off her white cotton panties.

She gave a little gasp as she realized she was naked. "Showing off your vampire speed?"

"Sweetheart, I've only just started." He wanted to love her all night, but he'd taken so much blood. He knew how weak she was, even if she didn't, but he owed her satisfaction after all she'd done for him.

And she was so ready!

The scent of sexy woman filled the room, or maybe it was his own pent-up desires that magnified her blatant need.

"Are you going to grin at me all night or are you going to . . ." She broke off with a gasp as his mouth fastened on her breast.

Her gasp gave way to little sexy mewls as he suckled one nipple, while his fingers played with the other one. They were hard, pert and sweetly warm.

Just like Vickie Anderson.

She was woman. He was vampire. And he wanted her more than he'd wanted a second chance at life.

She was so marvelous: her gasps, her little sighs, the way she arched on the bed while his hands caressed her belly. When he reached her pussy, she let out a deep, long sigh as he parted her folds and spread her open, so he could feast his eyes and senses.

And his vampire desire.

She was so ready, how could he withstand her want and his need? Setting himself between her spread thighs, he held her hips steady as he eased into her warmth. Her sighs greeted his slow entry. Her cries and gasps of pleasure matched his thrusts. They came together in a wild crescendo of joy that left her limp and sweaty, and him astounded.

She lay spent and gasping on the bed, her eyes misty, and her body flushed with the after-ripples of her orgasm.

Pete rested his hand on her face. "Sleep, Vickie," he said. "Sleep."

She was softly snoring by the time he pulled on his clothes and let himself out of the house.

Chapter Six

Sunshine woke her. How late was it? Not that it mattered. She was in no hurry to wake after her fantastic—and verging on the incredible—dreams. Her night had been filled with Pete—nothing wrong with that, apart from the awful images of his mangled leg caught in a bear trap. But in the way of dreams, his leg healed, and that was when it really went wild. He told her he was a vampire and had carried her home. And made passionate love to her, if her memory was to be trusted.

Come to think of it, she must have climaxed in her dreams. She was wet between her legs and more relaxed than after a full-body massage.

She'd also thrown off her pajamas while she slept.

How on earth had she managed that? She got out of bed to retrieve her discarded jammies, and noticed the damp towels on the bathroom floor.

She never dropped towels on the floor. As she bent to pick up the wet heap, she recognized them as the spare towels she'd set out for Pete in her dream. Either she was sleepwalking to act out her dreams, or Pete *had* been in her house last night. Which meant . . .

Vickie sat down on the toilet lid, staring at the bundle of damp towels. It could not be true, but as she looked around, the clothes she'd worn last night were spread over her bedroom floor. She never left her clothes on the floor.

Had Pete really been here? Nonsense, it had to have been a dream. It couldn't be true. Vampires? Self-healing wounds? Mind-numbing sex? No! She'd just been without it so long, was attracted to Pete, and her subconscious had done the rest. She ought to thank her subconscious for the best sex she'd never had. Or had she?

It was too damn real to be a dream and her sated, relaxed body was not her imagination. But it couldn't have happened. Pete did not carry her home and sit at her kitchen table drinking mint tea, his glorious dark hair damp after a sojourn in her shower.

This needed some good, hard thinking about. A drive up the road to the old fishing cabin where Pete claimed to live might not be a bad idea. On the other hand, perhaps going straight home was a wise move. No way! Whatever had or had not happened between them, she needed to know for sure. Sure about what? That her nearest neighbor was a vampire and she'd had sex with him and yearned for more?

She had been dreaming!

And right now, someone was hammering on the door. Vickie was tempted to ignore it, but she reached for clean shorts and T-shirt. Might as well see who it was.

One glance through the glass panel in the door and she regretted that decision. It was Sonny Adams.

Vickie left the screen door latched. Just stood in the doorway. No way was Sonny crossing the threshold into rooms that held thoughts—or dreams—of Pete.

"You been having trouble up here?" Sonny asked, after barely acknowledging her cool greeting.

"What sort of trouble?" She restrained herself from saying, *None, until you knocked on my door.* Grandma would have said it was rude.

"Outsiders, people who don't belong. Poking around where they have no business."

"Sonny, you're the only person I've seen this morning."

"What about last night?"

She'd like that answered herself, but Sonny Adams was not the one to help. "What was there to see?"

He shrugged. "Just wondered. Looks as though someone's been up this away. That guy up in the old fishing place, you seen him?"

Quite possibly, everything there was to see of him. "I saw him go by on his motorcycle." Complete truth, that. She gave a sigh. "Why not ask him?"

"He int there. The place is all shut up. Sure you int seen him?"

"You're the first person I've seen since I woke up. Besides, what are you getting upset about? It's summer. There's bound to be people about. We're darn lucky we don't get campers and picnickers up here!"

That prospect wiped out Sonny's measly attempts at a smile. He muttered on about people poking where they had no business. Which was a bit rich considering the reputation his family had for poaching. With a parting exhortation to be sure to tell him if she saw anyone, he shambled back to his battered pickup.

Vickie was about to shut the door on him when she spied her backpack. Crammed inside were the flashlight, first-aid kit, and blanket she'd taken out last night. Pete must have brought them back after he left. Which meant she hadn't dreamed it all.

Two empty mugs, still smelling slightly of mint, sitting in the kitchen, pretty much confirmed things. One cup she might have made for herself, but two . . .

She plugged in the kettle. This needed some good, hard thinking about. Maybe she'd think better after a dose of caffeine. Maybe she needed something stronger, but it was only—she glanced at the clock over the range—eleven, and she needed a clear head.

Given that last night was not part of her REM sleep, then

it really happened. She did find Pete Falcon in a bear trap. He did suck her blood. She watched his ripped and torn flesh heal. He carried her home, and they ended up having incredible sex for hours.

Was she hallucinating? Suffering delusions?

If the answer was *yes*, she'd better hotfoot it back home and make an appointment with the police psychiatrist. If the answer was *no* then she was facing a new perception of reality.

So, her nearest neighbor was a vampire and she'd had sex with him. And yearned for more. Somehow there was a connection between Pete and her, an understanding, and intimacy she'd never known before.

Dammit, Pete owed her a few explanations.

Not even stopping for the much-needed coffee, Vickie delayed only enough to slip on socks and sneakers, and grab her car keys. Minutes later she was heading up the mountain towards the old fishing cabin.

She should have listened to Sonny. There was no reply to her knock. Shades were pulled down on the closed windows. She noticed recent repairs to the siding and roof, but wherever Pete was, he wasn't at home.

Yet she couldn't push away the conviction that he was nearby.

It was a nice day. He might be out fishing. Vickie walked around the back and headed for the pier. Pete's motorbike stood gleaming in the lean-to out back. He couldn't be that far, but a short walk up and down the lake bank showed no sign of him, and the boat was still anchored on the dock.

She gave up.

Pausing just long enough to tuck a note in the screen door, asking Pete to drop by later, Vickie drove back down the mountain, going right on past her house when she saw Lucas Adams sitting on her front steps.

She pretended not to see him or hear his call as she sped around the bend.

Cowardly perhaps, but she'd had her fill of that lot.

Lunch had been a good idea. She was ravenous and thirsty. Hadn't Pete warned her to drink to replace the fluids he'd taken? The movie matinee wasn't quite so smart. With a choice between *Interview with the Vampire* and a *Terminator* movie, she opted for the vampires. She might have been better off with the shoot-'em-up. True, she'd always had a thing for Brad Pitt, but as a means of sorting out her confusion over the past night, it was a lousy choice.

And pretty much convinced her she'd dreamed the whole affair. Pete had as much in common with Louis and Lestat as he did with Sonny Adams. Besides, vampires were fiction. Except that Pete was one. There, she'd thought it! Pete Falcon, the man up the mountain she rather hankered after, was a vampire. And if what happened last night happened, she'd also had rather glorious sex with a vampire. In that case, real-life vampires differed greatly from the fictional variety. If "real-life vampires" wasn't an oxymoron.

She'd give herself brain strain in a minute!

What she needed was a nice, safe brush with normalcy. She'd asked Pete to come by. She'd fix him dinner and see if she couldn't get some answers about whatever the hell was going on in her neighborhood. A trip to the Winn Dixie gave her the fixings, and a couple of hours at home, frying chicken, making homemade lemonade, and cutting up potatoes for salad, kept her mind away from thoughts of vampires, and the nagging anxiety of the Adamses. She did not want to dwell on the very possible connection between Sonny and his felonious father and the bear trap, but she couldn't block out the odd encounter in the drugstore. Maybe she was being too much a cop on holiday, but if she'd seen that in DC, her first thought would be *crystal meth production* and she knew the

Adamses well enough to know they were capable of just about anything.

Vickie's brief note perplexed Pete. *Please drop by this evening* could mean anything from: *I'm pissed and want an explanation* to *You're going to get lucky again, fella!* and everything in between.

It didn't help that an evening with Vickie, even if she intended to chew him out, was infinitely more welcome than a session reporting to John—with little to report. He was not much further on than when he arrived, other than knowing that there were people out to discourage exploration in a certain area of the woods. Very determined, in fact. After he'd recovered Vickie's backpack and Florence Nightingale package, he'd spent what was left of the night searching the area and found two more equally nasty traps.

He wheeled out his bike, and headed on down the road.

"Pete!" Vickie said with a sexy smile as she let him in. She looked at him shyly for a second or two and then reached out.

He wrapped her in his arms, pressing her warm, living body close. "Vickie, my love," he muttered against her mouth, as he closed his lips over hers.

She let out a little sexy sigh and invaded his mouth with her tongue. He was tempted to race across the mountaintops with her in his arms but settled for kissing her back and easing his hand down to her waist. Her soft flesh was warm as happiness. She had not rejected him. Maybe she didn't understand the ramifications of his life. How could she? He was only learning the advantages and drawbacks of revenance himself. But with Vickie in his arms, nothing else mattered. He shifted the angle of his mouth, cupping the back of her head with his hand, holding her steady, while he took over the kiss, easing into her mouth, brushing the tip of his tongue over hers, and caressing her lips. He let out a groan as she met his need with her increasing desire. Damn! He could smell her need. He had his arms wrapped around a woman who wanted him. He wanted to shout his love aloud until it echoed off the mountains. He wanted to stay with her. He wanted to make love to her until he sensed dawn in the offing. He needed her as male needed female. He wanted more. Much, much more, and he was due in Roanoke in John's office in forty-five minutes.

"What's the matter?" Vickie pulled back as if sensing his irritation.

"I can't stay."

Her disappointment blew like a cold draft across his soul. She didn't ask why, or why not. Just looked at him with her big, gray eyes. "I'd fixed us dinner."

She had! He caught aromas of fried chicken, and something sweet like the pies his mother used to bake for the family. Vickie didn't understand.

"Never mind," she said with a shrug. "If you can't stay, you can't."

"It's not that at all," he said, his need to make her understand but not compromise his cover, warring in his head and heart. "I'd give anything to stay, Vickie, but I have to go. It's work."

She nodded. "I know about work taking over," she said. "That's why I came up here, to get away."

He pulled her close and dropped a soft kiss on her forehead. "Vickie, love, I don't eat—at least not solid food. I feed other ways."

She pulled back, staying in the circle of his arms, but giving herself space to look up at him. "Yes. I learned that last night, didn't I? I half-thought I'd dreamt it all, but I didn't. You're a vampire, you feed off blood."

She sounded resigned, angry, and perplexed all at the same time. "Do you mind that much?"

"I honestly don't know. I don't know what's real, fictional, or utterly impossible anymore."

He framed her face in his hands. The pulse at the base of

her neck beat under his thumb, underscoring the vast gulf between their existences. He should probably go down to John's, demand a new assignment and never come back. But to do so would kill his soul the way that enforcer's bullet had killed his body. "Vickie, there's a lot I have to tell you, things I have to explain, make you understand. If I come by tomorrow, will you be here?"

The kiss she gave him answered that question.

Chapter Seven

"You've been busy, Falcon."

At least John wasn't complaining—yet. "I wish I'd actually found something, but we're talking about covering a lot of ground. I'll concentrate on the area beyond the traps."

"Be more careful next time. You can't count on that young woman rescuing you again, and why the hell weren't you wearing ankle boots?"

Pete treated the question as rhetorical. "When do you want me to report back?"

"Same time next week—but before you nip off to the backwoods, we need to do something about this young woman."

Every nerve in Pete's body bristled. "Such as?"

"She broke your cover. She could blow the whole thing apart."

"Rubbish! She knows I'm a vampire, that's it." Okay, it was a leap beyond most people's reality, but . . . "It will be fine."

"You can't be sure." He could. His cop's instincts told him so. "Maybe she set the trap, so she could playact the rescue." Yeah, and playacted the rest of the evening—not that he had any intention of sharing those details with John. "What do you think?"

"I think it's a shame I can't break your nose so it stays smashed."

John raised both eyebrows. "Like that, is it?"

"Like what?"

"You took a live feeding from her and the effect went to your head."

It hadn't been his head. "I needed her blood, damn it. My ankle was cut to the bone. Without her sustenance I'd have been crawling home."

"And with it?"

Pete refused to blush. Dammit, why was John acting as if consorting with Vickie was a crime? "She saved me, John. Without her intervention, I'd still have been lying there when the sun came up. You might forget that. I never will."

"I don't deny you owe her a life debt, but that's not all between you, is it? This isn't just feeding or a sense of obligation."

"What the hell do you mean?" Pete growled.

"I'm three hundred years old, Pete. I can recognize a man in love when I see one."

John's almost gentle words hit like a blow between the eyes. Was he in love with Vickie? Was it possible? He barely knew her. She'd saved his life. Her blood sustained him. Didn't that create a bond? Hell, yes! A bond he wanted to renew repeatedly for eternity. John was right, this could get tricky. "What the hell do I do now?"

John gave a little smile and rested his hand on Pete's shoulder. "Only you can decide, but take it from me, it's smart to stay uninvolved with mortals. It avoids endless complications."

Now he told him! No, he'd told him before, many times. "I never realized I'd feel this way about her."

"Time will soon resolve it, Pete. Once this job is over, you could be across the country somewhere. The break will come naturally enough."

His face must have shown exactly how much that prospect slammed into his guts—like a spiral twisting up to his heart. It might no longer beat, but hell, it ached.

John shook his head, sadness in his eyes. "There's no other way, Pete. Trust me. Wind this assignment up. Soon. Get us a nice arrest and you'll have your pick of assignments."

Pete stood. "I'll hold you to that."

John nodded. "Before you go there's a couple of things . . ."

Pete raced home, ignoring trivialities like speed limits, and wishing Virginia was one of the enlightened states that didn't legislate about helmets. Hell, he wasn't worried about head injuries and a little wind in his hair might clear out his confused thoughts.

John had made it darn clear: somewhere out there was a meth lab. All Pete had to do was find it and grab the operators. Might as well be looking for a needle in a haystack! It was only just past one A.M.; he had a good few hours before dawn. Time to scout out a few more square miles.

First, he had to see Vickie. This late she was no doubt fast asleep, but . . .

As he neared the bend just before her house, he cut the engine and wheeled his Monster bike. No point in waking her if she was asleep. He'd have no trouble getting in.

John was right. Pete Falcon had it bad, and it was fantastic. He and Vickie did need to have a good long talk. If she felt the same, he'd damn well find a way for them to be together.

He left his bike in front of the porch, peeled off his jacket, draped it over his bike and had one foot on the first step, when he heard a noise.

Every vampire sense alert, he stopped. He wasn't the only one here.

He rounded the corner of the house, fury boiling his brain. A dark figure, perched on a box or crate, was peering in Vickie's window. The head shifted from side to side, trying to sneak a peek between the gap in her curtains.

Pete only just remembered to rein in his strength. He leapt forward. Instead of killing—which the asshole deserved—

Pete grabbed him by the shoulders and threw him to the ground. The intruder fell in a heap, felling the upended trash can he'd been perched on. Pete was tempted to shove him in it, and cram the lid on—permanently.

Instead he left him lying on the ground, and turned away. Mistake, that.

Two sweaty hands closed around Pete's neck just as he heard Vickie call, "Who's there?"

She was awake, and no doubt terrified. As Pete broke the bozo's hold with one hand, he grabbed his shirtfront and recognized the younger of the Adams pair. Typical! Add peeping Tom and stalker to his other crimes.

Reminding himself not to strangle the scuzzball, Pete hissed, "Get lost!"

Sonny snarled and brought his knee up to Pete's crotch. Pete let him, grinning as Sonny hit home.

The look on his face made Pete laugh. "That's enough." As he muttered promises of the alterations he'd be delighted to effect on Sonny's anatomy, he heard Vickie call out, "What the hell is going on out there?" Without waiting for an answer, a shotgun blast exploded just feet away, and a spray of lead shot stung Pete's back and shoulders. Damn, if he'd only kept on his jacket.

The shot burned like fire, but he was strong enough to keep hold of Sonny and drag him to the front porch. "It's okay, Vickie," he called. "I'm here."

The front door opened with a blaze of light, and a blazing Vickie, in a short sleep shirt, shotgun at the ready. Sonny seemed to think she was there to be ogled. A quick thump upside of his head fixed that.

"What the hell is going on?" she repeated.

"Miz Anderson," Sonny began. Out of curiosity, Pete let him continue. "I was just walking down the road and caught this here outsider, lurking round the back of your house. Now, worrying about you being a woman all alone, I ax him what he's doing, and he went for me like a wild coon." He tried to shake off Pete's hold. Pete let him try. "I don't know what it's coming to when a woman can't be safe in her own home, and when a little neighborly concern gets greeted with violence. Why, he threw me plumb to the ground and . . ."

Pete couldn't hold back the guffaw any longer.

"What the hell's so funny then?" Sonny demanded. "If you ax me, Miz Anderson, you should call the cops."

"No need, Sonny. I *am* a cop."

That was news to both of them. Sonny gasped in the night. Pete would learn more later. He'd ask. Come to think of it, what did he know about her?

"Well then," Sonny went on, "you should be arresting this here outsider for prowling. I'd seen him! You need to know what's been going on here . . ."

Vickie's burst of laughter rang in the warm night. "Sonny, I can guess. You used to stand under the monkey bars at school to look up the girls' dresses and you haven't changed."

"Lookee here . . ." Sonny started.

"Vickie," Pete asked, "you okay?"

"Other than being disturbed by flying trash cans in the middle of the night? Fine. I'll be even finer when you get lost, Sonny. Be glad I'm not arresting you. Aren't you still on probation?"

Seemed even thickos like Adams knew when they were beaten. He slunk off down the road, muttering to himself, and casting snarls over his shoulder that would have done credit to Frank Langella.

And just in time. Pete's back and shoulder stung like hell. A couple more minutes and he'd have had a hard time keeping hold of the sneak. "I'm glad you believed me," he said, putting his foot on the first step. He was going to have to take care of his back, or rather she was.

"It wasn't hard." She grinned. "Want to come in?" She held open the door.

"Please!" He smiled at her and walked towards the light.

"Pete," Vickie gasped, putting her hand on his shoulder and turning him. "What happened?"

"You nailed me with that buckshot of yours."

He heard her intake of breath and her quickened heartbeat.

"It's metal. It's hurting you, isn't it? Have a seat in here." She helped him into the kitchen, turned on lights, and filled a kettle with water. "I'll get them out. Oh, Pete, I'm so sorry! I heard noise and the trash can going over and thought it was a raccoon until I heard voices..." She paused, grabbing towels and a bowl, and leaving for a minute to come back with tweezers and gauze.

"I'm going to have to use metal tweezers to take it out. Will that hurt worse?"

"Just get them out, Vickie, please. I'd do it myself but I can't reach back there."

She unbuttoned his shirt and eased it off his shoulders. Had to be the best thing that had happened to him all evening. "You're bleeding like nobody's business, Pete." She paused for several seconds. "Will you need blood?"

Just as well she was behind him and couldn't see the grin on his face. Saints and angels bless her. She was offering herself . . . later, please later. After he stopped hurting and she stemmed the slow sapping of his strength. "Later, love. How about get the stuff out first? I'm not much use to you with my strength oozing away like this."

She'd done this to him. She'd thought she was shooting *away* from the noise. She'd spared Sonny Adams and clobbered Pete. Her mouth went dry. It was done; she had to fix it. "Let me sterilize these and . . ."

"Don't waste time, Vickie! Sepsis is not a concern. Just wash my back off and get digging."

Despite that, she bathed his back with peroxide. Not that it helped a great deal. He was still bleeding like a stuck pig.

She picked up the tweezers, wiped off the first wound and poked.

Digging into his living flesh—okay, unliving flesh—was not exactly her idea of fun, but she had to get them out.

The first bit was easier than she expected. So was the second. The third one took a bit more digging, but as she dropped the little pellet on a pad of gauze, she gasped. The first wound was completely healed! Spurred on, she worked faster after that, marveling as his flesh healed over once the little lead pellet came out. But it still took her ages. She never realized how many little lead balls they crammed into one shotgun shell.

Pete said little, just gave the odd grunt or wince as she dug deep for a tricky shot. With his fast healing, it was easy to see progress. She dropped the last little pellet onto the gauze, stood back and watched as the final injuries healed before her eyes.

He looked over his shoulder and grinned. "Thanks. I'm glad that's over."

So was she. "You know," she said, crossing to the sink to wash her hands, and dump the bundle of gauze, bloody towel, and shots into the trash, "if I had any doubts about the vampire, undead, revenant issue, this evening cleared them all up. You really *are* a vampire!"

Chapter Eight

Right now, he held the future of their relationship in his hands. Forget mind games, glamours and dreams. She deserved the truth. All of it.

Pete nodded. "Yes, love. Does it bother you?"

"I really don't know," Vickie replied. "I half-convinced myself I dreamt last night, but I know darn well I'm not dreaming this."

He stood up and crossed the yard or so between them. "It's all real, Vickie. Very real. Can you handle it?"

She thought about that as she washed and dried her hands, folding the towel carefully to give her a few more seconds. She smiled. "Pete, love. I have no idea if I can handle it. Heck, I barely know you. But I do know I want you."

"Maybe we need to have a good, long talk."

"Afterwards!"

He knew better than to argue. He swept her into his arms. "So glad we're in agreement. Let's go check out your bedroom. Make sure there are no bogeymen under the bed!"

"I can walk, you know."

"I know, but I like having you warm in my arms. Gives me all sorts of naughty, sexy ideas."

Her giggle felt like a warm breeze over his skin. She was

everything he'd ever dreamed of, sexy, loving, courageous, and if appearances were to be trusted—his. She leaned her head against his chest, her soft hair brushing under his chin. "How nice," she whispered.

He couldn't agree more. But just in case she changed her mind about messing around with a vampire, Pete darted across the sitting room and into her bedroom, pulling back the bedclothes with one hand, before laying her gently on the pillows. Her nightshirt was rucked up at the top of her thighs, giving him a tantalizing glimpse of her pussy. One peek was nowhere near enough. The sweet scent of her arousal stirred his mind—and his cock to immediate attention. "This comes off," he said, lifting the hem.

With a grin and a little sexy sigh, she lifted her hips and half sat up, as he pulled the soft cotton over her head. He'd thought her fantastic last night. Renewed acquaintance cemented that opinion. He sat on the edge of the bed, and grinned.

"Going to sit there all night smirking?"

She had to be kidding. "What do you think?" He trailed a finger down the side of her face and tilted up her chin.

Her eyes glowed with desire and a sexy little smile quirked the corners of her mouth. And what a mouth. Time to stop lollygagging around. He bent over. She raised her head to meet his lips. A wonderfully enticing sigh escaped from deep in her throat as they kissed. Her lips were every bit as sweet as he remembered. The caress of her tongue sent wild ripples through his mind.

He deepened the kiss, as her sighs and her quickening pulse echoed in his ears. He lifted his mouth. "Vickie, you are incredible. Wonderful. My beautiful mortal, I love you."

That was the goddamn crux of his dilemma and for right now, John's admonitions could go hang.

"This is almost too much," Vickie gasped, as her breasts rose and fell with her breathing. "You, loving you. Loving a vampire!" She gave a gasp.

"Get used to it," he said, putting a little growl in his voice. "Because I need you."

"You do?"

"Hell, yes! You saved me twice, after all. Not many mortals manage that."

"True," she agreed, the corners of her mouth twitching a little. "Doesn't that mean you owe me?"

"Owe you what?"

She leaned back on the pillow, meeting his eyes with a steady gaze and an unmistakable smirk. "I'll think about that while you kiss my breasts!"

With an invitation like that, what hormonally inspired man or vampire could follow John's advice?

Her nipples were warm and sweet to his lips, and soft— but not for long. They hardened alluringly under his tongue, coming to ripe, firm points that just begged to be sucked some more. He took her left nipple in his mouth, suckling as if to draw life and sustenance. Her heartbeat was steady against his ear as his mind and soul basked in the warmth and love that was Vickie Anderson. He moved to her right breast, marveling at the joy to be found in her arms. Her hands tunneled through his hair, stroking his head, as she crooned soft sighs of need.

He'd be only too delighted to oblige.

He kissed the pale skin of her rib cage, and the fullness of her breasts, trailing a line of kisses down her chest to her navel, resting his face against the softness of her belly, and relishing the headiness of her arousal.

Sweet moonlight, Vickie desired him! He'd never disappoint her. He stroked her thighs and she opened her legs. Wide. As if in need of more embrace. In need of him.

He slid lower on the bed, until he lay between her thighs,

her beautiful pussy just inches from his face. Gently he opened her soft folds, and smiled at the sight of glistening, aroused woman.

His mouth came down. She let out a groan of pleasure that became a cry as his tongue found her core. Her body rocked, her back arched, and he grasped her hips to hold her where he wanted her.

It didn't take long. Her need was as tightly wound as his. All it took was a few gentle strokes of his tongue, his lips soft on her aroused flesh, and she came, yelling aloud her satisfaction, as her hips left the bed. Her body stiffened with her climax, and then sagged limp and lovely on the mattress. Her breasts heaved with her hastened breathing, her racing heartbeat echoing in the little room. Limply she rolled on one side, and propped herself up on her elbow. "That was incredible!"

"Just like you, my love."

"Why, thank you." A little dimple appeared in her left cheek. "Yes, it was wonderful, but please don't tell me it's all over."

No way! "What more do you anticipate?"

"For starters, I'd like to see you naked."

Sheesh! He'd been so hot for her, he'd not even stopped to take his pants off. And they were so damn tight they verged on uncomfortable. "I can take care of that."

Pete was off the bed, his shoes kicked off and his pants unzipped, in seconds. A couple more and he was back on the bed, leaving everything in an untidy heap on the floor.

"Better?" he asked, kneeling up.

"Much," she agreed, rolling over to get a better view. Her eyes widened with shock as she looked at him. "What happened?" She reached out to his cock, pausing a few inches from him.

Feeling the warmth of her hand, he looked down. Dammit! No wonder she'd hesitated. He was lucky she wasn't gasping with shock. He was bruised purple from nuts to knob and most places in between. "What the hell happened?" she repeated.

"Sonny Adams kneed me in the family jewels."

She stroked him with the soft tips of her fingers. "Does it hurt?"

He shook his head. "It's a bit tender, but that's all." Her blasted buckshot had burned, his cock felt tight, but that could just be because he'd never been this hard in his life.

Her mouth quirked up at the corners. "Sonny knees you in the groin and you stay standing?"

"Yup!" He had to grin. "I think it rather nonplused him."

She let out a lovely, sexy laugh. "I imagine he's still trying to figure that one out. It was no doubt supposed to lay you flat."

"Didn't work."

"No," she agreed, her breath catching as she closed her fingers around him. "Sure it doesn't hurt?"

"You don't have to treat it like spun glass. Don't let looks deceive you. I bruise up as fast as I heal."

"I see." He doubted it, but he could explain—later. "Sure it doesn't hurt?" He shook his head. "Isn't there something I can do?"

"You could kiss it better."

She rolled her eyes, her breasts jiggling as she chuckled. "For that smart-ass comment you deserve to be thrown out into the night, but . . ." She rolled on her belly and scooted to face him. "I'd miss so much!"

He almost cried out as her mouth closed over him. Holding her head, he closed his eyes, threw his head back, and lost himself in sensation. Sweet moonlight, she had a magnificent mouth.

And it went on and on . . .

How could her mouth be soft, firm, sweet, wet, and demanding all at the very same time? How could she reduce him to a quivering mass but make him feel like a warrior or a king, with a single sweep of her tongue along the side of his cock?

She moved her head back and forth as her lips circled his cock in a glorious, dragged-out caress. It was enough to make a man shout to the skies. Hell! His groans were echoing off the low ceiling. He straightened his neck and smiled down at her. As if sensing his gaze, she looked up, and he almost lost it there and then. The sight of his cock, all but hidden by her sweet lips, and the sparkle of delight in her eyes, just about finished him.

He couldn't last much longer. Didn't want to!

"Vickie," he muttered, easing off. "You're undoing me. Can't wait any longer."

He settled her back on the pillows. Spread her legs. Knelt between her thighs and, lifting her hips slightly, drove deep into her warmth.

She was so wet, so ready and so . . . his.

He stroked slowly at first, hoping to prolong the pleasure for both of them, but she was as ready as he was. Her hips rocked with his rhythm, and when her inner muscles tightened around his cock, it finished him.

He drove in deeper, hearing his own groans echoing inside his skull, until he came with a great burst of joy, shouting her name. Vickie came seconds later, surrounding him with warmth. Staying deep inside her, he wrapped his arms around her soft body, and rolled them both on their sides. She smiled up at him, eyes misty with satiation. "You're not stopping there, are you?"

"I took blood twice last night," he replied. "You can only spare so much."

"What about doing it for me?"

"Tomorrow," he promised.

"Don't you need it? You said metal weakens you. Lead shot is metal."

He nodded. "Vickie, between your shooting at and having your wicked will of me in bed, I am what you might call . . . depleted." He grinned. "But I'll last. All I have to do is ride my Monster a few miles up the road. Even a mere mortal could do that."

"Casting aspersions on mere mortals?" She frowned. "You've just had a very nice time with a mere mortal."

"Vickie, you're no 'mere' anything. You're mine." To prove his point, he shifted his hips and moved inside her. "Remember?"

"As if I'm likely to forget in a hurry." She kissed him full on the mouth before rolling on her back and letting him slip out of her. "I can wait until tomorrow." She grinned. "Wouldn't want to deplete you."

His hand eased over her breast. "I'll be full strength when I return."

She kissed him again, leaning into his shoulder, sighing with utter pleasure and satisfaction. "Pete, this is the wildest thing. I come up here to get away for a few days, and meet you. Three days ago, I didn't believe in vampires, and now . . ."

"What were you trying to get away from?" Sneaky perhaps but, heck, he wanted to know more about her.

"I'm a cop in DC," she went on, "and just once in a while I have to get clean away."

"That was lousy shooting for a cop."

"That old shotgun shoots low. I'd forgotten. I aimed high but not high enough. Sorry."

"It wasn't your gun?"

"My grandfather's. This is my grandparents' house. After my parents died, my grandparents raised me. They moved to Hilton Head six years ago, and I promised to keep an eye on the house. It makes a wonderful bolt hole. I love my job, but sometimes, I need a total break."

"Yeah!" That he knew only too well.

"What about you?" Vickie asked. "You said you were

down here working for an environmental group. As a vampire?"

Time for a bit of the truth. "That's my cover, Vickie. I'm a new vampire, a friend lent me the cabin."

"How new?"

"I was killed a little over a year ago." There, he'd said it.

Her heartbeat raced in the silence. "Hell almighty, I've just had sex with a dead man!"

He longed to wrap her in his arms but hesitated. "I'm not dead, Vickie. I was, for a few hours, but I'm not anymore. It's a different level of living."

Vickie let out a nervous laugh. "That's one way of putting it."

She was upset, but not upset enough to pitch him out of her bed—not yet at least. "Does it bother you more than it did last night?"

"Last night I thought I was dreaming. I woke up convinced I was. But now . . ." She looked up into his eyes. "I'm not." She paused. "Not wishing to sound snippy or anything, but all your talk of loving me, and me being yours. How exactly does a vampire handle that sort of thing?"

"Since I'm new at this vampire lark, I'm doing it the way I always have—except I never met anyone quite like you, Vickie. I'm feeling pretty poleaxed one way and another."

She wrapped him in her arms, drawing him close so his head rested against her luscious breasts. "Oh, Pete." Her voice caught. "I've never met anyone quite like you either." She let out a little laugh. "And they say cops see everything!" It didn't sound like a complaint. "Think you can come spend a weekend in DC?"

Could he? "Got a nice, safe, light-proof place for me during the day?"

"Dracula could go about in daylight, why can't you?"

Should have expected something like this. "He was a few hundred years older than I am." He hadn't even had his first rebirthday yet. "Plus, he was fiction. I'm stuck with the night for a while." Like the next fifty years, if John was right. He'd break that to her later. "I don't turn into a bat, or a large dog either, don't float around in a mist, and can't fly."

A little furrow appeared between her eyes as she pondered that added data. "I'll admit I was curious about the flying bit." She kissed him on the nose. "I'll be happy to settle for what I've got. And yes, I think I can fix up a light-proof room. I live in a duplex, and there's a finished basement a former tenant set up as a darkroom. I'll put a cot down there or do you use a coffin?"

"Another myth."

She snuggled close. "Seems I've got a lot to learn about vampires." She chuckled. "*The cop and the vampire*! Sounds like a title for a romance novel."

Sounded like problems with the division, but heck, he'd cope. Nothing was keeping him from Vickie. "You've been a cop long?"

"Seven years. I joined right after graduating from college." And to think he'd suspected her of being involved in the local drug trade.

"And you come up here when you need a break?"

"Yeah. I was beginning to think this was turning into a busman's holiday though."

"Why? Meeting me?"

She shook her head. "No . . ."

"What?"

"There's something going on up here. I've been of two minds to call the sheriff, but I've nothing but a suspicion." He waited for her to go on. "Could be I just dislike them so, I'm ready to suspect them of anything, but I saw Sonny Adams buying the drugstore out of lye and cold capsules."

Heaven help him! "Sure about it?"

"Sure I saw him? Hell, yes. Could be they are spring cleaning, or stripping furniture and someone in the family has severe allergies, but they're ingredients for crystal meth. I should call the sheriff and ask if it's a problem around here. I wouldn't put it past that lot to be manufacturing."

Time to fill in the blanks. "There is a local problem. I've spent the past six weeks scouring the woods for the lab. Either it's well-hidden or they keep moving."

That appeared to shock her more than the revelation he was dead. "Why would you be looking for a meth lab?"

"I'm with the DEA."

"I see." He suspected she really didn't. "Vampires work for the DEA?"

"Paranormal division of the DEA." No point in mentioning the werewolves and ghouls yet.

He heard her swallow. Well, he'd have a hard time believing it, if he wasn't already dead.

"What happened?"

"I was a DEA agent and got shot. One of the team working with me was a vamp. He turned me."

"Does it hurt?" she asked after a long silence.

"Being shot? Yes, worse than buckshot, but not for long."

"No, you big lug. I mean getting turned into a vampire!"

He stared at her. "Not hurt," he replied cautiously, "but there is a lot of sensation."

Her eyebrows rose as she considered this. "Pleasurable sensation?"

He nodded. One more time when he needed a deep, calming breath. "Don't give me that look, Vickie! It wasn't *that* sort of pleasurable!"

"I see." She pursed her lips like his second-grade teacher when she'd caught him and a buddy throwing a toilet roll around the boys' bathroom. "What sort of pleasurable was it?"

Fair enough question, he supposed. Putting it into words wasn't easy. "Remember when you were a kid, and you'd lie on your back on the grass in summer, and look up at the sky until you felt light-headed? Everything was quiet and the sun warmed you and if you shut your eyes you could feel the earth rotate. You'd be perfectly happy and utterly relaxed."

"Until someone called you in to dinner, or told you to go clean your room."

He grinned with relief. She understood! "Right. Apart from the bit about cleaning your room. I was totally relaxed and utterly peaceful. I didn't hurt anymore. Everything went quiet and misty, until it went black, and later I woke up, as a vampire."

She rolled away from him, settling on her stomach. "Sounds awfully easy, but I bet it isn't."

"Not easy, no. I miss the sunlight, even dream of sunsets sometimes. And the diet gets monotonous. You can't imagine how I felt when you offered me fried chicken—used to be one of my favorite meals. We can drink, but no longer digest solid food," he paused, "but all in all it beats the alternative."

"Yeah." She went very quiet again, running her hand through her hair. "We should be comparing notes about the Adamses, but I don't want that lot in my bed. All I want is you!"

How could any man, alive or undead, refuse that invitation?

He pulled her close, so they lay like spoons in a drawer, her ass curled nicely into his belly, his erection fitting perfectly in the crack of her bottom. He cupped her breast with one hand. With his other he ruffled her short hair back and forth. She let out a contented sigh, and pressed closer.

He thought he'd burst with the emotion burning inside. He was in love up to his eyeballs. Drowning, smothering in it in fact, and had never been happier—alive or vampire. Right, and he was slap-bang in the middle of an investigation, had just about compromised it (at least from John's point of view) and was utterly and totally content. And horny again.

He wanted her. Needed her. Not just for her blood, or her wonderful body. He needed her spirit and humanity. He needed Vickie. His hand eased down her belly and cupped her pussy. With a little sigh, she moved one thigh over the other, opening herself to him. He'd be a churl to refuse her obvious invitation and their mutual need.

Brushing her neck and shoulders with soft, feathery kisses, he had her moaning with pleasure as he eased inside.

A low groan of sheer wonder echoed inside his skull. Never had he known such joy. When had any man, living or undead, felt such utter bliss? He rocked his hips against her butt, pressing deeper and using his muscles to rock his cock inside her. Her arousal peaked as she made little sexy grunts. Her hands reached back to clutch him, as he held her shoulders steady and drove in deeper. She came with a shout of exhaltation, his own cries of satisfaction melding with hers.

They both sagged on the bed. As he eased out of her, she rolled over, nestling her head against his chest as he curled his arm around her shoulders. "I love you, Pete," she whispered, her eyes bright with fatigue and satiation.

She fell asleep in his arms.

Her breasts rose and fell under his hand. He tasted the saltiness of her skin. She was so gloriously and deliciously mortal. He should leave. He was dead beat. He needed blood. He couldn't take more from her. The woods teemed with wildlife, thank goodness. He was in dire need. Between the bear trap and Vickie's exploit with the shotgun, his body was depleted. Lesson there: wear a bulletproof vest at all times. Heck, if he'd just kept his jacket on it would have helped. It was still sitting on his Monster. He'd fetch them both in a minute, after he spent a little more time with Vickie. How could he walk out right after making love? Impossible!

He wanted a little longer with her warmth curled against him. After feeding from a deer and a good day's rest, he'd be fine. Tomorrow he'd get back to searching, but it was like looking for a needle in a haystack. He'd be better off trying to buy the stuff, and tracing backwards. This tramping through the woods was less than productive—apart from getting rescued by the love of his life. Or should it be "love of his death?" "Love of his revenance?" Whatever it was, it complicated things, but if John thought he was giving Vickie up, his supervisor had another think coming.

If need be, he'd take a vacation. Spend the next few weeks with Vickie.

Pete found himself relaxing against her sweet warmth. Finally he gave up even thinking, and dozed beside her.

It wasn't day sleep, it wasn't rest. It was pure contentment.

Chapter Nine

The smell of the coming dawn brought him back to his senses. He had five, at most ten minutes before sunrise. As he leapt out of bed and reached for his clothes, Vickie stirred. "I wasn't dreaming. I'd offer to cook breakfast, but . . ."

"I'd offer to stay and keep you company, but dawn is coming. I have to get back to safety."

She was out of bed and reaching for her robe. "Ohmigod! You have to go."

"It's okay. The motorbike will get me up the road in minutes. No prob. I'll be back tonight. Go back to sleep."

Typically, she ignored him. Pulling on her robe and running after him. She reached the top of the porch steps as he stood, shocked, staring at his Monster.

"Pete!" she called. He only half-heard her. He was still gawking at his slashed tires when she ran up beside him.

"Sonny," she hissed.

He didn't doubt she was right. The man intended to inconvenience him and like as not was terminating him. Pete looked up at the ever-lightening sky. "I'll never get back there in time," he said, half to himself. He wouldn't even have time for regrets or a proper good-bye. He grabbed Vickie's hand.

"Can't you leave the bike here and run?"

If only. "I'm weakened. I planned on resting to restore myself. I'll never get up there in time."

Her hand tightened in his. "No prob. Come back to my house."

"No good, love. I need a sealed room where the sun can't penetrate." He wasn't letting her witness this. Better find a spot deep in the woods and wait for the end. Dammit. He wanted to live, for Vickie.

"Come on, you big lug." She stepped away and yanked his arm. "Get a move on. I've got the root cellar. It's as dark as a dungeon. Gramps used to call it 'the coal mine.'"

It was so slender a hope. But more than he'd had a second earlier . . . "Where?"

He ran back with her, hand in hand, into the house, slamming the door behind them, shutting out the warmth of the slowly rising sun. "Vickie?" What if it didn't work?

"Help me!" She was tugging at a corner of the worn carpet. "I've got to move this and the table."

He pushed the table and chairs aside. She rolled back the carpet and reached to the floor, pulling open a trap door. "It's damp, and probably full of spiders," she said, "but it's dark."

She wasn't kidding. He stared down at uneven wooden steps and blessed darkness. "Can you see enough to get down there?" she asked. "I'll get a flashlight and blankets."

"I don't need a flashlight."

"I do. I'm not risking a broken leg. I don't heal like you do."

He ran down the rickety steps. Definitely cool and underground but dry and, more importantly, dark. As he looked around the packed earth floor for a resting place, a wavering flashlight beam showed where Vickie was descending the steps.

"Be careful," he said, crossing back to the foot of the steps.

"I am. Catch!" She threw him a bundle of blankets.

"I'll get you a pillow."

He hadn't the heart to tell her that when he was deep in day sleep, he'd not notice if he lay on a bed of nails. He spread out the blanket against the northern wall and settled on the pillow she brought from her own bed, a pillow still smelling of Vickie and lovemaking.

She knelt beside him, the flashlight beam playing on old stone walls and dark corners. "What should I do about the bike?"

Good question. He told her how to slip it into neutral and move it off the road, adding the number of Mike the Bike Man in Roanoke. "He'll come fix it." He could smell the approaching dawn. "Better close the trap door."

Her lips brushed his. "I'll take care of everything." The air around him shifted as she stood up and walked toward the steps. The light beam danced and receded. The trapdoor came down. He let the dark embrace him. As the sun rose in the heavens, day sleep engulfed him.

Vickie rolled the carpet back over the trap door and prayed the root cellar was as dark as she remembered. Used to be the only light was from chinks in the trap door. With the carpet and a couple of extra quilts she spread on top of it, the light was blocked—she hoped.

Not much she could do about that now.

Better save her energies for what she could do.

She pulled on shorts and a T-shirt and walked back down the road, taking Pete's ignition keys with her. She picked up his jacket, damp from the dew on the grass. Slipping her arms in the sleeves brought back memories of sleeping in the circle of his arms.

The bike was massive and very red in the morning light. She hoped he was right about it being easy to move. Vickie turned the grip on the handlebars, put the Monster—most aptly named—into neutral, released the kickstand, and gingerly wheeled the bike towards her house. It wasn't that hard. Awkward, and bumpy over her graveled drive, but she managed, wheeling it at last around the back of the carport.

She wanted it out of sight. No point in letting Sonny even think he'd inconvenienced Pete.

She put the coffeemaker on and collapsed into a chair. She was dead beat. Making love half the night took energy. She'd need that coffee. She had work to do while Pete slept.

She called Mike the Bike Man, who promised to send someone up as soon as possible. That taken care of, she took her coffee and cornflakes onto the porch to think. Where, in the hundreds of acres around her, would a couple of felons set up a meth lab?

Back in the house, she opened the drawer at the base of the bookcase and pulled out all the large-scale hiking maps. They were old and yellowed but showed all the trails, some long overgrown.

Some while later, Vickie stood up and stretched. And grinned. She might be wrong but it was worth a look. She was tempted to go on her own, but would wait for Pete. This was not a solo job.

It was hours before dusk, and she'd been up all night with Pete. Might as well catch up on sleep, as she doubted she'd get much after he woke. Grinning at that prospect, Vickie slid between the sheets that still smelled of Pete.

She was halfway to dozing when the doorbell rang.

If that were any sort of Adams, even old granny from the nursing home in Boones Mill, she'd spit.

It was Joe from Mike the Bike, complete with spanking-new tires.

At least she'd sorted that out. Joe's truck bumped off down the mountain and Vickie finally got her nap.

It helped. She woke late afternoon, refreshed, ravenous and deeply conscious that Pete was asleep under her feet. Or was he dead? He'd called it "day sleep."

She took care of her hunger by making a nice, thick ham sandwich. If Pete were a different sort of man, she'd be thinking of fixing dinner, but as it was . . . At least he was darn easy to feed. Her heart seemed to catch. Twice. He would feed— off her. Her body warmed at the prospect. Her heart raced. If she didn't get ahold of herself, she'd need to change her panties. She'd never been this needy or aroused before.

She'd never made love to a vampire before!

Good thing she was sitting down. Just thinking about that sent her head into a spin and her need a notch higher. If she went on at this rate, she'd be leaping his bones the minute he woke.

Meanwhile, she might as well give a last look over the maps. She spread the one she needed on the table, held it down with one hand, and set the sandwich plate on the other corner.

She was in mid-chew when the cellar door opened.

She looked up and there was Pete in the doorway. Her mouth went dry. It took a huge effort to swallow the half-chewed chunk of ham and Roman Meal.

"Hi," she said, when she finally downed the mouthful. "Did you sleep well?"

"Best day's sleep I've ever had. Knowing you were close made all the difference."

She'd made the mistake of taking another bite. It was almost the end of her but worth it to have him cross the room in a nanosecond and pat her on the back. The kiss on her cheek wasn't half bad either.

She swallowed fast and gulped a mouthful of tea to clear her throat. "I'm glad you're okay. The bike's fine and I've been thinking." She looked up at his eyes. He'd obviously been thinking too—and having a few interesting dreams himself, to judge by the front of his leather pants. "About the Adamses."

He raised his wonderfully dark eyebrows. "Do we really have to? I've got a good hour or so before I need to start my prowl."

It was a distinct temptation, but she was a cop and the law came before wild, animal urges. "I have an idea where they might have set up their lab."

"Assuming there is one." He pulled the chair out beside hers and sat down.

Having Pete this close was wondrous, and wondrously distracting. "I doubt Sonny is refinishing furniture for a living."

Pete nodded. "Wouldn't argue with that."

She stood up and held out her hand. "Let me show you."

He glanced at her spread map and shook his head. "Vickie, my love, I've gone over the ground umpteen times. I even caught a whiff that had me hopeful, but decided it had to be a pack of feral cats."

So he'd smelled it, had he? Bingo! "It wasn't. It was the lab."

"If it's out there, it's hidden damn well."

"It's hidden damn well."

He had the grace to listen. He was definitely a man—okay, vampire—to keep. But right now . . . "I know these woods. Grew up here until I was sent away to boarding school and still roamed them in the summers. You've searched the woods, several times, okay. Have you looked under them?"

His face lit with interest. "In caves?"

"Let me show you." Pete held down one side of the map, watching intently as her finger traced up the line of the old logging road and off on a marked footpath, to a faded, inked-in circle. "Here's the ruins of an old cabin. My grandfather always said the chimneys dated from colonial days."

"I've been over the ruins, Vickie. It was close to there I caught a whiff." He paused. "The caves are near there?"

"The cabin was built over the caves. I only went in them once. Grandpa took me but made me promise never to go inside on my own. There's one large chamber. They must have used it as a cellar once. It even has rough-cut steps leading down. There are other chambers leading off but we never explored those. They have to have it vented somehow, but the caves aren't deep, they probably cut a few outlets."

"Damn lucky they haven't blown the side off the mountain."

Couldn't argue with that. "I don't think safety is any more of a concern than abiding with the law."

"Can you explain how to get into these caves?"

"I can do better than that. I'll show you."

"It's too dangerous!"

"Pete. I'm a cop."

Pete felt his forehead crease as he scowled. He didn't like the option one iota but she was right. And he'd bet she was a damn good cop at that. She'd make a good detective by the look of things. "Show me, and then you come right back, agreed? This is out of your jurisdiction."

"You'll need a good flashlight and a helmet if you're going in."

"Vickie, I can see in the dark. I'll carry the flashlight for you."

It took over an hour, walking through the woods, rather than the road, to avoid notice. By the time they reached the ruined cabin, Vickie needed the flashlight even if Pete didn't. The moon hadn't risen and it was pitch dark.

"Show me where the entry is," he said. "Then I'll take you home."

It was on the tip of her tongue to argue but this was his investigation. "Okay."

It took her a while. Without the flashlight, she'd never have found it at all. The tree her grandfather had used as a marker was fallen, and undergrowth—she hoped it wasn't poison ivy—covered the old doorway. She paced around until she noticed a cluster of fir trees, with broken and bent branches. "Here. I think."

He pushed aside the branches and crawled through, motioning her to stay back. She compromised by peering over his shoulder. There, quite improbably, was an old door weighted down with boulders. Pete lifted one corner and peered in. The whiff of cat's pee pretty much suggested they weren't growing mushrooms down there. He set the door back down and eased back under the trees. "Vickie, you are incredible! I'm off to report this. You stay inside and safe, okay?"

Vickie nodded and didn't even cross her fingers. She'd keep her word. It wouldn't be easy, but getting in the way of a bunch of vampires wasn't a wise move. "What are you going to do?"

"Take you home." He scooped her up in his arms, planting a rather splendid kiss on her mouth. Just when she was thinking about distracting him from his job, he lifted his mouth. "Right now."

He held her tight against his chest, one arm under her knees, the other around her back. She'd be a liar to say she didn't thoroughly enjoy the sensation. Last time he carried her, she'd been halfway to shell-shocked. This time, her mind and senses were in top gear. As he ran through the woods, she did the frail female thing and clung to his shoulders. She relished the security and power of his body. It wasn't just her mind that appreciated him. Her body was keyed up, aroused and ready. And from what he'd just told her, he was going to drop her on her doorstep and run.

He should. He was a cop—okay, a Fed—a bit of an irregular one, yes, but still he was on a job. She wished roaring success to his investigation. Putting the Adamses out of circulation for a good long while could only benefit the entire country. Plus, what this would do for his career.

She was jolted out of her thoughts as he set her on her feet on her porch. He'd run the hour-or-so walk in ten minutes, if that.

He was leaving her. Right now. He had to. He should. He . . .

"I've got an hour," he said. "Then I must go."

She didn't waste time asking what he planned for that hour. She had the door unlocked in seconds, and all but dragged him inside. Not that he needed much enticing.

He pushed the door shut with his elbow, took her key and locked up, and whisked her into the bedroom.

Her breath jammed up tight in her throat as she looked at him: tall, male and imposing, an almost-feral gleam in his eyes, and his wide lips curling in a grin. "Got something on your mind?"

He nodded slowly. "Bet I can get naked before you can."

Blatantly unfair advantage! He was half-naked before she kicked off her shoes and unzipped her shorts. Why complain? While she pulled off her T-shirt and unsnapped her bra, she had an eyeful of naked, aroused vampire. Not a sight one came across every day of the week. Might as well make the best of it. She glanced up at the clock. They still had fifty-six minutes.

Pete lolled on her bed, leaning against the head, one foot flat on the bed, his other leg dangling off the mattress, toes brushing the hooked carpet. Astoundingly male and arrogant, yes, but not without justification. He was magnificent, and all hers!

Resting her right hand on his nice, firm thigh, she knelt by his knee, eyes fixed on his impressive erection, and moistening her lips in anticipation. Heart thudding with excitement, she leaned forward and took the head of his cock between her lips. Excitement shivered through her, as he hardened even more under her gentle touch. Breathing hard, she held her lips around him for several moments, before she took him into her mouth.

He was so strong, so firm, so male. Her heart thudded with joy, as he muttered, "Vickie, you are fantastic!"

A groan escaped him as she ran her tongue over the smooth head of his cock and up the side. His hands stroked her hair as she worked her mouth up and down. His need matched her own. She could taste his desire, and sense the rising passion between them. She'd make the most of every minute they had.

"Vickie!" he said, easing her head up and away from him. "Better stop, my love, or this will be the shortest fuck in history."

She grinned. "Think so?"

"Right!" He yanked her up onto the bed beside him. Holding her chin between his fingers, he brushed his lips against hers. "Think I can't make it last, do you?"

"Fast or slow, Pete Falcon, you're worth the trouble."

"You said it!"

His mouth came down, hard, certain and determined. Melding his need and her want. She opened to him, welcoming the caress of his tongue and the sweet touch of his lips. She was adrift in a sea of passion, an ocean of desire, pressing against him in her need. A little moan slipped out, as her hands caressed his chest and eased over his shoulders. She wanted him, all of him, his being and his body. She had to break the kiss to catch her breath—and met his gleaming eyes as she tunneled her hands though his dark curls, pulling off the band that held his ponytail in place. Midnight-dark curls spilled over his shoulders in a soft wave of sensuality.

He pushed her down on the pillow. "My turn."

"Fast" was woefully inadequate when it came to describing Pete Falcon. He had her thighs apart before she took another breath. He bent down, his hair brushing her thighs, pausing a minute as he looked up. "You are so goddamn sexy, Vickie, I'm having trouble lying on my stomach!"

"That's my fault? And it's a problem?"

"I can stand it."

She bet he could! Whether she could stand it was another matter entirely. One touch of the tip of his tongue and she all but came off the bed. He fastened his mouth on her and her hips bucked and her back arched. His strong hands grasped her hips, holding her still, as his mouth worked its magic.

By the time he finished, she was a quivering mass of female need, and begging him for more.

That delighted Pete to the very depths of his vampire soul. Vickie needed him, did she? Hell, it was mutual. It raked him to his soul that he had to walk away from her bed, and cope with some of the sleaziest criminals in creation. For now, he'd ignore what awaited him. Vickie was a cop. She knew. She also knew what she wanted. She propped herself up on her elbows, her hair deliciously on end, face flushed rosy with her inner heat. The heat he'd just tasted.

"I'm not kidding, Pete. I hurt for you."

"I can make that better, my love. No trouble at all."

He moved up the bed, so he rested between her wide-spread thighs: her beautiful, creamy-smooth, wondrous thighs, and drew her close as he kissed each breast in turn. He stroked each hardened nipple with his tongue and had the satisfaction of hearing her groan, and feel her hips jerk with sexy little mortal movements. Yes!

She was in need and so was he.

He positioned his hips above hers, teasing her by rubbing his erection over her sweet, soft belly. He watched her face.

She was enjoying this, but it wasn't enough—for either of them. Fast as he could move, he shifted, eased her legs wider apart, and entered her in one, fast move.

A long, slow, delighted groan came from her parted lips. "Pete!" she cried, and wrapped her legs around him.

The second groan might have been his. They were joined: one in need, desire and love. Nothing else mattered, not the Adamses, not the agency, only what existed between his love and his soul in this small room.

Her panting resounded in his ears, her speeding heartbeat echoed in his mind, as her feminine muscles tightened around his cock.

He stroked in and out, gently, slowly, wanting this to last, but longing for completion: a completion he was sure was mutual. He'd give her all the joy that ever passed between mortal woman and vampire. Her eyes were afire with lust and need. A sweet sheen of sweat glistened on her pale skin. She was moving as one with him, her hips rocking to his rhythm, speeding with him, slowing as he eased, until she took the lead. What a woman. What a love! Vickie set the pace, working her hips faster, easing and tightening her hold on him as her body rocked with rising passion. It seemed they moved forever. It was bare seconds. Could have been all night. He was past worrying. Vickie was his. His love. His connection with the mortality he'd lost. His everything.

Little gasps came from her open lips. "Soon, Vickie, soon," he promised. He'd give all he could take, fulfill her desire with his need. She arched her shoulders and dropped her head back and the sight of the beating pulse at the base of her neck drove him to the edge. He pressed his cock in harder, felt the first ripples of her climax, and set his lips over her pulse and bit. She cried out, the slight pain lost in the crest of her climax. He closed his mouth and tasted.

With the heat of her mortal blood, his climax peaked and hers burst in wild ripples that shook every nerve and sinew in her body. She was still shaking as he lifted his mouth. He stayed deep inside her, savoring every last ripple of her orgasm as her wondrous body shook in his arms.

As her heartbeat eased and her breathing slowed, Vickie opened her eyes and smiled: a slow, sated, sexy smile that had him wanting to start all over again, but she had mortal limits, and besides, they had to talk.

"Satisfactory, love?"

She had such a damn sexy chuckle. "You bet!" She let out another little gasp and tightened round him again. "You're still hard."

He wasn't about to argue such an obvious point. "It's what you do to me, dear."

"I'm still thinking about what you did to me."

"What we did together."

"I didn't bite you."

"No," he agreed. "How was it?"

Her face gave him the answer to that one. "It was"—she paused, as if searching for words—"orgasmic!"

"It was intended to be." He slid out of her and drew her to him so they nestled together. "I want to have a thousand nights like this."

"Is it really possible?"

"Yes! I'll get them to post me to DC. I'll be close, we can live together or apart—whatever suits you."

"My place is big enough for two, and I've even got the darkroom basement, if you like."

He did like, very much, and told her so.

She kissed him, but he sensed she was still insecure. "It will work out, Vickie."

"But you get posted around, right? You won't be in DC forever."

"I'll talk to my project supervisor and see if we can't find you a place with us."

That got a skeptical raise of eyebrows. "You put mortals in the vamp squad?"

"We need a few trusted mortals as support. People to take care of things while we sleep in the daylight hours."

"Hmmm. Don't tell me you call them Renfields."

"We call them assistants. Renfield, indeed! Please, my love, this is not some hack's fiction. This is reality. You can forget the nonsense with crosses and consecrated hosts too."

"What about mirrors?"

He raised his eyebrows. "How the heck do you think I shave or brush my teeth, if I can't use a mirror?"

"Just wondered." She curled close, resting her hand on his chest, and went quiet. Worried, no doubt. He'd thrown a lot at her in the past couple of days, and now he was leaving—for who knew how long and . . . "What about me becoming a vampire? You bit me, right? Does that mean I'll be one?"

She'd tried to hide the fear but her voice betrayed her, as clear as her heartbeat. "It's not like that. I could take from you for the next fifty years and that alone won't change you. Transformation comes about after mixing and exchange of blood, and certain rituals. It's magical."

"I'm not sure whether to be relieved or let down at that!"

He loved her honesty. "If you do decide you want to turn, it can happen. It's not a decision to make on the spur of the moment if you can avoid it. It changes a lot. Everything, in fact. For me it was easy. I was dying from multiple gunshot wounds. It wasn't too hard to say good-bye to the sunlight when the alternative was death, but for a healthy mortal . . ." He left the rest unsaid. She had brains enough to work it out.

"I truly don't know, Pete."

"When you do know, then we'll make that choice." He wrapped his arms around her, rejoicing in her mortal warmth. They lay entwined for several minutes. He hated leaving the welcome of her body, but he had a job to do. "I have to go, Vickie. I'm going to nip into the shower. You doze until I'm ready."

She let out a sleepy, very sexy mutter, and lifted her head just enough to kiss him. "Don't leave without saying good-bye."

As if he could.

Chapter Ten

Warm water cascaded over Pete's head and down his body. It was torture to have to leave Vickie. Who knew how long the stakeout might last? Leave he had to, and come back he would. Even the Adamses couldn't do what was needed to douse a vampire. Pete borrowed her shampoo, rinsing well. He doubted lavender scent would impress John.

By the time Pete toweled himself dry and gathered his discarded clothes from the bedroom floor, Vickie was fast asleep, a contented smile on her flushed face. He hated to wake her but he'd promised, so he bent over the bed and kissed her.

Vickie felt his lips on her cheek and the gentle pressure against her skin. She opened her eyes slowly, her mind reluctant to disturb the sweet, hot memories that wrapped around her sleep. But Pete was leaving. She pulled herself to sitting.

"Take care of yourself, please," she said as she swung her legs to the floor and stood. She was buck naked and delighted to be so. Might as well give him a good memory to take with him into the dark.

"I'll be okay," he said, sounding almost smug. "Bullets can't harm me—at least not for long."

"So I noticed." She had to kiss him for that, managing a very nice one, considering she was worn out. Of course, Pete did a good bit of the work. She'd dream of his mouth all night. When she wasn't having fantasies over the rest of him. She was going to miss him like hell. "You might be immortal but you're not invincible. Watch out."

"Vickie, there will be a team of us on the stakeout. Vamps and others. I'll be fine. You're the one who needs to take care. Might be best if you leave for a few days."

"I'm staying put. I'll stay busy." *And try not to worry myself sick.*

"It might take days."

"Then I will wait days. And no, I will not do anything to compromise your investigation." That was a given, but it never hurt to point out the obvious to a man.

He kissed her again, slowly, full on the mouth. "I hate leaving you." He grinned down at her and cupped her right breast. "Seems such a dumb thing to do: leave a lovely naked woman to ride down the mountain but . . ."

"You've got to go. Stop dilly-dallying, Pete. The job awaits."

"Lock the door after me and slide home every bolt. I want to be sure you're safe."

"Perfectly safe. I'll keep the shotgun handy in case Sonny comes around."

"He won't be around much longer."

He disappeared into the warm night. Vickie bolted the door, but stood listening as Pete started the engine and the sounds of the motorcycle faded as he rode down the mountain.

She expected to lie awake and worry but she was asleep in minutes, her mind and body sated and content with loving.

Cleaning out the attic, and Grandpa's old shed out back, kept her busy, and provided some intriguing insights on her grandparents. What had they planned to do with all those carefully preserved empty coffee cans? And Vickie was half-tempted to call the Historical Society down in Roanoke to gauge the interest in a collection of number plates dating back to 1933. But on reflection she tossed them in a bunch of boxes and took them down to the recycling center, along with a mountain of yellowed newspapers and an astonishing number of dusty mayonnaise jars. She lost count of how many trips she made down the mountain, her car stuffed with bulging trash bags, but eventually, she surveyed the neat and empty attic, and the shed that was tidier than she ever remembered. It kept her busy, not that she hadn't thought about Pete at least once every five minutes, but the work kept at bay her urges to stroll through the woods towards the old ruined cabin.

Evenings and nights were the hardest, knowing when the fireflies came out, he was out there, watching, waiting, and hoping—as was she. She did wonder how a bunch of vampires managed daytime surveillance. That must be when they called in the mortal support, or the old vampires.

A stakeout could take days, weeks. Her heart didn't want to accept that. She needed Pete, wanted him in her bed, longed to watch his hair spring out in dark curls as he pulled off his helmet, hankered for the sound of his Monster coming up the mountain.

She had to settle for the local news and summer reruns. It was no substitute.

On the third lonely night, Vickie was brushing her teeth, ready to curl up in bed and read awhile, before turning out the light and sharing the dark with her memories. As she replaced the lid on the tube, two helicopters overhead broke the night quiet. Helicopters with searchlights.

Unlikely to be coon hunters. Could only mean one thing: a manhunt. She jettisoned her toothbrush in the basin, pulled her clothes back on, and for luck, grabbed the shotgun and a handful of spare shells. She was debating the question of iced tea or coffee to keep awake, when the first car came up the mountain. Dammit, she was not staying inside. If she didn't turn on the porch light, no one would notice her in the dark. She flicked off all the lights, opened the front door and slipped outside. A veritable convoy of cars, marked and un-marked, were roaring up the mountain, passing her house in a cloud of dust and gas fumes, and harrying up the mountain.

They could only be going one place.

Definitely coffee. A whole pot of it. It was going to be a long night.

It wasn't as long as she'd expected. She was only on her second cup when the convoy started back down. More slowly this time, as if now aware of the hazards of driving an unmade mountain road on a moonless night.

Three cars passed: one unmarked, two from the sheriff. The fourth stopped, just yards from where she sat on the darkened porch. She knew she wasn't visible from the road. Not to anyone with mortal sight.

The passenger door opened.

A leather-clad leg appeared.

Vickie couldn't contain herself anymore. She jumped up and ran to the railings, spilling coffee on the way and not giv-ing a hoot. "Pete!"

He was there.

Pete Falcon: her man, her lover, her vampire.

He paused at the bottom step, a dark outline in the night. "We got them, Vickie! And a truckload of evidence. We'll have it sewn up tight." She all but jumped the four steps, landing in his arms.

"I never doubted you would."

"Your tip-off was key. Without it, I'd still be tramping around the woods."

"Pete," a voice called from the car.

"I'll catch you up. I need a few minutes here."

"Okay, bud."

The door slammed and the car followed the others down the mountain.

As the last engine sounds faded into the dark, they were

still standing there, wrapped in the night and each other's arms.

"Are we staying out here?" Vickie asked.

"We've only got a few minutes. I'll have to run after them and catch up before they all get to the field office, but I needed to see you."

She needed more than seeing, but Pete was worth waiting for. "You're coming back soon?"

"Might not make it back by morning. If not, I'll be headed this way the minute the sun sets. I want you, Vickie."

The last four words he whispered, but the certainty and hunger in them matched her own.

"You've got me!"

He might not be able to stay but dammit, she'd give him something to remember her by. She stood on tiptoe, pressing her lips to his, opening his mouth and kissing. Deep. Pouring need and love from her soul to his. His arms tightened around her, until her breasts flattened against his chest, and her hips angled into his. He smelled of outdoors, and maleness, and desire. And he was all hers.

It was going to be a long twenty-four hours.

He met her kiss, his tongue caressing hers, working with a passion that demonstrated his need. She had to break the kiss. She needed to breathe. He had no such handicap. Just grinned as she gasped for air and her heart thudded in her chest.

"When are you going back to D.C.?" he asked.

"In a couple of days."

"Should work out nicely."

Yes, it would! Now all she had to worry about was introducing him to her grandparents.

Midnight Court

Linda Thomas-Sundstrom

Chapter One

It was a nightmarish world of shadows separating at the seams, of unending darkness live with the promise of more of the same, Dante thought. The devil take it all—if the devil himself hadn't already done so.

Eyes closed, he took a languid breath, inhaling deeply, filling his lungs. He then wondered why he bothered. The perfumed candles, hundreds of them in this salon alone, thousands of them lining the castle's hallways so its honored guests wouldn't trip or lose their way, had long since ceased to intoxicate. The whirling, bejeweled, corseted bodies of the men and women supplicating themselves on the polished marble floor in time to the music seemed now little more than a bore.

Food was folly, wine a tasteless affectation. The woman bending low over his shoulder to whisper in his ear, breasts plump, rosy-hued nipples clearly visible above emerald green brocade, failed to elicit a manly response. Her air of innocence, real or feigned, was wasted. She had no idea how close she had come to peril, to a twilight beyond despair. Would she invite him, taunt him, breathe upon him if she knew? Would she offer up her fullness for him to suckle? Might she spread her round thighs in a flurry of skirts and lace and guide his tongue to the dark-haired place between them—a private place heretofore penetrated only by her secret thoughts and longings? Perhaps so, he decided. Innocence was wasted on the young. Pathetically. One move of his eyes, the tiniest portion of a smile upward, and this ridiculous creature would be his for the ride.

The tedium was unending, the turn of time merciless. And yet, he thought as he glanced at the untouched plate on the table before him . . . and yet through it all, beneath it all, down deep in the pocket of the place where his soul once resided, a sharp, dire, incomprehensible hunger raged.

Oh yes, he might have this girl, this tease, this would-be whore, he knew. Just as he knew his hunger would tear him apart, turn him inside out and leave him to burn, if unappeased. He might take her now, here. On the table. On his plate. Next to the costly linens and Belgian lace soaked in the wine he would spill as he laid her there. Think of the chaos that would surely ensue if he were to strip her over-tight bodice from the quivering flesh beneath it with his venison dagger. He could easily pin her sleeves, thus rendering her thin arms immobile, with a well-placed fork or two struck to the gleaming oak slab.

Would he have her slowly, basting her thighs delicately in the honey so graciously supplied by his host? Kneading her pink flesh with his thumbs as his mouth followed the trail of the sticky, sugary delicacy en route to the door to her womanhood?

Womanhood? That was a laugh. This female was nothing more than a girl—silly, inconsiderate, not yet ripe enough for a true mouthful. She wouldn't be able to stand up to his careful ministrations, nor comprehend what was really happening to her. She would be wearing layer upon layer of undergarments, carefully provided by her benefactor or maid to thwart any such action as this. Any such situation as this.

The girl would squirm, were he to cut her free of her fabric barriers. More wine would spill. More food. She would grow tentative as he crawled his way upward, as he unleashed his stiffening manhood, weary of her fidgeting and her cries.

Stunned she would be as he entered her plush, wet, convulsing canal with a brutal, uncaring shove. Her mouth would open. Whimpers would erupt when he ruptured the last shreds of her innocence. Screams would follow, echoing each plunge he made. Then, a last gasp deep in her throat as he withdrew from this gift of maturity to drop his face between her trembling legs. She would pray, silently, lips moving, when his own lips stroked the wound his shaft had created. She would faint as he lapped at the last visage of her lapsed virginity—as he sampled a moistness almost sweeter than wine.

Blushed flesh. Emerald brocade, stretched out like a patch of verdant grass. White lace in shreds. Vaporous candlelight, trailing the scents of musk and malaise. Whispers of onlookers with lustful, envious scowls puckering their painted faces. All of this before dessert.

His chin lifted. His eyes rose slowly from the imagined scene before him, hesitating on the heaving bosom so very near to his mouth. The silly girl's heavy, buxom bosom. He glanced up, meaning to look at her face . . . meaning to focus on something to ease the endlessness. Anything to end it.

But he caught sight of something else. Something dazzling in the distance. Something that nipped at his attention.

For the first time he could recall, there came a stirring sensation inside of his chest.

A soft thud not unlike a real heartbeat.

A true heartbeat.

Chapter Two

"Dante?"

Someone spoke his name, parlaying for his attention, but Dante did not want to be disturbed. He wanted nothing to get in the way of this wave of sensation.

A gloved hand covered his on the table. He held his breath.

"Dante? Is something wrong?"

It took all of his willpower to turn his head, to gaze politely at the woman seated next to him, a woman whose features he barely recognized but whose touch he knew intimately well.

"Is something wrong?" Elizabeth repeated in a voice tainted with the grit of jealous inquisitiveness.

"Wrong?" he returned benignly, purposefully regulating his breath and choosing to ignore the subtleties of her warning.

He was staring. Staring at the most beautiful woman he had ever seen. A woman who glided into the room like a liquid moonbeam, pale gown glistening like grated jewels in the candlelight; blue-black curls tumbling across naked shoulders. An apparition, Dante guessed. An apparition come to ground?

The vision's hair was like midnight, loosely gathered around her white face. Thick, shiny, buoyant, stray tendrils of darkness caressed her cheeks—the cheeks of an angel—ageless, timeless, pale and perfect.

Dante sat up straighter in his chair, feeling his body shiver with a vague yet poignant ripple of surprise. He strained for a better look at the radiant creature. His ever-whirling mind grew still.

"Dante?"

Not now, he directed silently to Elizabeth, beside him. *A moment, please.*

A strange scent flooded the room. Exotic. Floral. Unearthly. Otherworldly. Like the creature's trailing gown, the perfumed air wafted—gauzy swirls of scent caught in the flickering candles, drifting over his face.

"Dante," Elizabeth said more adamantly, but Dante couldn't reply. He couldn't speak.

The apparition's cheeks were tinted with the faintest trace of color—an almost fragile flush of pink. Not from a paint-pot or too much drink, Dante knew instinctively. This was the palette of innocent heat, of untried fire. Christ, he could feel that fire from where he sat.

"I see," Elizabeth hissed, removing the hand she had placed atop his and slipping it beneath the table, into his lap. She uttered a sharp, muffled cry. Her features rearranged like water in a shallow pond upon her discovery of what he had swelling there.

"Perhaps I should leave you to it," she snapped, eyes glittering with malcontent, softness dissipated.

Dante looked across to the angel's eyes, and found her hiding hers. Creaseless lids framed by dark lashes closed slightly over light blue globes, the color of daylight. Her action had been demure, wistful, but her eyes were keen, he decided, and symmetrically placed. Her nose was narrow above a full, febrile mouth glossy with the latest tincture of oil. A mouth no doubt tasting of rose or pomegranate. The kind of mouth a man prayed for, longed for, and then used mercilessly for his own purposes. The kind of mouth which could enslave a man and very nearly drive him mad.

"Bloody hell, Dante," Elizabeth whispered as his gaze

swept over the angel's smooth expanse of neck, coming to rest on the hollow of her throat.

His erection pulsed.

She wore jewels, great stones of citrine linked with gold, though she needed no such diversions. The gems vied for attention. He wanted to see her flesh undecorated. A more inexperienced eye than his might have seen little past the necklace's all-too-obvious value. A less experienced eye might have stopped there, missing altogether the beauty of the blue veins spreading gracefully beneath the lustrous white skin, toward the graceful slope of her shoulders and the unconscionably immodest cut of her gown.

Dante's gaze lingered seconds more. A twinge of something quite akin to pain took root deep inside of his body. Unable to name this pain, helpless to tear his attention from the angel, he sat mesmerized, knowing he had been lost from the moment he had first beheld her. Lost, as would be the moon without the stars. A strange fever heated his face and his motionless limbs. His head echoed inside with the sound of summer thunder.

The only hope, he knew, was to find a flaw—one single crack in the seamless composition of her glorious whole which would allow him room to breathe. A flaw which would enable him to rebind his rapidly fragmenting composure.

"You're a fool," Elizabeth said.

"Am I?" he returned casually.

"Do you know who she is?"

"I haven't a clue."

"Then I will tell you."

"I'd rather you didn't."

His reply seemed to give Elizabeth pause. "You can't have everything you want, Dante. Not everything," she said a moment later, withdrawing her hand.

"I take that back," Dante said, catching hold of her fingers before she could rise from her chair, his tone so serious that Elizabeth stayed quite still for several seconds more.

"Take what back?" she asked at last.

"Who is she?"

The strength of his left arm was the only thing retaining Elizabeth as she said petulantly, "No. I don't think I shall tell you after all. And when you do find out, *my* door will be locked."

She wrenched her arm free of his hold and stood. Sliding a finger into the tight space between her own partially exposed breasts, she leaned forward, allowing him a whiff of lavender as well as a closer view of her greatest assets—a frank reminder of things he would be missing if he strayed too far. Her cool cheek brushed against his as she placed something in his hand. A key.

"Then again," she whispered, skirts rustling as she turned, "I do love it when a man *begs*."

As quickly as that, he was alone. Though he noted Elizabeth's exit, he did not turn to watch. Instead, he took a sip of wine and sat back, fingering the key in his hand, wondering if he shouldn't feel guilty and if he shouldn't pursue something tried and true.

To test himself he looked up and across the lavishly decorated room, this time to meet the blue-eyed stare. He stood with a sharp, unconscious move brought on by the unmasked intensity of her gaze. Caught up in the moment, he failed to notice the man at the angel's side until the man moved. Taking her slender elbow in his hand as if she were mere flesh and blood, this companion ushered the angel across the marble floor toward the far door, passing in and out of candlelight so that her gown sparkled like disseminated dreams. *No*, Dante thought, sending his message silently and adamantly to her as the door opened and a guard moved aside.

Don't go.

The angel hesitated. Her chin lifted regally. She glanced back over her shoulder, as did her companion, whose angular face was illuminated briefly in a light which bathed him with a reddish glow.

"Damn it to hell!" Dante swore as he bowed his head to the angel's comrade in mock fealty. "Damn it to bloody hell!"

It seemed he had found that flaw he had been searching for, and it was a formidable one.

Lord Alan Fucking Rothchilde.

Chapter Three

"Dante?" Elizabeth called out victoriously as he closed the door behind himself.

"Were you expecting someone else?" Dante said.

"It would serve you well if I were."

Elizabeth floated from the shadows and into the light of a solitary candle, scantily clad in something colorless. She tugged upon the ribbon holding the front of her gown, and Dante watched, feeling suddenly sorry he had come, feeling uncommonly disinterested in the yellowish gleam of her naked body.

Elizabeth's creamy drape fell to the ground soundlessly as she floated closer. The lush extravagances of her voluptuous torso filled his vision, blocking the light.

She smelled now of cinnamon.

"You are magnificent," Dante said, reminding himself that he had always considered the lavishness of her curves a delight, and the quickness of her wit a just reward. How now could he ask her for the information he needed? How, in the face of her renewed pursuit, could he insult a woman who had become an ally in a world gone sour?

"Perhaps you're feeling overdressed," she suggested.

He closed his eyes, trying to rid himself of the sensation of having made a terrible mistake by using her key. When her long, warm fingers rested on his arm, he stirred. Though his thoughts had recently flown through the damp air and through each wall of the castle searching for the brilliance of the moon, Elizabeth's touch, as she rubbed up against him, as she carefully removed his coat, seemed merciless in its promise.

"You are quiet," she purred, slipping slender hands inside of his shirt, massaging his chest lightly. "It is hardly like you."

"Too much wine," he murmured, cursing the fickleness of the effect she provided.

"Wine? Is it so?" Elizabeth's mouth nestled close to his ear. "I did not see you finish a single glass."

"You were occupied elsewhere, as I recall."

"I?" She laughed throatily. "That is uncommonly good."

Her breasts were soft against the middle of his back as she leaned still closer, as she thrust her arms beneath his to grind herself tightly to him, confident in her ability to rouse a man.

"No," Dante whispered, sensations coming in ripples as her hands dropped slowly downward, angling toward his waist, "*this* is uncommonly good."

"You see," Elizabeth whispered triumphantly. "You need me, just as I need you. We complement each other, do we not, while demanding so very little?"

With her out of sight he could almost imagine . . .

With her body against his he could almost believe . . .

But her eyes were not of a blue hue, and not so innocent. The flush of color on her cheeks came from a porcelain box, one he had in fact given her.

"Yes," Elizabeth purred as he reached behind with both hands to pin her body to his. But Dante knew he could not yet afford to look upon her face or into her wizened eyes. Not just now. Not as obsessed as he was with the angel.

He had to let the angel go.

Had to.

Didn't he?

As if in answer to his inward question, Elizabeth's fingernails raked across his neck, drawing, he knew, a thin line of blood. Though he winced, the thought arose that he would not long have to withhold the tremendous rise of physical power coursing through his limbs. Nor would he have to be gentle in this taking.

With a single, graceful move, he turned and lifted Elizabeth into his arms. Finding her light in weight, for all her ample graces, he dragged his gaze across her nakedness. He smiled when she moaned. Elizabeth was aware of him as a man, rightly enough, amid all the other things he might be. She still seemed to need what he had to offer, and wasn't afraid. What man could resist this boldness? What beast could turn away?

Yet the bed was not close. Not nearly close enough. If he moved, even a step . . . If he had time to think clearly about what he was doing and who he imagined doing it to . . .

Elizabeth's lips found his earlobe. Her tongue, torturously deft, darted into his ear and retreated maddeningly, defying him to pursue his current path of thought. If she knew of his treacherous lusting and the new direction of his desires, she made a good showing of pretending not to care.

That was it. She didn't care.

Why didn't she?

He deposited her on the old hinged chest. Shoving its contents aside with a sweep of his arm, he pressed her back, across the trestle's smooth, polished surface. Elizabeth made another sound, faint and guttural. His action had pleased her.

"Dante?" she murmured, spreading her arms so that her breasts, nipples drawn like peach silk, lifted with the slow rhythm of her breathing.

"Yes?" he queried, watching her shapely legs open just enough to reveal what lay between them. "Yes?" he repeated, hunger now straining at his pants.

Elizabeth reached for him, pulled him down on top of her. She wrapped her arms and legs around him, driving thoughts of the angel deeper into his mind. His mouth hovered above hers.

"She is not for you," Elizabeth whispered. "Not this one. Not this time."

A strange, oddly profound light shone in Elizabeth's eyes as she said this. The light of challenge? Would he rise to it?

Her mouth was still open when he found it. Her exquisite tongue, so recently removed from his ear, so hot and experienced in the finer pleasures of lovemaking, lay in waiting between her parted lips. He brushed his mouth over hers briefly, felt the accompanying swell below his waist, then bore down. He took her mouth in the name of passion, kissing her with a fury that would have terrified any lesser woman. He bent her backwards over the edge of the chest with his hands on her shoulders, holding her tightly, allowing her no time for a breath. And suddenly, behind closed eyes, came a flash of light. A white face formed in the twilight, illuminating his actions, slowing him down.

He hesitated, lips removed from Elizabeth's.

"Now, Dante," Elizabeth said throatily. "Now, or never."

Slender fingers moving like liquid fire found his belt. Without a glance at what lay unleashed, Elizabeth smiled. Dante smiled back. Cupping her full, ponderous breasts in both hands, Dante leaned forward to take one sensitive bit of her gently between his teeth. With a slow, circular motion of his tongue, he closed in, drawing her flesh into his mouth with a slight sucking sound.

Elizabeth's head dropped back, as he knew it would. Her face was alight with ecstasy. He knew how to pleasure her, all right, and she, in turn, knew exactly what it took to allow him to do this. It was a cunning game of erotica they played, with the leader never truly revealed. Give and take. Lunge and retreat. Artful maneuvering, with sensation as the ultimate goal.

But Elizabeth demanded something more this time. He could smell it, sense it. Her blood was up, her life-pulse fast. She would skip all the pleasures between the kiss and the taking. This is what the rapid beating inside of her chest told him. This was the source of the scent radiating from her—the slightly acrid odor of secrets withheld.

What secrets?

Aware of his hesitation, Elizabeth shoved him back so that he might observe the further opening of her legs. She did not quiver, nor feign any such naïveté as she did when they played games in the hallways, or with their tumbled assignations in other places. She would not let him discern what she wanted. She would allow him no time to scrutinize the symptoms he had sensed.

Cautiously, his hand slid between her warm, damp thighs. There came an answering throb between his own. He grunted aloud. Again, she smiled.

He parted the petals of her desire with his finger; it was a pale flower surrounded by a forest of fine, brown fur. Another throb hit him, distant, insistent. He worked his finger inside of this flowering of femininity, inching the surrogate shaft upward. A wave of moisture met him. Hot. Creamy. Smelling of dark, forbidden places. A shudder of delight shot through his limbs. His enlarged staff pressed tightly to her naked hip.

What secrets do you possess, dear Elizabeth?

He sent the question silently to her, yet adamantly.

Why the rush?

What is in it for you if the pleasure is quelled?

Though he entered her body roughly, she made no sound. One hard thrust into the heat of hell's inferno itself, and Elizabeth closed herself around him as only she had the mastery to do. He found her blisteringly heated and hazardously tight, though he had sheathed his sword in this scabbard enough times to wear her skin raw.

"Now," she said, as if he had done nothing, as if she felt nothing of his initial thrust.

Her eyes were exceedingly bright when he looked there. Green eyes flecked with gold. Something unsaid was delicately wrapped in that gold. He nearly pulled back.

"What are you waiting for?" she asked throatily. "Some

206 / Linda Thomas-Sundstrom

pathetic virgin who hasn't the capacity for dancing with danger? Some yearling who can't treat a cock properly? Perhaps a vapid version of a woman who doesn't know what kind of things lurk in the darkened hallways of castles like this one? Someone unused to the shadows?"

"You do care, then?" Dante returned without any softening of the cock she had hoped to tease into submission.

"Care?" Elizabeth tossed back, maintaining a tight hold on the edge of the chest as Dante plunged into her depths yet again to prove a point.

"If you care, why don't you say so?" Dante suggested wryly, slamming himself into her with all his might, reaching, he knew, the very core of Elizabeth. And she laughed aloud and opened wider still.

"Why don't you make me," she challenged.

All right, he thought. *You will play this game to the hilt, and I will join you in it. Or,* he added insightfully, *was it the other way around, and Elizabeth is meeting my challenge?*

She began to move. Her sleek buttocks undulated. Her insides massaged him, drew him in, compelled him. Her pliant, determined body demanded he take heed, for the juices of her passion were flowing, game or none, luring him, surrounding him, trapping him in spite of everything.

He yanked her from the chest with his prick still buried deeply inside of her and stumbled to the wall. She cried out as her back met hard with the stone. She groaned as he gripped her thighs roughly in his hands. Yet she clamped her thighs around his waist, making it difficult for him to ease himself back.

Her smile was but a memory now. Intensity had overtaken her. Her eyes were closed. Dante stroked her dark, furry patch at the point where he had and was still penetrating her body. She loosened her hold on his back. Her eyelids flapped.

It was enough. He had won this battle, surely?

He jammed himself into her. And again. And again. Over and over, without hesitation or mercy, hearing the slap of her back against the stone, feeling the impact of his body meeting with hers with each breath he took. And Elizabeth rode the storm, wave for wave, refusing to scream or give in, seeming to revel in the excruciating intensity of the pleasure they shared.

Locked together, they tumbled to the floor, crying out for a satisfaction neither of them seemed yet able to find. Faster and faster, harder and deeper still Dante went into the maelstrom, needing to move her, seeking to make her back down. And then she lifted her chin. She turned her head slightly, exposing a glistening patch of pale skin across her throat.

My God, Dante thought fleetingly. So provocative. So white and smooth. So *bloody* smooth.

When the sky exploded, it was not with stars but with fire. Red fire. The flames of lust, greed, and maybe even hell itself beat against Dante's nakedness, bending his mind, drumming at his temples. He thought he heard himself cry out as Elizabeth pressed herself to him, as he took her skin between his teeth. With an ache of monstrous proportions that barely gave credence to her gesture, he poured every last bit of himself into Elizabeth Rothchilde. His final thrust shook them both to the bone.

And then with the heartiness of a conqueror, he bit right through her soft white flesh.

Chapter Four

Elizabeth's cry was inward, silent, and stuck in her throat. Ecstacy? Yes, she thought fleetingly, and then the sensation was replaced by a stab of pain that seared her flesh and scalded her blood to the point of boiling.

Her skin and stomach were alive with fire. Fire so vivid as to be insufferable. Was she dying? Was this what the shadow of death felt like?

Her body seized, muscles rigid with the faintest trace of fear, and then the mouth on her neck tugged harder still, sucking, drawing the fire upward through her arms and shoulders. Her blood rushed to meet *his* demands.

Dante's demands.

Blackness swallowed Elizabeth soon after shadows leaned in. Even the flicker of the candle could not hide what was taking place: Dante's dark head against her cheek, Dante's teeth embedded into her flesh. And yet she seemed somehow removed from these things, curiously distanced from the action she had invited.

Oh yes, she had invited it. Him. This. She had asked for Dante to show himself, and now she had gone beyond the realms of couplings and torrid sexual assignations. She had wanted to know. She had *had* to know. So why now fight what she had gathered to her? Surely it was too late to struggle? Much too late to protest? The fire had reached her throat. Everything below was lost to feeling, to sensation, having been forsaken in the name of love. Sense had been abandoned for this one man, for this particular creature.

Christopher Dante.

Should she give in? Elizabeth considered this. The thought fled. She brought it back again. And then feeling suddenly reappeared, as though it had not truly been distanced for good.

A throb accompanied the drawing of her life's blood. Faintly it came on, the sensation similar to catching and holding a man's eyes for the first time after secretly lusting for him. A sensation exchangeable for the impact of lips touching for the first time.

Flames rushed downward through her chest, abdomen, thighs, and over her heated skin, the fire now coursing, singeing, insistent. Down the heat went, toward the site of her sexual pleasures, toward the door whose key she had distributed to one man only. To a man who was not merely a man.

Could there possibly be any blood left to engorge the organs driving her desire? Yes. She felt it now. God, how she felt it. Waves of heat burst, then retreated, flaring white-hot, darting in and out of the space between her thighs. God. Oh, God.

What was he doing?

She shook, moved, undulated. Still, she had no control over her arms. Her back arched with an audible crack. Her legs opened. Only then did she notice that Dante's mouth had left her neck, and that Dante's eyes—his great dark eyes—were peering into her own.

She went into those eyes, felt herself drowning, slipping.

"Elizabeth," Dante whispered.

As if he had control over her very consciousness, Elizabeth's attention returned to his face. Dante's features filled in where only paleness had reigned. Black eyebrows arched severely over his luminous eyes, eyes as bottomless as her greed for him had been. His full lips opened, revealing the dagger-like sharpness of his teeth. But there was something else. His cock grew steadily harder against her thigh.

Elizabeth wanted that great hard shaft inside of her. She had never wanted anything so badly. The desire nearly drove her mad, and yet she was helpless amid the intensity of the heat and loss of control. She could not pull him close, nor could she press herself up against him to show him how much she needed what he could offer. She could not move her lips.

But Dante knew well enough what she needed. Perhaps he had read her mind? He rolled on top of her, seemingly weightless. His shaft once more entered her heat. She could feel this! This was what she wanted!

Dante began to move, slowly, rhythmically. All the while, he looked into her eyes, never leaving her, his expression sober, almost pained.

"And now you know," Dante said, velvet voice mingling with the blaze and the sizzling juices her body produced without her help. "You know what I am."

Elizabeth tried again to form a word. She tried desperately to move her lips. Dante laid a finger against them as he plunged again into her body's waiting inferno. And again.

Breath caught at Elizabeth's throat, stuck. Dante's hands encircled her throat, gently closing in.

"And what will you do with this knowledge?" Dante asked, body continuing its furious dance with hers, fingers massaging her throat softly.

He would not kill her, Elizabeth decided. He would have done so already had that been on his mind. Of course, she had considered the fact that this night might very well be the end of her. What beast would want his secrets brought to light? Nevertheless, she had to take the chance, had to see if he felt anything for her. She had to keep him occupied—with her, inside of her—long enough for Dante to lose sight of the other . . . woman. Her brother's vermin. Satan's bride.

"Ah." The sound escaped from her closed throat. Dante drank in her cry by placing his mouth over hers. His hips stopped moving. He eased himself back.

No! she wanted to shout.

Dante's expression rearranged as he stared at her face. In a graceful rise to his feet, he scooped her up into his arms. He held her against him, while her own limbs dangled uselessly over the carpet like things disconnected.

Her head lolled. She could not lift it, could barely breathe. Had the fire grown dimmer? Was life draining away after all? Is this why he'd stopped?

The room began to spin, slowly at first, then faster. *Dante!* she thought, before losing the shape of his name.

He looked down at her, his face still pale, still white, not at all flushed from his conquest. "Yes," he whispered. "You are alive, my dearest Elizabeth. Foolish, but alive."

She floated downward. Softness met her. Pillows. Bed. His angular, deftly chiseled face came closer. "This is what you wanted?" he asked. "To be sure of what I am? To hold my secrets so completely as to have me a slave to your future wishes?"

Could the devil be so perfectly chiseled? Elizabeth wondered. Was Dante's beautiful countenance held together by magic? Beauty to draw beauty? Perhaps his face, his wide shoulders and narrow waist were carefully chosen from the pools of the blood of his victims. Perhaps the sheen of his rugged beauty was outward only, and inside of him only hunger persisted.

His dark expressive eyes now lacked spark. The white spaces surrounding them were swimming with red. "Rest, my beautiful and foolish Elizabeth," Dante said, sweeping her hair back with his fingers, laying his palm to her cheek. "Your strength will return on the morrow if you care for it. We shall see then what *your* secrets are."

Leaving a kiss on her forehead, he then distanced himself. Without his attention, Elizabeth could think more clearly. The fog began to clear. Secrets, he had said. But he had not gotten them from her, even though he had shared his own. Christopher Dante had no idea what she had protected him from this night and what she might have given up to do so. He had no idea *who* she had saved him from.

But that was not all, not the extent of things, she reminded herself. Not by the half. Dante might have her lust, her love, her loyalty, and even a taste of her life's blood, but Dante did not know everything.

She closed her eyes, drifted, and fell.

Chapter Five

Rothchilde castle's halls were mired in the fading echo of his own shout when Dante slipped quietly from Elizabeth's rooms. The sound seemed deafening; it seemed to rumble through the very stone and mortar surrounding him.

He paused to lean against the thick stone wall and found it icy after the warmth of Elizabeth's bed. He found the hallway air dank after the luscious scent of Elizabeth's naked limbs.

He inhaled, coughed, wiped a thin trickle of blood from his lip with the back of his hand. He stared at the blood, then glanced toward Elizabeth's closed door, able to feel her in there, able to hear her breathing. Able to hear the rush of blood in her veins.

He almost smiled—until he remembered that he had not pulled her secrets from her, after all. He had not won, nor even been a player in this latest game of hers, it suddenly seemed. Damn it all to hell. The round belonged to her, didn't it?

Most disturbing.

Arms lowered, Dante stood straighter. What had she kept from him, and how had she kept it? Why was he grinning, in spite of himself? It very well could be that he, plainly, simply, had succumbed to Feminine Mystique. Him. After all this time. And though he had tried to fight it, he knew now for certain that he was not immune to the lure of Elizabeth's wiles, no matter how much his thoughts intended to stray. Worse yet, as Elizabeth lay nestled in the great bed, he had found her strangely fragile. Almost compellingly vulnerable.

"Pah!" he spat. "Elizabeth, vulnerable?" But his thoughts refused to reassemble in any kind of usable order once he had considered this. Elizabeth had done this to him, had taken from him his wits. She had robbed him of his manhood—whatever of his manhood he still retained—and he couldn't even guess how she had done it. Mightn't the loss of superiority he suddenly felt be due to the fact that Elizabeth hadn't been satisfied with his performance?

A wave of apprehension washed over him.

Why?

Again, he looked to her door. Had Elizabeth expected something more from this dark union?

How long had she known what he was?

"Bloody damn and blast!"

What was Elizabeth trying to do? Why would she seek out a member of the devil's clan, she who had long survived without succumbing to it? How could she invite him into her bed and then trust him to leave her soul the way he'd found it? Well, almost the way he had found it.

Grinning wickedly, he recalled the shape of Elizabeth's luscious hips. The feel of her seamless skin. The way she had used both of those things to ensnare him.

And now she knew what he was. She would have no doubts about it. Devil's spawn. Nightshade. Predator. He had been called many things in many places, but no voice had ever raised against him twice. No one had ever withstood his careful scrutiny. Those who strayed, those who had rallied against his kind had died terrible deaths. Unspeakable deaths. Yet . . . Elizabeth Rothchilde had offered herself up. Sought him out. Elizabeth Rothchilde, for all her obvious guile, was indeed a formidable woman. The exception.

Or else it was some kind of an elaborate trap.

"Duke?"

The hallway darkened for Dante. His smile dissolved.

"Duke?"

The approaching scent was of youth, of sour, unbathed flesh.

"A note for you, my lord," a young lad said in a voice that wavered as much as his image did in the flickering candlelight.

Dante tilted his head, wary of the interruption. Then he stretched out a hand to accept the bit of parchment the lad held at arm's length. A roar of hunger pounded in his chest. A bit of leftover dampness gathered on his brow as he worked to keep this hunger at bay—hunger for the lean muscle and strongly pounding heartbeat inside of the lad's scrawny chest.

"What is it, I wonder?" Dante pondered, staring at the paper, unable to focus.

"I do not know, Duke Dante. Will you require anything further?"

The lad's tenor was nasal. His arms shook as though they had just been plunged into a bucket of ice water.

"Have you anything warm to drink?" Dante taunted.

"No. No, my lord. Shall I—"

Dante held up a hand to cut off the lad's excuse. Something else nagged at him. He closed his eyes, lifted the paper closer to his nostrils. Perfumed paper. Exotic. He opened his eyes, waved a hand at the waiting lad. "Off with you then."

The lad nodded, bowed his head, and took two steps backwards, still facing Dante.

"There is something further?" Dante inquired, lowering the parchment, wondering who would miss this lad in the morning when he didn't make himself available for work.

"She . . . she bid me make certain you read the note, Duke Dante."

Dante fingered the parchment but did not take his eyes from the lad's ashen face. "Whom do you speak of, then?"

"Lord Rothchilde's . . ."

"Bride?"

"'Twas the woman who gave me the note."

"Ah, I see. And where does Rothchilde's future bride reside, lad?"

"His future bride is in the tower."

The tower. So close to the light when the sun needed to rise, Dante thought. How long had he spent with Elizabeth? How much time was left until sunrise?

"The lady bid you wait at this hour?" Dante asked. "Well then, we cannot have you miss your beauty sleep, can we?"

Sensing the lad's nervousness, able to smell the lad's malaise, Dante lifted the parchment. The paper was sealed with a stamped crest. Blood-red wax bound the edges of the paper.

At the sight of the wax, Dante's hunger flared. The lad's heartbeat became infuriatingly loud.

"Do you belong to the woman in the tower, the sender of this note, or to the castle?" Dante asked the lad.

"I serve Lord Rothchilde," the lad said bravely enough, for all the weakness of its conviction.

"Have you served him long?"

"A fortnight only, Duke Dante."

Another step back. The lad's hand went to his head before remembering himself and his position.

"You can take me to this woman in the tower? You know the way well enough?" The words sounded odd to Dante as he said them, as if they had been sifted through his tight throat. Hunger raged now, nearly driving him to his knees. Elizabeth had been but a fine wine preceding his necessary supper.

"The woman said you would come," the lad offered humbly.

"Did she, indeed?"

And she had sent him a package, all tied up in sinewy muscle and reeking of fear. The question was: Did she send the lad on purpose? Had Rothchilde already turned his future bride? He did not think so. He had seen her, sensed her innocence, smelled that innocence from across the room. If Rothchilde had turned her without Dante knowing it, Christopher Dante had lost his edge.

And the devil had put the angel in his tower.

The devil, as did most men, preferred toying with the divine.

As Dante looked up at the lad, he felt his smile return. If the lady had sent him the lad unbeknownst to her circumstances, or his, and unbeknownst to the dangers of Rothchilde castle after dark . . . well. . . .

"You may tell the lady I will come."

He almost did so now, just thinking about her. Both his cock and his cravings were swelling beyond containment. And so soon after being appeased.

"You have not . . ." the lad began before remembering himself.

"Yes?" Dante said, moving closer to the boy.

"Read the note," the boy finished.

"Yes, well I find I need that warm drink after all," Dante said. "It will only hurt a little," he added with a swift, graceful lunge forward.

Chapter Six

Dante sped through the complex castle corridors. As he walked, he removed his bloodstained coat and tossed it aside. Visions of the angel filled him, now that his hunger had been appeased. He had regained some control.

Angel. Her skin would be as white beneath her gown as it had been above it. He might inch that gown over her bare shoulders slowly, deliberately. Torturously.

The angel's doe-like eyes, so bright and blue amongst the bottomless blank eyes of the night creatures, might plead with him to desist. Angels might imagine that men and their devilish counterparts might obey.

So senselessly naïve.

Ah, and angels should not yet be experienced to a man's hand, gentle or otherwise. They could not be ethereal if they had ever closed hand or mouth over a suitor's engorged shaft. These very deficiencies would be the reasons Alan Rothchilde had chosen her. Virgin. Simple. Perhaps a sacrifice from her family, her village, her own castle? A barter for days of safety from the Rothchildes and their kind? Such things were common near to a nest.

Rounding a corner, Dante came up short. Senses on high alert, he grabbed hold of the coat of the servant halted there.

"Where would a man keep a star, had it fallen to the

earth?" Dante asked the poor frozen man who obviously knew nothing of him other than what he could discern from Dante's clothes and noble bearing.

"You do not know the answer to my riddle?" Dante taunted. "Then perhaps you can tell me what part of darkness we are in. After midnight, or before sunrise?"

"Early," the servant said. "Or late, as the case may be. The sun is not just yet above ground."

"Is something amiss that would cause you to be about in the dark?"

The man looked up at Dante, two heads taller than himself. "I am waiting for a changing of the guard."

"Guards? For what?"

"Protection."

Dante released the man. He must be close to her now. Close to the angel. "Guard, is it? Then you must see to your task. And mind that you look around corners before you entangle yourself for good."

"By your leave, sir."

"No. By yours."

Dante glanced past the man, up the stairway from whence the man had come. The stairway to the tower. Smiling fully now, he repeated, "Where would someone hide a star fallen to earth? The answer is, the nearest place to heaven."

Hands raised, ready to push open the tower door, Dante hesitated. A question arose to plague the living daylight out of him and dampen his spirits. Though virgins were indeed rare in his travels, would a virgin's blue eyes truly compare to the emerald, intelligent, sometime belligerent stare of a paramour? His incredible paramour?

Elizabeth.

Would this angel so willingly give in to the darkness just to keep him close? More likely she would scream her bloody lungs out and he'd have to take care of that right off.

Another thought came, intrusive, blurring his way to the

angel. Why had Elizabeth been so willing to sacrifice herself? How had she known about him?

Secrets.

Bloody hell, what did Elizabeth Rothchilde think she was doing? What was she keeping to herself?

Chapter Seven

The tower room lay in darkness. An acrid odor of burned-out candles permeated the air. A tapestry had been flung back to allow in the cold outside air.

Dante looked to the window, where a pink shadow tinted the stone. The sun would soon rise. Time was fleeting.

Despite the danger of approaching daylight, he was pleased with himself. He felt lucky. A note from the angel remained in his hand. The guard had conveniently removed himself, saving Dante the trouble. And the round room was empty, save for the person lying in the over-large oaken canopied bed in the center of it.

The angel was alone.

"Do angels need beauty sleep?" he whispered.

Without caution, he strode to the bed and swept back the heavy draperies. The benign action sent a thrill to the tip of his boots. There she was, luminous in her dark coverlets, long-necked body curled into a ball.

Angel.

Dark hair flowed across the pillows, uncoiffed and natural, like a waterfall spilling over sand. The angel's face was hidden by her hands. No jewelry adorned her fingers or wrists, contrary to the common practice women preferred of keeping their baubles to themselves. The tattered lace of a frivolously gauzy shift lay against her neck; not at all proper attire for the season.

Hand outstretched, Dante rested his fingers upon a strand of her hair. A shudder rocked him. Her hair was as black as midnight. Her skin was pure white, like goose down, like he remembered. Without touching her, he traced the outline of her cheek just inches above it, then drew back. A familiar pain shot through him. His stomach churned with a familiar heave.

The angel's bed was hung with garlic.

Dammit to hell!

Alan Rothchilde would surely have ordered it placed there to make certain no hands touched her until his did. That no one making use of the open window could stomach a long look at his future bride.

"The devil take you, Rothchilde," Dante murmured.

But though the garlic was a minor setback, it did provide one answer on his list of questions: Rothchilde had not yet turned her. The angel was intact.

Fingers to his lips to keep from laughing, Dante considered this further. The angel must indeed be special for Rothchilde to have withheld his infamous hunger. The cad. The brute. The bugger. His appetites were legendary.

Face lowered to hers, Dante took closer stock of the angel, holding his breath so as not to inhale the garlic into his lungs.

The angel, it seemed, might have skin like down, but she possessed no feathered wings. Too bad about the wings, he thought. It would have been a nice touch.

Still, this angel seemed completely vulnerable in her fetal pose, knees drawn up, back rounded. A position of self-protection. A little ball of naïveté. Did she realize to whom she was betrothed, and what would soon befall her? Had she any idea what she would become, if deemed worthy of Rothchilde's hand?

Undoubtedly not.

"Perhaps the same thing that keeps Rothchilde away from his future bride, at least temporarily, is what holds my own hands back," Dante reasoned as he stared. Though he was experienced in the art of making love to women and in shunning old superstitious devices used to keep creatures such as himself out . . . though he was twice this angel's weight and several hundred years her senior . . . she had the one thing they all coveted. True innocence.

"I will have you, my angel, if I so desire." Dante crooned so quietly, the words were a sigh. "I cannot remember what your thoughts must be like. I cannot conceive of a time when walking in the light meant life without the threat of peril."

She stirred. He stepped back.

A sound escaped from her lips. Her eyes opened. But she was blind in the dark. Dante covered her mouth with his hand to stifle a second sound.

"Not yet, my beam of starlight," he whispered, feeling the presence of the garlic as a humming inside of his head and a heaviness in his limbs. "I will not force myself upon any woman. I respect your kind, and hold you in the highest esteem."

He could rip her from the bed, of course. He could remove her from her sacred temple, away from the restraints of the beastly weed that surrounded her. So, why didn't he? What was wrong with him? He had fed. He had been sexually appeased. He always took what he wanted.

This was Elizabeth's fault, he knew with sudden certainty. His thoughts flew back to her, to the way he had left her. What he had done to her. And to the secrets he had been unable to unlock.

Elizabeth's infernal secrets.

Pain was beginning to spread from his stomach to his head. Particularly potent garlic, or merely the insufferable remembrance of having left loose ends in a room below?

With a glance to the window, to the angel, to the door, he backed away from the bed. At the door, he stopped.

"Vulnerabilities are deadly in this court. You must come to realize this or you will not be safe."

He tugged at the door, considered that toying with her might be more fun than a quick conquest anyway, then turned once more toward the angel. "It is only with extreme caution that one can truly be free. You may trust me well on this."

Chapter Eight

Elizabeth lay where he had left her, tumbled and wrapped in her blankets of fur. Robbed of so much of her life's force, Dante knew she would be unable to challenge.

He sat down beside her, found her shivering.

"I suppose it would be useless to ask where you have been," Elizabeth said in a voice emerging as little more than a whisper.

"I cannot explain," Dante said.

Carefully turning Elizabeth over, Dante slipped his arms beneath her shoulders to lift her from the pillows.

"You have never professed love for me and I have never demanded it," Elizabeth said, words taking some time to get past her bruised, swollen throat. "Have you returned for the information you seek? Shall I give it to you for leaving me like this? As a reward?"

"A reward for what?"

"Unraveling your true nature."

Dante looked closer at Elizabeth's wan face and waited for her to go on. He knew how sick she must feel. His own throat tightened.

"Her name is Dominique. But I am afraid, my beautiful lover, that my brother owns her, body and soul."

"Does he, indeed?"

"Rumor has it he won her." Elizabeth paused to cough. Dante wiped the speckles of blood from her chin with the back of his hand and refrained from touching his lips to the stain.

"She was a lavish gift from a bad debtor," Elizabeth continued weakly. "Plucked from a nunnery, they say. Well educated in some things, while sadly lacking in others. One can see this in her eyes, can they not? Would you be thinking her an unlikely candidate for the wife of my brother?"

"That depends on what comes with her."

"You assume there is more to her than a pretty face?"

Elizabeth struggled to breathe, to speak. Dante laid a cool hand to her throat to ease her discomfort. Elizabeth looked up to see the frown he was wearing.

"I have heard some mention of properties, true enough," Elizabeth confided, rallying, determined not to faint as the pain in her throat increased. "Yet the way my brother looks at her . . . The way *you* looked at her . . ."

She closed her eyes, fighting hard to finish what she had started. "What is it about her, Dante? What is her lure? You know nothing of her. Surely you do not crave her professed innocence? Every woman is innocent once in her life. Only once."

Dante ran a hand slowly over Elizabeth's silken shoulder, remembering what he had given up this night to return here. Conquest could wait. Elizabeth was an unfinished detail.

He said, "She is beautiful, is she not?"

"Ah," Elizabeth sighed. "Beauty. Is this your answer?"

"I am no poet, Elizabeth, nor am I likely to become one at your request."

"Yes, and my brother has gotten to her first, my keen friend. You would do well to remember it. His plans include nothing less than marriage."

Elizabeth observed his reaction, warded off light-headedness with a turn of her neck. "Whatever it is that you see in her, my brother also sees. He watches over her carefully and has set others to the task of doing the same. Do not be fooled. The girl is as much a captive here as she was in that nunnery, and nowhere near as safe."

Unsafe? Didn't he know it, Dante thought, allowing his fingers to drift to the swell of Elizabeth's breasts, observing the faint rise and fall of her breath.

"The bad debtor. The one who gave her away," he said. "Who was this?"

"Her father."

Dante's fingers hesitated in their exploration.

"It would seem that we are not the only dismal family in England," Elizabeth added laconically.

"Has this father of hers a name?" Dante asked.

"He does."

"What might that name be?"

"Wallace."

A small storm gathered upon the outskirts of the ivory sheets that surrounded Elizabeth's body as Dante heard the name. Conscious of nothing but the implications of this, he went inward for several seconds, reemerging only when Elizabeth's cough returned.

"I have every right to be jealous," she said.

"I'm sorry."

"As you cannot have her, I suppose your apology matters little."

"I am sorry, nonetheless."

Elizabeth's expression had dulled. With the dawn's light gaining strength in its battle over night, Dante could see her eyes less clearly, but found them round and bright, despite what he had done to dilute their color. For the first time that he could recall, he felt truly displeased with himself. He felt guilty. And then there might be a small bit of anger thrown in. Had Elizabeth merely allowed this . . . for love?

Slowly, he placed her back on her pillows, eyes locked to

hers. He thought her suddenly younger than her twenty-two years, and much less wizened and callous than she pretended to be. Had she been drained of those trappings?

"I'll not help you," she stated faintly.

"I have not asked for your help."

"You will soon enough."

"On the contrary, I would ask of you nothing of the kind. I would do nothing to jeopardize your position here."

"I do not give a damn about my position here."

"One of us has to."

"I do not love you, Dante."

"Not even a little?"

Her green eyes softened, Dante imagined. But had she read his mind? Remnants of long-strained and departed heartstrings pulled at his chest. Elizabeth was correct in that he had never professed to love her. He could not love her, could not love anyone. He had no heart for such things.

"I stay here because of you, but I do not necessarily love you," Elizabeth told him. "Your feelings for Alan's bride are merely a nuisance."

Unable to find the strength to sit up, Elizabeth sagged back down to the covers. Her hand found Dante's, briefly, resting lightly. She said with complete directness, "My brother will kill you if you touch her."

"I have no intention of allowing him such an opportunity."

"I know you better than you think, Dante."

"Yes, I believe you do."

"You will leave?"

"And miss the festivities? I wouldn't think of it."

"My beautiful Duke, devil, scoundrel. You must be careful. My brother already fears you. He fears anyone with a better title and a bigger . . ." Elizabeth coughed, went paler, closed her eyes.

"Yes, Elizabeth?" Dante pressed, bringing his face nearer to hers.

"My brother wishes he were half the man you are. He will not take kindly to your attentions."

"No? Then the Rothchildes have very different tastes, do they not?"

Elizabeth smiled. The smile dissolved into pain. "My brother allows me freedom in this castle because he fears me. I am able to do as I please because I am discreet."

Her expression grew clouded. Her lips glistened beneath the lick of her tongue. Dante watched her carefully.

"Alan will not be as lenient with *her*. You must promise me something, Dante. I will not help unless you do."

"What will you have of me, Elizabeth?"

"I would have you come to me each time you think of her. In this way, everyone will be safe."

Dante searched the outlines of Elizabeth's face, observing how close to fainting she was, how transparent she seemed in some areas, while maintaining her infuriatingly secretive world. Safe? he thought. She could not possibly believe being with him could be safe. Had she no idea of what he had done to her merely minutes ago? Or the battle he had faced in trying to keep her alive once he had had a taste of her?

Safe? He leaned forward, inhaling the smell of her fatigue, discerning no scent of fear. It came to him in that moment that her lack of fear was what made this union so thrilling.

He laid his lips on her cheek, touched her chilled skin with his tongue. Her skin was alive, though pale. Elizabeth was a creature who fed on sunlight.

The smell of dried blood on her throat floated to his nostrils, producing a strange mixture of pleasure and guilt. More inner battles.

His hands shook slightly.

"Perhaps it is a pity you can read me so well," he concluded, mouth moving over the bones of her chin, hands sliding into her thick, tangled hair.

"Yes, perhaps," Elizabeth whispered.

Dante felt the vibration of her reply against his lips. He felt her skin quiver.

"If my brother truly knew me well, he would shake in his boots," she said. "My mere thoughts would bring him to his knees in despair."

"Then it is better he gets no wind of your talents, dearest Elizabeth. That is a fact."

Had Elizabeth become deranged, Dante wondered? Had her loss of blood confused her? Why would Alan Rothchilde fear any woman, let alone his own sister?

"My fee, Dante," Elizabeth muttered.

"Fee?" His mouth hovered above hers, where the scent of blood came to him on the air she exhaled.

His hunger returned. Desire strained at his breeches.

Elizabeth looked up at him wearing an unreadable expression.

"My fee for the help I will offer is that you must come to me when I call. Always. Regardless of whom it is you envision beneath you, I will have your . . ."

"Yes?" Dante prompted.

"Friendship. Fealty. Will you swear to this, Dante?"

"It is something you needn't have wasted a wish on, Elizabeth."

Words seemed to bubble deep within Elizabeth's chest. A rivulet of blood, now nearly slowed to a trickle, would be inhibiting her breath, Dante knew. The loss of blood would be choking her, weakening her.

"We have a bargain, then," Elizabeth whispered, voice rattling, then trailing off into oblivion.

"We have, indeed, my fair one." *At least until I know what you are about.*

"Dante?" Elizabeth called, barely.

"Yes?"

"I will kill you myself before I will allow my brother to do it."

"A comforting pledge, dearest Elizabeth, to be sure. I feel much better already."

Dante ran his fingers over her neck, brought a bit of caked blood to his lips. But he did not taste what lay upon his finger. His hunger was too dire. He was too needy. And she could lose no more of her life's essence.

Elizabeth's lips parted. She strained, winced, spoke in hushed phrases. "I wonder," she said.

Dante leaned in closer to hear.

"I wonder . . . why no one . . . saved me."

As Dante stared down at her peaked face, and swept the honey-hued hair back from her dampened brow, he made a vow.

No further harm could come to Elizabeth. She was much too valuable. Much too endearing . . . and delectable.

No harm would come to her.

He would see to it.

Chapter Nine

The steward, carefully chosen for his discretion and similar nocturnal appetites, opened the door to Dante's rooms. The space was dark, its walls heavily concealed by burgundy draperies, its windows boarded by thick wooden shutters.

Dante brushed past.

"My duke," the steward said, "you have a visitor."

Dante paused, said wryly, "Dessert, perchance? How thoughtful."

The steward's face was covered by the glow of an uneasy sweat. "The lady would not hear a word of protest." A gold coin lay exposed on his open palm. "Little enough use the coin will do me when you have me hung for admitting her."

Dante sniffed the air, where a strange scent floated. Soap? Lye? Old bruised skin?

He turned.

A woman stood in the corner, barely discernable in the dark, save for an expanse of light-skinned face. An old woman, Dante saw, dressed in black. The black of a nun's habit? The black of mourning?

"I am distressed to have disturbed you, Duke Dante," the woman offered in a seraphic voice.

The skin on Dante's arms chilled. His nose wrinkled.

238 / *Linda Thomas-Sundstrom*

"I have but little time here," the woman added. "The guards will soon find me."

"Are guards after you?" Dante inquired.

"Protection is what they suppose. From what, one might wonder?"

"Thieves? Assassins? Monsters?" Dante suggested.

"You know of such dangers in this castle?"

Dante smiled.

"You find my plight amusing?" the woman queried, showing, Dante thought, some bravado, though her hands were clenched and her teeth chattered.

"I know nothing of any plight," Dante said, smiling more.

The woman's lips parted as if she would protest, though she did not. Her lips were, Dante noted, thin and dry, and no doubt an example of what else lay beneath her dress. She smelled of leather.

"Is this the way people behave at court?" she demanded at length. "Does everyone here find amusement in my girl's torment?"

"Your girl?"

"Lady Wallace."

Most interesting, Dante thought. Most interesting, indeed.

"Has Lady Wallace sent you here?" he asked. "Is it not an unusual time to come calling?"

"She has not sent me. I seek answers."

"Ah, it is not to be a rendezvous, then?" Dante countered. "How disappointing."

"Rendezvous?"

The woman spoke the word with a perfect French accent. Dante knew her tongue had wrapped around this word in her mouth. He imagined what her withered tongue would feel like wrapped in such a way around his cock. An image came to him of how her grainy flesh would hang shapelessly from her brittle old bones. Like a plucked chicken.

He grimaced.

"Does the term 'rendezvous' not mean, in actuality, mystery and false alliances?" the woman said, wary of his light-ness.

"Why yes, I suppose it does," Dante agreed. "But I am tired. Get to the point, if you will."

"I have come to ask your help."

"And how might I be of help to a woman such as your-self?"

"Rumor . . ." The woman paused, started over. "I have been forewarned about you."

"Nothing too dire, I trust?"

"At the same time, I have also heard tell that you are a gentleman. Is this true?"

"Not particularly, I'm afraid. A title is never a guarantee, you know."

How many years had it been since he had been a gentle-man? Too many to count. Too far to go back.

The woman sidled toward the door as far as she could without passing Dante. He now caught the scent of her fear. Pungent, fermented, withered.

"Your lady sent me a note," Dante said.

This seemed to startle the woman. Her head came up and tilted, as if she would look at his comment from all angles. Her cheeks were strained above her black collar. "She sent no note to you, sir. She would not dare do such a thing."

"Then it seems I was mistaken."

And who could have sent the note? Dante wondered now. If the angel had not, who had? Why hadn't he read the blasted thing?

"Perhaps Elizabeth Rothchilde sent it," the woman said.

Dante's eyes crept slowly up her wrinkled face.

"It was she who suggested I gain your confidence," the woman explained.

"Elizabeth is a thoughtful woman," Dante confirmed, fin-gers curling, back rigid with the mention of Elizabeth's name.

"You did see Lady Wallace tonight?" the woman asked. "It was you who came to her?"

Dante observed how her hands went to her throat, and then, catching him watching her, the woman dropped her hands to her sides. She would be the angel's servant. Perhaps even a relative less fortunate than the angel. Unless one considered where the angel was and what her fate would be.

"What is it you want here?" Dante asked impatiently, hearing in the thick walls the resonance of Elizabeth's voice imploring him to stay well clear of Alan Rothchilde's bride.

The woman across from him reeked of dread. The room stank of it. The odor was all too familiar. Ten foot–thick walls sealed them off from the rest of the castle and its occupants. No one would hear if she shouted, Dante reasoned. These rooms had been chosen with care. No one would come to her rescue.

But then, he was tired beyond belief. And the old woman held no promise. Dawn had arrived beyond the wall. He could feel it. He could sense the heat of the sun, though his room had never been exposed to it. He could taste the light.

Somewhere above, Alan Rothchilde would be settling in for a nap, as would the others of Lord Rothchilde's dark entourage, his "Midnight Court." The beasts would sleep, as he would. The rest of the world might turn, but the night creatures would not be a part of it.

"Will you help her?" the woman dared to say, interrupting his musings, disrupting the pull of sleep that lay over him.

Dante felt his crossness coming on. His need for rest is why he would forego the pleasure of throwing this woman to the wolves, he told himself. This is why he would allow her to escape. He was fatigued, drowsy, uninterested. His mind was occupied elsewhere.

In spite of that, he could save her for his steward. He might easily best her with an arm tied behind his back. Two arms. But then the pleasure would be halved if he hadn't the ability to touch her, to inflict his tongue and his teeth upon her puckered skin. And she would no doubt whine ceaselessly.

His fingers closed. The crackle of paper seemed uncommonly loud in the quiet. He followed the noise, found the note still in his hand. If the angel had not sent it, who had?

"Does Lord Rothchilde know about you?" the strange woman asked, taking from her pocket a sprig of garlic and holding it before her as she backed into the door.

"Are these the kinds of questions they teach servants these days? More's the pity."

Dante held his ground.

"I came here to discern what kind of . . . man you are, and to beg your aid in my lady's escape."

"I'm afraid I have no such aid to offer."

"You are Lord Rothchilde's ally? One of his . . ."

"There is no love lost between your angel's betrothed and myself, I must admit. Still, and all in all, I cannot help you."

"Perhaps Lady Rothchilde was mistaken in her allusions to your honor?"

"Maybe you are too inquisitive for your own good."

The woman nodded, held the garlic higher. "I would do anything to help my lady."

"Even if it means asking the likes of me to participate?"

"Even such a thing as that."

Dante's body beat with a strange irregularity. His feigned nonchalance was wearing thin.

"Lady Rothchilde said you exhibited honor about all else, though you would feign to its opposite," the woman said. "She did not tell us you were a demon. That was not made clear. We knew not that you are a creature of the night. The stench of what you are pervades this place."

"Might you say how you come by such knowledge? How you have judged my countenance so quickly?"

"My village was small, though not isolated from the rest of the land. We were taught whom to fear, well enough."

"Yet the angel's father would sell her to such a creature as you're discussing?"

"Her father is dead. Lord Rothchilde saw to that."

"Ah."

"Lady Rothchilde does not know about you?" the woman said. "She was wrong in her estimation of your character?"

"Wrong?" Dante repeated, closing in on the garlic, fortifying himself against the discomfort such a small plant could inflict.

"Lady Rothchilde told me you were the only one to be trusted here, and that you would help us."

The old woman was close enough for Dante to have caught her. But his arms would not move. His head would not turn to follow her progress toward the door—toward freedom from what might have otherwise overtaken her. It wasn't the garlic that caused his lethargy. It was the sun.

The woman's heavy-lidded eyes were veiled by the scarf she wore over her head. She had the door open. "Perhaps Lady Rothchilde does know about you. Perhaps love is indeed blind."

Dante knew he should stop her. The saggy old defiant thing knew about him, or thought she knew. Secrets like this could be pried out of an old woman. Their bones snapped like twigs when pressure was applied.

So, why did he hold back? Was it because she watched over the angel? Because she had real concern for the angel's plight? If so, then she would merely be in the way. His way.

But then . . . she was such an *old* woman. Not a worthy adversary. She knew nothing for certain. She knew no one at Rothchilde's fortress. She would never be chosen as an appetizer by anyone in Rothchilde's party. No one here would care about her fear. Therefore, she had some time left.

"Your angel will not escape," Dante said, stifling a yawn. "Rothchilde is thorough, if nothing else."

But his words echoed in the cavernous room.

The old woman had gone.

Chapter Ten

"You desire me to go after her? Detain her?" Dante's steward asked.

Dante's gaze settled on him. "Was there not something odd about her?"

"Decidedly so. Now, will you drink before your rest?"

"You have someone in mind?"

"I have someone in the next room."

Dante turned his head, heard no sounds, looked back in question.

"Lord Rothchilde chose his fortress well. The walls are thick."

Dante nodded. "And Lord Rothchilde will begin to miss his servants and other minions who lose their way in the night. Though, I suppose, those absences will not be as noticeable with such a gathering as this."

Dante tossed off his shirt and crawled onto the bed. He closed his eyes, not wanting to sleep. Sleep brought visions of blurred white flesh. Faces came and went, as always. Victims. Names from the past. Yet the hunger was upon him. His shaft still throbbed with the remembrance of Elizabeth's willingness, and the moist heat between her thighs. Or was the throb leftover from his sighting of the angel in her bower?

He wanted to sleep the dreamless sleep of his kind, not

bothered by visions and contemplations. Not bothered by fantasies of wings or the scent of Elizabeth's hair. Such things should be left to mortal men.

"I will dream of the angel," he muttered to himself. "A much simpler pastime."

After all, how many delightful ways might he invent to snare her?

How could an old crone protect her, really, when her fate was sealed?

"I'll have this angel, all right." Elizabeth had most assuredly seen to that. He would take up her challenge and return triumphant. He would part the angel's fur . . . Surely angels possessed the same attributes real women did?

Then he would slap his cock into her tight little slit until she begged for mercy, or begged for more.

Upon that pleasant thought, he drifted.

"Steward?"

Dante rose to his elbow. The room was dark. He had overslept.

"Steward?" he called again as a sound came from the vicinity of the door. A bolt sliding into place?

Senses alert, Dante's surroundings formed around him. Stone walls, draped and shuttered windows, tousled bed-sheets. The room's single candle, now spent, sputtered softly. From some distance came the sound of a thin trickle of water seeping through cracks.

He inhaled, sat up, held back a spasm of distaste. Someone had brought garlic back into the room. The odor invaded the quiet, chasing away the remnants of sleep.

"What is it you want here?" Dante said, voice ringing through the thick, moist dark. "Have you nothing more imaginative to offer than insidiousness?"

A flash of white crossed his eye, hovered in the corner, then moved forward. Slightly. Enough.

"How did you get away, angel?" Dante said, recognizing

her scent beyond the garlic she would use to ensure her safety.

Muscles gathering to attention, Dante's eyes opened wider in surprised disbelief. Quite phantomlike, a woman glided toward the bed, head bowed, eyes hidden. A humming began in Dante's ears as he stared. His chest tightened.

The angel looked up. Even in the last of the light, Dante could see the curious brilliance in the gaze. But . . . these were not the eyes of the angel. He knew these eyes.

His wits were momentarily eclipsed by the stink of the plant. His sight dimmed considerably. His eyes stung. Bloody hell! Who first considered that a plant could inflict so much damage on a beast? Did they try other talismans before settling on this particular one? Did everyone at Rothchilde castle know of its properties? One would assume, after all, that this particular host would have seen to clear the halls of it.

"My dearest Dante," Elizabeth said, voice low-toned and earthy.

From his position on the bed, Dante looked up to eye Elizabeth levelly. "You are well enough to move about, Elizabeth?"

"Out of necessity," Elizabeth returned, working to keep her face passive and her expression hidden, knowing she would succeed only if she adhered to her plan. Yet the smile Dante offered was devastating. The sight of him in the bed made her heart lurch.

"You have the smell of her about you," Dante said.

"You recognize her scent already, then?"

"Are you unfamiliar with the senses we beasts possess, you who have lived within your brother's inner circle?"

"Scent before sight," Elizabeth quoted. "Even in the night."

Dante's eyes went to her throat, she noticed—to the black velvet ribbon of jewels she wore tightly wound around her neck to hide the wounds he had made. He signaled her closer.

"Why does her essence linger upon you?" he asked.

"I have brought you a token."

Dante watched as Elizabeth sat on the foot of his bed. She was dressed in a dazzling display of green brocade trimmed with ermine. In spite of the richness she exhibited, her skin was alabaster-white. When she blinked, there was hesitation.

"Token?" Dante narrowed his own eyes. Elizabeth's necklace shone in the candlelight. Egg-shaped emerald stones flared with an inner darkness. But the flare and exuberance of her countenance masked a remaining translucency, he thought. Her green eyes were feverish.

"Another reward?" he asked as pangs of guilt reassembled.

"You did not kill me," Elizabeth said. "You do not profess to love me, but you let me live. Then you went to her."

"Do you have eyes in the back of your head, dearest Elizabeth?"

Dante got to his knees on the covers and crawled toward her. Elizabeth did not draw back, as he half-expected her to do. She showed no signs of retreat.

"Where is she?" Dante asked. "What has been done to her?"

"You do not know these things?" Elizabeth countered.

"Actually, I have not put my mind to it."

"Why ever not?"

"Is it not a waste of time, when you will tell me?"

Elizabeth laughed, coughed, put both hands to her throat and closed her eyes. Dante reached her side.

"Careful, Dante," Elizabeth whispered. "It will seem as though you care."

"I do care."

Elizabeth attempted a smile, failed to affix it.

"What is it you expected me to do?" Dante asked.

"Reason that it is not worth the effort. That *she* is not worth the effort."

"Whatever effort are you speaking of?"

The green eyes accosted him suddenly. Dante frowned. Was Elizabeth's secret that she was a witch? Could she see down into him so completely as to know what he might be thinking? Had she cast a spell upon him? Used the ancient incantations to keep him unbalanced?

For what purpose?

He considered this question.

Elizabeth leaned in to rest her head on his shoulder. Her soft masses of curls brushed against his face. So soft. So pale. The hue of summer wheat, an image only remembered in the deepest recesses of his mind. The darkest recesses of his mind.

This reminder was uncomfortable. He had made a vow. He would keep her safe.

But he was so hungry.

Elizabeth's head came up, realigning on her smooth regal neck with a swanlike grace.

"You told her I am honorable?" Dante said. "And that I would help her."

"And you turned her down."

"Was it a game, then? A tournament of wills?"

"Something perilously close."

"Did you send the old woman?"

"Yes."

"To tempt me further?"

"To see if you would keep your promise."

"What promise would this be, exactly?"

Elizabeth's eyes flashed in place of a reply.

"Hadn't I done enough to you already?" Dante asked.

"Not enough, by far, it seems."

In an attempt to dissect her remark, Dante tilted his head. "You are speaking of love?"

"Do you love my brother's choice?"

"Would you keep me from others so that you can continue *not* loving me in the future?"

"So that I can keep you close, whatever there is or isn't between us."

"Selfishness doesn't become you, my green-eyed challenger."

"Do not insult my intelligence, Dante. Look upon these walls. This is where I live."

Dante felt the lines of a fresh frown deepen the furrow on his forehead. Was she being so subtle as to have made clear her position in her brother's nest? She was perhaps the only woman to remain outside of Alan Rothchilde's clutches, while existing in the very center of the debauchery and evil.

How *did* she accomplish this?

Back to that.

"Elizabeth . . ."

"I am a woman, Dante, in case you have not noticed."

His frown deepened further. "I have noticed."

Ask her, he thought. *Just ask her how a mere woman might survive here amid her brother's lair.* Wasn't that what he had come to Rothchilde's castle in search of? The knowledge of who this sister was? And how she withstood all this? Were these answers not the reason for being here, where danger reigned even for such a creature as himself?

"You touched her," Elizabeth remarked before he could ask anything.

And Elizabeth's intake of breath caused her breasts to swell above the heart-shaped neckline of her gown.

Throb. Pulse. Rise in his breeches. But this was not supposed to happen. He did not love her, he reminded himself. He was incapable of such emotion. In all of his years on this godforsaken ground, he had never felt the need to love.

"You left her because she was protected, and out of necessity rather than any choice you might have deemed to make," Elizabeth charged.

Guards. Garlic. Hindrances, one and all, all right, Dante thought. But those things had not unnerved him.

"Now who is insulting whose intelligence?" he returned.

"He knows about you," Elizabeth said. "Need I tell you how my brother knows?"

Dante grinned. Once again her breasts swelled above her bodice, along with her anger—though she kept a loose leash on that anger. Her breasts were luminous, plump with life and longing. In turn, he longed to hold them, lick them, caress them. He reached out, ran a finger across the delicate bones beneath her chin, and fought off a shudder of delight. No, not delight. Something more.

"I do hope that scrawny lad was not your brother's intended bedtime snack," Dante said. "I can understand how this might have upset him."

A patch of pink the size of a thumbnail flushed Elizabeth's cheeks. *Fascinating,* Dante thought. *Demure, despite her challenge. Alluring.* He barely noticed the garlic now. He barely thought about the angel.

Perhaps his hunger was tainting his viewpoint.

"You needn't bother telling me anything about your brother," he said. "I know him well enough."

"Do you?" Elizabeth countered. "Then you know *she* told him."

"Actually, I reasoned that she might be too frightened to do anything of the kind."

"Just as you reasoned that the promise I extracted from you was a joke?"

"On the contrary, I believe you knew your warnings would challenge me to go to her, to see for myself, up close, what caused your brother to choose her." Dante eyed Elizabeth closely. "Was I wrong in assuming this?"

"Yet you did nothing to her."

"There is an abundance of time left to change the outcome, is there not?"

"Garlic had been placed in her room, Dante. Perhaps its effects are not lost on you?" Elizabeth tried another smile, this time with a fair amount of success, though her lips did not long remain upturned.

"I placed the garlic there," she said.

"Ah. I believed it was your brother."

"I removed the guard, so that you wouldn't."

"I had already met a scrawny lad."

Elizabeth could not fully hide her distaste over this comment, Dante saw. He said, "You sent the note?"

"The note was a warning, not an invitation. Had you stayed but a while longer in the tower, you would never have left it."

"You would warn me, and at the same time make a present of the angel?"

"A trial, merely. A test. My brother's choice is no gift."

"A test of what? The sharpness of my wits? My fighting skills?"

Yes, and in which way had he failed, Dante wondered? What was she getting at? He hadn't taken the angel. He had not dragged her from the bed and clamped his teeth to her neck, beating Alan Rothchilde to it. Elizabeth had been victorious in this, surely? And he had allowed her victory.

The look in Elizabeth's eyes was stirring up something deep within him. Something discomfiting. The beat in his throat had become a nagging question. His thirst was now a viable craving.

Then an idea slipped in beneath the other thoughts. A new scent came to him, stronger than Elizabeth's, mingling with Elizabeth's. Token. She had mentioned a token. Something belonging to the angel, perhaps?

He looked at Elizabeth questioningly.

She was no longer smiling.

Chapter Eleven

Dante's lungs were near to bursting, though he supposed he did not actually breathe. Habit, maybe, that he inhaled through his nose? Old traditions were so very hard to break.

"Yes. I brought you something," Elizabeth said.

Dante's limbs took on the burn of being internally heated. Perspiration broke out on his brow. He could discern the reason, well enough, of course. Though the stink of the garlic pervaded, swirling through the air, tainting everything, it masked a thing beyond it.

Elizabeth had brought the angel.

Here.

To him.

Elizabeth watched his reaction, felt near to swooning. Weakness pervaded her body, still. She was drained, suffocating. After everything she had offered, Christopher Dante dared to look beyond her now.

With a limp hand, she signaled.

Surprised, speechless, Dante stared. The angel, in a blur of white, stepped into view. Simultaneously, Elizabeth reached for his hand. She placed it across the exposed portion of her breast, held it there for several breaths, then drew her soft, full lushness completely free of the cloth surrounding it.

There were others in the room, Dante knew suddenly. Not

just the angel. Dark shapes drifted in the shadows, in the corners, near the door. And Elizabeth, seemingly impervious to them and to the angel's presence, molded his fingers around her.

"You were right," she whispered. "Innocence is alluring." Her fingers squeezed his. "You are right in that I have never given in to the weaknesses that bind other women. I have not been allowed such leeway. But I was innocent once, and untried. You, of all . . . people . . . know this for a fact."

She manipulated his hand so that his palm rubbed across her raised pink nipple. "Imagine me here, amid the nightmares of my brother's court. Imagine what a nightmare I have been living, Dante. Until you came."

The emphasis she placed on the last word was not lost to him. Elizabeth leaned in, ran her mouth across his.

"My brother searches for her as we speak," she said. "He will, of course, find her before long."

Her lips lingered on his, slid softly across his as she spoke. "You must help her. But not for the reasons you assume. First, there is something we must do. There is a thing *she* can do."

Elizabeth drew his head downward, so that his mouth rested upon the nipple that lay exposed, so that he could no longer see the angel. Above him, Elizabeth leaned her head back, whispered, "Drink."

He was ravenous, nearly insane with hunger. But his vow not to injure Elizabeth further rang in his ears, alongside the beat of her heart. Meaning to speak, he opened his mouth. His tongue touched her skin. She sighed, then her hand went to his breeches. She had found him hard. Decidedly hard. Deliciously hard.

"Yes," Elizabeth whispered. "You know."

Affected by her brash invitation and the slickness of her oiled skin, Dante half wondered why she had brought the woman he called his angel here to watch. His tongue, seemingly of its own volition, slipped sideways, over the mound of her breast. But he did not draw her into his mouth. Instead, he straightened. He looked into her eyes.

"You can smell innocence," Elizabeth said. "Can you not?"

"What are you doing?" Dante whispered.

"It is too late, don't you see?" Elizabeth said. "He noticed. He will come for you."

Dante was confused. Allowing Elizabeth to turn her head, he followed her attention across the room—to the angel. But Elizabeth's faint cough brought him back.

"So you will kill me? Is that it?" he said. "You will give her to me as a parting gift before you let your brother have me?"

Elizabeth was deadly serious. "I told you I would never let my brother kill you."

Dante laughed. "Then you will do so yourself? How many men have you brought with you, dear one? Or do you assume the angel will keep me so occupied that I might fail to notice the plan you have in mind?"

His laughter subsided. "Does *she* know what you are planning?"

"Oh yes, my dearest Dante," Elizabeth whispered in his ear. "She knows some of it. You did not actually believe a woman could lack both the power and intellect to fool you?"

Dante studied Elizabeth's oval face. "Whatever do you mean?" he asked as the angel took a step forward.

Chapter Twelve

The angel's eyes were downcast, as he had first seen them. But her pose was not one of meek compliance. It was merely tolerance. He watched avidly as she took a second step.

She wore a gown of pink. Not the white he had imagined, but the color of a carnation. The color of a rose that hadn't the benefit of the sun to deepen its lividness. The gown seemed to float in heavy pieces, failing to denote the lightness or airiness he had imagined. Long cords of rope dangled from her shoulders from a collar around her neck, like an overlong necklace.

Dante swallowed, stunned. It was not rope that dangled, but an intricate braiding of garlic stems.

His hand went to his mouth in an involuntary gesture. Mesmerized, he stared harder.

The garlic was also wound into a cornet, and intertwined in the black hair that hung to the angel's waist. His limbs tingled. His head swam as all that garlic came closer, as the angel came closer. The puzzlement of it kept him still.

"I do not wish to demean you," Elizabeth whispered into his ear, and yet the words seemed to come from his own mind rather than from any external source.

"I merely question the validity of your judgment," she

continued. "I question the intelligence of my brother, who thinks he can deal with a creature like this."

The candle sputtered. Elizabeth lifted a hand, and another candle was placed in it, wick lit, before Dante could even see what had happened.

A pool of light bathed Elizabeth, tossing long shadows across her face. The expression she wore was one of determination. The flush had disappeared from her cheeks, leaving her wan. Though Dante wanted to speak, his attention moved to the angel. His own limbs felt heavy. His head felt light.

"You are honorable," Elizabeth said. "I can think of no other way to end this."

"End?" Dante intoned, seeing now that the angel was beyond colorless. The pale dress seemed invariably darker by contrast.

"She will not willingly help us," Elizabeth explained. "She is beyond helping anyone, beyond anything you or I could imagine."

"What is this?" Dante said. But his hands began to shake with the nearness of the angel and her heavily odored, garlic-laced raiment. He could not lift his arms.

No, it was something else that bothered him, more potent than the garlic. He looked up with a ripple of shock to find that a cross had been hung on the post of his bed. Its silver facets gleamed in the candlelight.

Dante swallowed. Eyes wide, he faced Elizabeth.

"You thought her innocent, my dearest Dante," Elizabeth said. "They all did at first. It took a woman to see through the ruse. I tried to warn you."

Was this indeed a joke? Dante wondered, his mind grasping at anything that might explain or shed some light.

Was something wrong with the angel?

"Touch me," Elizabeth whispered, vying for his attention, demanding compliance. Her voice was silk, surrounding a harder substance. Her green eyes were once again flecked with gold.

Secrets.

Dante's hand went to her cheek. Elizabeth covered his fingers with hers.

Secrets . . . there in her touch, in her paleness, in each shallow breath she took.

"Bloody hell!" he exclaimed as she separated one of his fingers from the others on his right hand and pressed it lightly to her lips.

"Elizabeth," he whispered, feeling the throb below his waist, fighting the urges she had always brought out in him, despite the best of plans.

He watched with fascination as Elizabeth's lips parted. He nearly rose from the bed when she inserted his finger inside of her hot, wet mouth. He nearly burst as she drew on the finger, sucking it inside of her lips, covering it with her tongue.

He could barely move—caught between the garlic and the shadow of the silver cross that stretched across the sheets, between the angel's mysterious presence and Elizabeth's careful ministrations. Yet he felt curiously removed from those hindrances. One part of his body was reacting, despite the circumstances. Something seemed live enough . . . in his pants.

Chapter Thirteen

You will listen to me, Elizabeth sent silently to Dante. *I have not kept myself free of the nest for no reason.*

She tugged slowly on his hand, and his finger slid from her mouth, between her teeth, over her fevered lips. He was looking at her so strangely.

I have never interfered in my brother's pursuits, she told him. *Until now, Dante. Until I met you.*

He had some residual strength left, she knew. And she could take no chances. He had to be weakened more. Enough.

Climbing onto her knees beside him on the bed, she took his shirt into her hands. From her pocket she pulled forth a dagger and slit the white cloth down the center.

"You cannot kill me with that," Dante said.

His speech was slow, hesitant, Elizabeth noted. She smiled grimly and placed both of her hands on his chest.

"I don't mean to kill you," she told him, mouth moving over his skin in lazy circles, her hair falling across his lap. "I mean to have my way with you, and then some."

"Have you not chosen an odd way of going about it?"

"Yes. I suppose I have."

She felt his skin ripple. Pleasure, in spite of his defiance. Excitement, in spite of the garlic and the cross. It would have been much easier if he hadn't gone to sleep fully dressed, she thought. How long could she keep control of the thing that stood not far from the bedside?

But then, Dante's head was back when she looked at him. His dark, dangerous eyes were closed. She ran her tongue down to his waistband, heard him groan. Perhaps he was weaker than she imagined. Perhaps . . .

Confident now, with some of her fears eased, she glanced up again. Her heart skipped inside of her chest.

He was staring down at her.

There was nothing weak or remotely passive in the keen expression he wore.

"Perhaps," Dante said, taking her shoulders into his hands with a grip that made her wince, "you need a little help?"

Chapter Fourteen

Four guards rushed to Elizabeth's side. Dante held them back with a hand raised in warning. "Be gone. Do you not see that your mistress and I have things to do?"

"They will go nowhere on your command," Elizabeth said breathlessly.

"They are not here to protect you from me, surely?" Dante's eyes slid to the band at her neck. Did she think he would finish what he had started? Might she assume he would drain her dry this time, if pressed to the limits of his arousal?

If she thought so, why would she be here now? Why taunt him?

"They are here to watch over *her*," Elizabeth replied.

Dante's eyes went to the angel. "Whatever for?"

His question lingered in the stuffy air. He spoke again to Elizabeth. "You have trussed her up to protect her from me?"

Breath. Silence. A long stretch of unspoken excuses. *Yet so curious,* Dante thought. This new and mysterious Elizabeth was so damned intriguing. Why hadn't he seen it before?

"Why doesn't the cross weaken you?" Elizabeth countered.

"I have made it a point never to give away secrets that matter."

"I am here to change that."

Unable to help himself, Dante smiled in surprise. "Did you bring her here to bargain with me?"

"I brought her here as a last resort."

"For what, might I ask?"

"Siring."

"What?"

"Is that not what you call it? Does one beast not *sire* another?"

"I do not follow your line of thought," Dante said, smile fading.

"Can you not? How unfortunate, since both of our lives are now at stake."

Dante sat back, gazed down at Elizabeth's ashen face. He glanced to the angel, whose eyes were still downcast. "What has she to do with this?" he asked.

But he didn't like the expression Elizabeth adopted. It was one of someone getting the better of another. It was Elizabeth thinking she had gotten the better of him.

Had he missed something?

What the bloody hell could it be?

She leaned closer to him again. She looked up at him and he could swear that some of the keenness had left her eyes. He could swear she was waiting, expecting something.

He watched as she got to her feet on the covers, and as she lifted the cross down from its place. A need to back away nearly overwhelmed him as she brought the cross to him. With a fascination too great to retreat from, he stayed where he was as she pressed the silver cross to his chest.

The odor of burnt flesh filled the room. Dante's mouth opened in a silent protest. The ache was paramount, but he did not move.

"Are you not angry with me for doing this to you?" Elizabeth whispered to him, eyes wide and staring intently into his.

He took hold of her wrist, shook it. The cross dropped to the floor with a sharp, metallic sound. With a graceful bending of his elbow, he brought Elizabeth closer.

"I am not angry," he said, lips forming the words slowly, precisely, above the soft hiss of his scorched flesh.

"Then perhaps this will do," Elizabeth said, picking up her dagger, running its sharp tip down the length of his arm.

Dante's skin opened beneath the pressure of the razor-sharp knife. A thin line of blood gathered and then began to spill. Dark red liquid ran down his arm. A drop of it hit the sheets with a dull thud.

In an instant, he had Elizabeth on her back. Arms pinned above her head, he looked into her face. "I repeat, Elizabeth: What are you doing?"

Her lips were on his before he finished his query. Back arched, arms straining above her, Elizabeth rose to meet him.

There was a noise in the distance. A low growl. But Dante paid no heed. Nothing could get in the way of this moment. Not even the angel.

There was a score to settle.

Warm lips covered his, drew on his. Elizabeth's tongue, moist, usually compliant, darted across his teeth, then retreated. The sharpness of his teeth, rivaling her dagger's edge, would have startled her, hurt her, Dante knew. Yet she came on again, undaunted.

Blood spattered into his mouth. Elizabeth's blood. The scent of it filled him, sent his insides scrambling. The taste—thick, rich, a taste like no other thing—unleashed a portion of his inner beast.

Hold back, he reasoned as Elizabeth's mouth clung to his. *Hold back.*

But questions vied for his focus. His mind whirled. Did Elizabeth know no better than to tempt him in this way? Couldn't she reason how fine the line was that he walked? Blood was the key. Blood was his existence.

"Dear God!" Her hands caressed him with disturbing motions. Blissful ministrations. A murmur rose to her throat, soft, like her touch. Thrilling. Utterly beguiling.

He caressed her throat, slid his fingers over the velvet band of jewels she wore as a collar. The thing tore easily. Priceless jewels fell to the floor, discarded. Out of the way.

In full evidence were the two punctures he had made. There, near where the blood flowed its fullest. Beneath her jaw. Beneath her ear. The wounds were raised, raw, the flesh around them blackened and bruised. He had hurt her. It must hurt her, still. How brave she was for facing him after that.

"If there were actually to be a God, surely he would strike now, for doing this to you. For wanting to do it again," he whispered.

The two raised bumps of her wounds were an invitation to the most inhuman of actions. He had to keep the passions bound. He had to fight his very nature now. Elizabeth had become more than a mere vessel. Much more than that.

"What is it you have become?" he asked her throatily, rhetorically, vocalizing his uncertainty. "What do you mean to me, so suddenly? Are you a pathway to the truth? A mortal soul to balance the hole where my own soul once had been?"

He shook his head, going backwards against the tide of his desire. "No. If there were a God, the beasts would not be allowed to roam. There would be no place for what hides in the shadows. You are right to torment me."

"Dante."

The utterance of his name momentarily stopped the questions. He fell back into the moment. Into his own sweet torment. Heat engulfed him, spreading from Elizabeth's body to his, through her clothes, through the thin bit of air separating them. Heat. Maybe not the sun, but similar. Golden in feel. Bright. He longed for this sun, her sun. He longed to take her brightness in. He cursed the night.

Creamy skin moved beneath his hands, his cool fingers.

Wine-tinted lips, full, lush, moved against his with the murmur of an incantation designed to drive him mad with desire.
It mattered not what Elizabeth said, what she whispered, he
told himself.

With a slow, measured gesture, he slid his tongue around
the rim of her mouth. *Do not go further,* he warned himself.
*Do not go there. You will be sorry. Nothing will be left. No
comfort.*

No comfort.

His hands found her breasts, moved over the luxurious-
ness of her gown, seeking to bolster the warmth. A breath
later, a mere heartbeat, the cloth barrier came apart at the
seams with a sound that split the night and sent his senses
soaring.

Elizabeth's heart beat irregularly, loudly. He should have
covered his ears, blocked out the sound. Instead, he moved
to the rhythm of that beat, as if it were his own heart pounding. He explored her possessively. Pleasure arrived in waves.

"Now look what we have done," he crooned to her.

The pulse of her heart beat against his palm as his hand
lay upon her chest. Able to hear her blood's frantic journey,
Dante closed his eyes, recalled what the mingling of her fluids
with his had been like. Light-headedness returned. Extreme
hunger.

Suddenly and inexplicably haunted by Elizabeth Rothchilde, by everything about her, he got to his knees. With her
discarded dagger in his fingers, he slit her velvet skirts from
their laces. The sound was muffled, erotic.

Arms wrapped around her nakedness, he lifted her from
the dark green mass that had clothed her. He stretched her
long-limbed nakedness out on the bed. He burrowed his head
against her soft white belly and bit her gently, just above her
right hip bone. The merest dot of blood rose to the surface.
Dark red, on white. She muffled a cry. He did the same.

"Yes, look," Dante repeated, "at us."

Again a sound floated toward him, low and resonant. Again

he let it go. The angel and her plight did not matter now. Nor did it matter how she looked on. Perhaps the angel would learn something of use for her wedding bed . . .

Downward he went, lips hovering over every inch of Elizabeth's quivering smoothness. A nip here, there, with his teeth, and then he bit down oh-so-softly to break the skin. Leaving a trail. Marring the beauty.

She allowed this. Was it her victory over the angel she needed? Is that why she had the angel standing by?

He moved on to her thighs. Rounded. Gloriously unflawed. Hot to the touch. Flames to the tongue, fueling the fires raging within him.

Elizabeth.

Damn you.

Scooping both hands beneath her buttocks, he elevated her upward, high off the covers, needing to hold her and feel her next to him. Her legs opened, as they had opened for him before. Yet this motion felt new. Different. The unmistakable scent of musk, of flowering womanhood in a time of need, came to him on his intake of breath.

Dear . . . Elizabeth.

What do you have in store for me?

One thrust of his tongue to part her light brown fur, to beckon at the door to her desire, and she stiffened. But he would not relent. Could not. She had started this. She was expecting this.

He took the pink petals into his mouth, sucked lightly at first, then with a harder draw. Elizabeth fluttered, spoke, saying he knew not what. Undulating legs the color of pearls closed around his back as she rose to meet his torturous, treacherous mouth. Her heartbeat quickened, pounding in frantic thumps that resonated just beneath her skin, and near to her silky womb's entrance. He could see the beat move her.

Moistness flowed to meet him. He drank in the nectar of the inferno, darting his tongue across her sensitive threshold, listening to her little cries.

And it was not enough.

He would show her that he could satisfy her and leave no doubts to fill his mind.

He hauled himself upward, unleashing his engorged cock as he did so. Before Elizabeth could open her eyes, he was inside of her savory heat with a smooth, lubricated shove.

"I cannot bear it," Elizabeth said in a voice as raw as the wounds on her neck.

"'Siring,' you said," he whispered to her. "Yet this is as much of me as I can give. You are living, breathing flesh. Your womb will never carry my heirs. I can have no heirs this way."

But then, she must already know this, he thought.

"My touch will not heal you," he said. "My touch can burn, harm, maim. I am an abomination. I am darkness, you are light. I am merely shadow to your flame."

As if in deference to his statement, his hips rose, flattened, and pressed into hers. His prick slid deeper inside of her, was welcomed with the familiar dampness.

"By God," he said hoarsely, "if I am an abomination, what might you be—you who crave this unholy attention?"

Another shove. Deeper. Truer. And he went spiraling back to the one word he distrusted. *Secrets.*

He would get those secrets from Elizabeth. He would force them out of her, fuck them out of her. She would open her mouth and out the words would tumble. He would kiss her as he drank them in, as her power transferred to him.

His engorged, unsatisfied cock plunged again into her velvety depths. And again. It felt good. It was a start.

"Tell me," he said, looking into her eyes as he withdrew himself almost completely, and as he dipped back inside the pink petals, barely, lightly. "What do you need?"

Without awaiting her reply, he forced his shaft into her lushness with a slap of his hips against hers. He repeated the action, building in speed, listening to the sound of their bodies meeting.

Elizabeth's fingers curled on the covers. Her head turned side to side. He would take her soon, he knew—down past desire, down past rational reasoning, and into his realm. The realm of the beast. The seducer. The cheat.

For he, along with the other things that clung to the shadows, had cheated death. And now, he had become death.

And after everything he could have imagined, was death what Elizabeth ultimately wanted? Did this beautiful Rothchilde want to die?

He paused. She moved, wrapping herself around him from the inside out, adding fire to fire. Her body swallowed him up, sucked him in, held him there. She said, "I want it all, Dante."

Elizabeth's skin glistened with perspiration, though the room was cold. The cold of a tomb. Her voice was desperate. "I demand that you give it to me, or I can have no peace."

"Do not invite me in," Dante warned, understanding dawning, rage building. "Not beyond the flesh. Not beyond this."

Hot fingers gripped his back, his shoulders, then his buttocks, hanging on, urging him on.

"All of it," Elizabeth said. "It is why I have come."

Dante shook his head, shuddered with the thought. Elizabeth's face came closer. She held onto his rigid back. Her chin was lifted, her head tilted to expose her wounds. He could smell the sweetness, remember the taste.

Her blood had been free-flowing. Thick. She had given it to him willingly, and he was an idiot for not seeing what she wanted from the first. Who better than Elizabeth Rothchilde, sister of Alan the Terrible, would know just what it would take to die? How easy it could be for life to drain away?

Who better than she would know how difficult it would be for any creature such as himself to give up, once the taste and smell of a mortal had been sampled? It was her blood that sang to him now, dammit all to hell. That was her hold, her wild card. This was the power she wielded over him. It was the Blood Lure. Her mad face had taken on the pallor of the Undead already.

"Yes," was the sound that escaped from Elizabeth's mouth as he studied her.

Yes, the shadows urged in a swell of dank, fetid draft. *She requests this. She wants this. Is it not what you are? Is it not what you do?*

He wavered on arms that had begun to shake, wondering who in those shadows had spoken, and if he should listen.

Chapter Fifteen

The flicker of the candle seemed uncommonly loud to Elizabeth's ears. Louder than her heart's beat. Louder than the silence that lay heavily upon the cavernous room now that Dante had hesitated.

She was afraid to look away, afraid to look anywhere but into the dark, bottomless eyes that sought and held hers. Though Dante was still erect and firmly embedded inside of her, though his hips remained molded to hers, his eyes had clouded over.

Was the thing Dante had called an angel, so securely wrapped in her garlic streamers, calling to him in a way only creatures of their kind could hear? Could Dante truly not comprehend the essence of this queen of the damned that her brother had chosen?

"I can see down into your soul. Beyond the surface things," Dante said to her, moving slightly, letting her know he maintained full control of his body and his actions.

Elizabeth forced a grin, felt like doing anything but smiling. "I assumed it was another part of your anatomy that concerned you."

"Then you value my other talents too little."

"I have no delusions about your talents, or your desires."

"I will not play this game, Elizabeth. If Lady Wallace desires to be rid of this castle and her impending marriage, what is it to you?"

"More than you seem able to guess," Elizabeth said, arching her back slightly, elevating her rosy breasts, breath escaping when Dante's focus drifted downward.

"Yet you can have her now," Elizabeth added in a tone of challenge. "And you are inside of me."

Dante's eyes came back to hers. Not clouded over—at least on the surface.

"I offered her to you on a silver plate," Elizabeth said, testing him further. "Am I but a nibble, and she the main course?"

"Why is she here?"

"I told you, Dante. She is here out of necessity. It is your honor my brother will take from me this night. I cannot have that. I will not allow it. I must force your hand. It is the only way."

"What part does she play, Elizabeth? I mean to know."

"Then you shall, my dearest Dante. If you must. But first you must make a choice. You—"

"Ah. A choice." Dante withdrew from their intimate connection, disallowing her final remark. He turned on the bed to stare beyond the candlelight, covered meagerly in a shred of green velvet that had once been a part of her skirt.

Elizabeth could not move. She lay back with her legs still slightly parted, feeling the cold air return, suppressing a shudder. She watched as Dante signaled for her guards to step back from the dark-haired creature they hovered near. The guards obeyed.

Dante's eyes flicked to the creature, then back to Elizabeth's face. Once again a frown marred his pensive, chiseled features.

"You did not kill me," Elizabeth said to him.

"And you imagine it was honor that stopped me?" he returned.

"You did not try to take her. You did not even try, Dante."

Dante's furrow deepened. His eyes darted back to the dark-haired creature. "I thought her the most beautiful woman I had ever seen."

Elizabeth felt her heart slide against her ribs. She experienced a moment of what seemed very much like defeat.

"It is her power," she said. "And the reason my brother brought her here."

Dante wore a puzzled look now. He knew something of this, Elizabeth thought. He did not know enough of it to save himself from what was happening. Time was running out.

"You may sense her innocence, Dante, but it is not what you think. She is not what you think."

"Shall we cut the bonds you have placed upon her and see?" Dante countered.

"You would choose her, then?"

"If I had chosen her, you would not be here, I think."

Elizabeth lifted her shoulders and sat up slowly, careful not to move too quickly, thinking that hope now stirred where shadows had begun to dwell. Dante had said *was*. The creature *was* the most beautiful thing he had ever seen.

Dante caught hold of her right ankle before she could straighten. He gave her an inquisitive look.

"What is this, Elizabeth? What are these marks on the bottom of your foot?"

He ran his fingers over the bumps—old wounds scarred over. She flinched, not from pain but from the discomfort of a secret partially exposed.

His eyes were on her. His fingers stopped exploring. "My God," he whispered, as though it had been hidden text he'd found and read. "How long, Elizabeth? How long has your brother been cutting his teeth on you? How long have you been prisoner here?"

He looked up. "How could I not see what this angel is?"

Chapter Sixteen

Elizabeth's eyes searched his with a sudden seriousness.

"How long?" Dante demanded, feeling his rage rise, feeling his strength return in direct proportion to it. "I want to hear it, Elizabeth."

"Because you would save me now, Dante?" Elizabeth said. "The damsel in need fuels the mystery?"

"Why did you not tell me of this?"

"Why did you deserve to know?"

Dante's head thudded with a dull ache. He was not certain if it was Elizabeth's retort or the degree of his hunger that produced the discomfort.

He stood, turned to the angel.

"The nunnery?" he said to Elizabeth over his shoulder.

"Deemed by her family to be the safest place to keep her."

Dante grinned briefly at the suddenness of the ill news. "Of course. The nuns would keep locked up a woman sought by the devil, would they not?"

He waved Elizabeth's protest away without looking at her. "It is what I thought when you first told me the tale, though I can imagine another twist on it now."

The angel was within reach, eyes still downcast, arms bound behind her back. The stench of the garlic was overwhelming. She was wrapped tightly in the stuff, inundated by the odor-

ous weed that was the bane of all creatures he shared a similar circumstance with.

He nearly laughed at his stupidity. Of course this angel
would stand out in a crowd. Her lustrous, luminous skin, so
pale, so fragile looking, so porcelain-thin, was the result of
long years without the sun. The nuns had locked her away,
all right, but not for her own good. For the good of others.

Laughter bubbled from his throat. The angel looked up.
Her light eyes found his. "I thought you an angel," Dante said
to her. "However, I was mistaken regarding the venue of the
term, was I not? Is it an *angel of death* that stands all wrapped
up before me? Was my attraction to you due to the fact that
a part of me recognized what my mind could not firmly grasp?"

The low growl returned in place of a reply. The angel's
face remained smoothly passive.

"Are you not the perfect match for Elizabeth's brother? A
queen to his midnight kingship?" Dante asked her. "Do you
require all this . . . hindrance to keep you in line after so long
being locked away? I wonder what they fed you, how they
kept you alive? And why they kept you alive? Surely the nuns
could have killed you in the name of their God and all that is
holy?"

"Wallace," Elizabeth whispered behind him.

Dante nodded. "Ah, yes. No doubt your keepers were
paid handsomely by your father. Did he not have the heart to
destroy his daughter, in the end? No matter what she had become?"

Dante thought backwards, to the tower room and the gar-
lic-infested bed that had kept him away. Here, the angel was
also a prisoner. Pity welled up inside of him, though he usually had little of it to spare for others like himself.

He turned to Elizabeth. "Have you done this to her?"

"Only to safeguard you," Elizabeth replied.

"Why? When I am like them?"

"You are different. Everyone knows this."

"And your brother? Why would he kill me? Not, I assume, just because I am better endowed and higher in the ridiculous aristocracy he thumbs his nose at anyway? Those things are false for our kind now. We go on. We endure."

No answer or comment came from Elizabeth. Dante moved to the bed, pulled Elizabeth up by her arms, and swung her around the back side of a heavy burgundy drape separating the room from another. Holding her against the stone wall with his body pressed to hers, he ran his fingers through her tangled honey-hued hair.

"You might like his attention. Your brother's. You might want to keep that attention to yourself, and prefer not sharing him with anyone," he said to her.

Elizabeth looked momentarily stricken, but rallied courageously. "And you might as easily die with a stake through your heart this minute. Five men are prepared to do it if I cannot."

Dante ran the tip of his nose down her cheek, still alerted to the perfume of her blood, aware of the state of her undress.

"You could have accomplished this many a night since I arrived," he remarked.

"Yes," she agreed.

"Yet you did not. Neither did you stake your dear brother, and yet look what he has done to you. Are you a prisoner here, Elizabeth? Have I stumbled into the Midnight Court to find you trapped within it?"

The growl came from nearby. Candlelight flickered eerily against the stone. Dante considered what the angel was trying to tell him, and gazed deeply into Elizabeth's green eyes.

"We must let her go," he said.

"She has already roused my brother."

"I will wager on that," Dante said wryly.

Elizabeth's lips upturned briefly.

"I would have saved you, had I known you earlier," Dante

said. "I might have ridden off with you on a black steed at the crack of dawn, skirting the sun, basking in your arms in the darkness."

His smile returned. He could not help it. "However, I am not so certain you needed saving, for all the scars. I am not fully certain you would like dwelling in the shadows, for all the compliments you have bestowed upon me."

The gold flecks in Elizabeth's eyes danced.

"You mentioned that your brother would cringe and shake in his boots if he knew what you truly were about. You spoke the truth about this?" he said. "Why do I have the feeling I'm left empty-handed in knowing what it is that you want? You would now hide behind threats and fickleness and take the night's confidences back?"

"Use caution, Dante. I will only go so far, and they approach, even as we speak, stakes in hand."

"Yet you told me you were not going to kill me, and that your brother would not be allowed to do so. *You* would not allow him to kill me."

Her remark began to take on new meaning as he considered it.

"I am a woman of my word, just as you are a man of yours," she said.

"Nevertheless, I accepted your challenge, did I not?"

"You would not have lived if you had. You are here now because you didn't."

"And so you brought the *challenge* to me here? You brought the angel, all wrapped up, to see if I would betray you?"

"I brought your angel here to show you what she really is, and why my brother holds her so dear."

"I am all eyes, Elizabeth. And all ears."

"You did not kill me," she repeated.

"Yes, well perhaps I should have, thus liberating myself from this annoying game of yours."

Again, Elizabeth smiled. Her eyes shined in the near dark of the dank room that was his tomb, his salvation from the light. And suddenly, quite abruptly, Dante knew that *she* had become his salvation. Elizabeth Rothchilde had removed the tedium of the shadows, had dangled before him the promise of a fate he had not conceived of.

"Game," Elizabeth echoed. "Yes. I suppose you could think of it in no other terms."

Her face was infuriatingly earnest, Dante decided. Smooth, delicate, and lit from within. He had tried to spare her, attempted to keep her from this. From himself. And now she was smiling. Was this another victory for the mortal? The woman? The weaker sex?

Damn her hide. There was nothing weak about Elizabeth.

She stirred against him. She would be cold, of course. Chilled to the bone. Dante tore from his shoulders the remnants of his shirt and draped it around her neck, hesitating when his fingers touched her wounds.

"I don't kill for pleasure," he said before realizing he had spoken. "It is not much of a line separating me from the others of my kind. Still, it is somewhat of a line."

Elizabeth's eyes reeled him in. Her lips parted. "I brought her here," she said. "I found your angel for Alan. I hauled her out of the dungeons, relieving the nuns from their pact to protect the devil. I brought her to the devil himself and presented her with her fate—to escape mine."

Dante could not hide his surprise at this revelation. Seeing this, Elizabeth went on.

"It seems that *I* may not be the woman you thought I was, and that we all have things to hide."

Amen, Dante wanted to cry, even though he might have forgotten exactly what the damned word meant.

Chapter Seventeen

Elizabeth's hand was light on his—a puff of wind, so slender and colorless. Dante had to work to control himself from muttering more obscenities. There was a hardness to her expression he had not seen before. Yet another surprise.

"Do you know what the Midnight Courts are?" she asked him soberly.

"Every creature like me knows of them," Dante replied.

"You think you know. But you see what you want to see, and believe what you want to believe."

"I came here to find out for myself," Dante said.

"Yes. And you found me."

Dante grinned despite the change in her demeanor.

"It is well known that the Midnight Courts are gatherings of ostentation, debauchery, and greed," Elizabeth began. "Silver, gold, jewels, lust . . . an agenda that draws many."

"To their fates, as you have so aptly put it," Dante added. "Unless they are the *intended* creatures. The creatures the courts were designed for."

Elizabeth nodded.

"They were designed as traps, of course," Dante continued. "Creatures such as your brother brought the ignorant mortals here to trap and then feast upon them. The mortals were the supper, the entertainment, the embellishments; all of them fair game for any creature participating in a Midnight Court. Isn't that it?"

"It is what you were supposed to believe. But you see, my beautiful Dante, that is not what the Midnight Courts really are."

Elizabeth slid her hand to his face, caressed his cheek. Over the scent of the blood at her wrist, Dante caught a whiff of something more dangerous. It was the odor of excitement. Elizabeth was aroused.

Eyes locked to hers, he arched a brow in question. But a terrible idea occurred as Elizabeth's fingers moved to his bare shoulder, then dipped to his waist.

She was not the bait.

He was.

The idea took form as his skin moved beneath her touch. He voiced it.

"Ah," he sighed. "*We* are lured here. Not just the mortals. We are to be trapped, as well. Feast and then . . ."

"Die," Elizabeth said.

The idea was not so fantastical, Dante thought. It certainly was no more than his kind deserved. "We kill the mortals, and then your brother kills us. Less competition that way. More for himself. Perhaps he then takes on the property of the deceased, feeding his accounts and his gullet simultaneously?"

Insidious thought. Ridiculous, surely?

But Elizabeth's face told him he was not mistaken in this theory. And dread set in, starting in his toes and working its way slowly up his legs. Enlightenment accompanied the sensation.

"Or," he whispered, "perhaps you are a part of the game, and not its victim? Perhaps your brother's reputation is ill-gotten?"

"Bravo," Elizabeth said, eyes boring into his. "In truth, it is my brother who is used."

Staring hard at her face, considering this confession, Dante experienced a rush of coldness and a feeling akin to shock. He controlled his voice reasonably well. "You are a Hunter, Elizabeth?" he said. "A Slayer."

Gold flecks in the green.

Secrets.

Bloody fucking hell.

"You provide us with a last supper, and then put us out of our misery? This is the reason for the Midnight Courts? They are traps. Lures, all right. But death for the night creatures who frequent them."

Elizabeth's hands were on his thighs, precariously close to his crotch. Damned if he didn't feel himself swell. Damned if he had any control over what she had the talent to do to him, while allowing him to believe he was in control—even knowing what he now knew.

She had garlic in the room. She had a cross. She had guards standing by, no doubt with spears, and the angel in chains. He had to laugh. He had not seen this coming. And he had prided himself on his intuition.

And his cock was hard.

"So," he said with a quick exhale of breath. "You will have your way with me and more."

"I will not harm you, Dante. Not you. Not in the way you imagine. I have no grudge with anyone, mortal like myself or vampire, who is honorable, and who hates the feeding breed. It is simply that your kind is rare. You are rare."

"I am here at the court, Elizabeth."

"Because you could not refuse my invitation. You would aid the damsel in distress, while ignoring other pleasures."

"I thought it was the angel who needed my help."

"You were wrong there, of course," Elizabeth whispered, hand now firmly locked around his stiffened shaft. "You do not kill them, my mysterious Dante. Not even the foolish humans. I know this firsthand, do I not? You drink only as much as you need to survive. Somehow you get by on this. You maintain your wits. The lad you found in the hallway stumbled back to me after you left him. He was still able to speak."

"And your brother?"

"My brother is the prisoner here. He is alive because of my good graces. Oh, he benefits in his own way, I suppose, but his cousins do not leave the Midnight Courts. No vampire leaves this castle to inflict more torture and punishment on the land. I see to it, Dante."

"And why is your hand wrapped around me?" Dante asked. "Why have you offered yourself to me?"

"I have failed, after all the years, and all the work."

"But you do not love me, Elizabeth."

Dante found himself smiling, perhaps cruelly, perhaps only to cover what was taking place inside of himself.

"Well, I'll be damned," he whispered. "The Huntress would give herself up for . . ."

For what?

For love?

"I have merely to taste your blood. Is this not how it's done?" Elizabeth said.

She did not want to die. She wanted something far worse, Dante now saw. A lightness he had not recalled until now kept his gaze riveted to her face. Some of the light he had perceived in her seemed to cling to his skin. She would do this for him. She would sacrifice her life in the sun for his.

And what could he offer her? What would she lose by living in shadow?

Everything.

He would not allow it, of course. Could not bear it. Yet he could never let her go, could never lose her. Not now. Not when he loved her so utterly and completely. Not when he had met his match and his existence, no matter how much he detested it, suddenly seemed worthwhile.

"Join me?" he said with a laugh as he swept her into his arms. "I think not, dear heart."

His eyes glided over her paleness, her expression, her wide-open eyes. "I like you just the way you are, my fearless, dearest Elizabeth. Besides, if you were like me, who knows what I might have to put up with both night *and* day."

"Dante . . ."

"Elizabeth," he said, seeing that the room was now clear of everyone except the two of them, and wondering how she had accomplished that. "A man, vampire or no, must have some self-respect."

His lips upturned as he drew her closer, still, as he felt her nakedness next to him. Life with Elizabeth would be the test to end all tests, he thought as he eyed the bed with a calculation of just how long it would take to get her into it.

We don't think you will want to miss

JUST A HINT—CLINT

by Lori Foster coming in October 2004 from Brava.

Here's a sneak peek.

A bead of sweat took a slow path down his throat and into the neckline of his dark T-shirt. Pushed by a hot, insubstantial breeze, a weed brushed his cheek.

Clint never moved.

Through the shifting shadows of the pulled blinds, he could detect activity in the small cabin. The low drone of voices filtered out the screen door, but Clint couldn't make out any of the slurred conversation.

Next to him, Red stirred. In little more than a breath of sound, he said, "Fuck, I hate waiting."

Wary of a trap, Clint wanted the entire area checked. Mojo chose that moment to slip silently into the grass beside them. He'd done a surveillance of the cabin, the surrounding grounds, and probably gotten a good peek in the back window. Mojo could be invisible and eerily silent when he chose.

"All's clear."

Something tightened inside Clint. "She's in there?"

"Alive but pissed off and real scared." Mojo's obsidian eyes narrowed. "Four men. They've got her tied up."

Clint silently worked his jaw, fighting for his famed icy control. The entire situation was bizarre. How was it Asa knew where to find the men, yet they didn't appear to expect an interruption? Had Robert deliberately fed the info to Asa to embroil him in a trap so Clint would kill him? And why would Robert want Asa dead?

Somehow, both he and Julie Rose were pawns. But for what purpose?

Clint's rage grew, clawing to be freed, making his stomach pitch with the violent need to act. "They're armed?"

Mojo nodded with evil delight. "And on their way out."

Given that a small bonfire lit the clearing in front of the cabin, Clint wasn't surprised that they would venture outside. The hunting cabin was deep into the hills, mostly surrounded by thick woods. Obviously, the kidnappers felt confident in their seclusion.

He'd have found them eventually, Clint thought, but Asa's tip had proved invaluable. And a bit too fucking timely.

So far, nothing added up, and that made him more cautious than anything else could have.

He'd work it out as they went along. The drive had cost them two hours, with another hour crawling through the woods. But now he had them.

He had *her*.

The cabin door opened and two men stumbled out under the glare of a yellow bug light. One wore jeans and an unbuttoned shirt, the other was shirtless, showing off a variety of tattoos on his skinny chest. They looked youngish and drunk and stupid. They looked cruel.

Raucous laughter echoed around the small clearing, disturbed only by a feminine voice, shrill with fear and anger, as two other men dragged Julie Rose outside.

She wasn't crying.

No sir. Julie Rose was complaining.

Her torn school dress hung off her right shoulder nearly to her waist, displaying one small pale breast. She struggled against hard hands and deliberate roughness until she was shoved, landing on her right hip in the barren area in front of the house. With her hands tied behind her back, she had no way to brace herself. She fell flat, but quickly struggled into a sitting position.

The glow of the bonfire reflected on her bruised, dirty face—and in her furious eyes. She was frightened, but she was also livid.

"I think we should finish stripping her," one of the men said.

Julie's bare feet peddled against the uneven ground as she tried to move farther away.

The men laughed some more, and the one who'd spoken went onto his haunches in front of her. He caught her bare ankle, immobilizing her.

"Not too much longer, bitch. Morning'll be here before you know it." He stroked her leg, up to her knee, higher. "I bet you're getting anxious, huh?"

Her chest heaved, her lips quivered.

She spit on him.

Clint was on his feet in an instant, striding into the clearing before Mojo or Red's hissed curses could register. The four men, standing in a cluster, turned to look at him with various expressions of astonishment, confusion, and horror. They were slow to react, and Clint realized they were more than a little drunk. Idiots.

One of the young fools reached behind his back.

"You." Clint stabbed him with a fast lethal look while keeping his long, ground-eating pace to Julie. "Touch that weapon and I'll break your leg."

The guy blanched—and promptly dropped his hands.

Clint didn't think of anything other than his need to get between Julie and the most immediate threat. But without giving it conscious thought, he knew that Mojo and Red would back him up. If any guns were drawn, theirs would be first.

The man who'd been abusing Julie snorted in disdain at the interference. He took a step forward, saying, "Just who the hell do you think you—"

Reflexes on automatic, Clint pivoted slightly to the side and kicked out hard and fast. The force of his boot heel caught the man on the chin with sickening impact. He sprawled flat with a raw groan that dwindled into blackness. He didn't move.

Another man leaped forward. Clint stepped to the side, and like clockwork, kicked out a knee. The obscene sounds of breaking bone and cartilage and the accompanying scream of pain split the night, sending nocturnal creatures to scurry through the leaves.

Clint glanced at Julie's white face, saw she was frozen in shock, and headed toward the two remaining men. Eyes wide, they started to back up, and Clint curled his mouth into the semblance of a smile. "I don't think so."

A gun was finally drawn, but not in time to be fired. Clint grabbed the man's wrist and twisted up and back. Still holding him, Clint pulled him forward and into a solid punch to the stomach. Without breath, the painful shouts ended real quick. The second Clint released him, the man turned to hobble into the woods. Clint didn't want to, but he let him go.

Robert Burns had said not to bring anyone in. He couldn't see committing random murder, and that's what it'd be if he started breaking heads now. But in an effort to protect Julie Rose and her apparently already tattered reputation, he wouldn't turn them over to the law either.

Just letting them go stuck in his craw, and Clint, fed up, ready to end it, turned to the fourth man. He threw a punch to the throat and jaw, then watched the guy crumble to his knees, then to his face, wheezing for breath.

Behind Clint, Red's dry tone intruded. "Well, that was efficient."

Clint struggled with himself for only an instant before realizing there was no one left to fight. He turned, saw Julie Rose held in wide-eyed horror, and he jerked. Mojo stepped back out of the way, and Clint lurched to the bushes.

Anger turned to acid in his gut.

Typically, at least for Clint Evans and his weak-ass stomach, he puked.

Julie could hardly believe her eyes. One minute she'd known she would be raped and probably killed, and the fear had been all too consuming, a live clawing dread inside her.

Now . . . now she didn't know what had happened. Three men, looking like angelic convicts, had burst into the clearing. Well, no, that wasn't right. The first man hadn't burst anywhere. He'd strode in, casual as you please, then proceeded to make mincemeat out of her abductors.

He'd taken on four men as if they were no more than gnats.

She'd never seen that type of brawling. His blows hadn't been designed to slow down an opponent, or to bruise or hurt. One strike—and the men had dropped like dead weights. Even the sight of a gun hadn't fazed him. He moved so fast, so smoothly, the weapon hadn't mattered at all.

When he'd delivered those awesome strikes, his expression, hard and cold, hadn't changed. A kick here, a punch there, and the men who'd held her, taunted her, were no longer a threat.

He was amazing, invincible, he was . . . *throwing up*.

Her heart pounded in slow, deep thumps that hurt her breastbone and made it difficult to draw an even breath. The relief flooding over her in a drowning force didn't feel much different than her fear had.

Her awareness of that man was almost worse.

Like spotting Superman, or a wild animal, or a combination of both, she felt awed and amazed and disbelieving.

She was safe now, but was she really?

One of her saviors approached her. He was fair, having blond hair and light eyes, though she couldn't see the exact color in the dark night with only the fire for illumination.

Trying to make himself look less like a convict, he gave her a slight smile.

A wasted effort.

He moved real slow, watchful, and gentle. "Don't pay any mind to Clint." He spoke in a low, melodic croon. "He always pukes afterward."

Her savior's name was Clint.

Julie blinked several times, trying to gather her wits and calm the spinning in her head. "He does?"

Another man approached, equally cautious, just as gentle. But he had black hair and blacker eyes. He didn't say anything, just stood next to the other man and surveyed her bruised face with an awful frown that should have been alarming, but wasn't.

The blonde nodded. "Yeah. Hurtin' people—even people who deserve it—always upsets Clint's stomach. He'll be all right in a minute."

Julie ached, her body, her heart, her mind. She'd long ago lost feeling in her arms but every place else pulsed with relentless pain. She looked over at Clint. He had his hands on his knees, his head hanging. The poor man. "He was saving me, wasn't he?"

"Oh, yes, ma'am. We're here to take you home. Everything will be okay now." His glance darted to her chest and quickly away.

Julie realized she wasn't decently covered, but with her hands tied tightly behind her back, she couldn't do anything about it. She felt conspicuous and vulnerable and ready to cry, so she did her best to straighten her aching shoulders and looked back at Clint.

Just the sight of him, big, powerful, brave, gave her a measure of reassurance. He straightened slowly, drew several deep breaths.

He was an enormous man, layered in sleek muscle with wide shoulders and a tapered waist and long thick thighs.

His biceps were as large as her legs, his hands twice as big as her own.

Eyes closed, he tipped his head back and swallowed several times, drinking in the humid night air. At that moment, he looked very weak.

He hadn't looked weak while pulverizing those men. Julie licked her dry lips and fought off another wave of the strange dizziness.

Clint flicked a glance toward her, and their gazes locked together with a sharp snap, shocking Julie down to the soles of her feet.

He looked annoyed by the near tactile contact.

Julie felt electrified. Her pains faded away into oblivion.

It took a few moments, but his forced smile, meant to be reassuring, was a tad sickly. Still watching her, he reached into his front pocket and pulled out a small silver flask. He tipped it up, swished his mouth out, and spit.

All the while, he held her with that implacable burning gaze.

When he replaced the flask in his pocket and started toward her, every nerve ending in Julie's body came alive with expectation. Fear, alarm, relief—she wasn't at all certain what she felt, she just knew she felt it in spades. Her breath rose to choke her, her body quaked, and strangely enough, tears clouded her eyes.

She would not cry, she would not cry . . .

She rubbed one eye on her shoulder and spoke to the two men, just to help pull herself together. "Should he be drinking?"

Blondie said, "Oh, no. It's mouthwash." And with a smile, "He always carries it with him, cuz of his stomach and the way he usually—"

The dark man nudged the blonde, and they both fell silent.

Mouthwash. She hadn't figured on that.

She wanted to ignore him, but her gaze was drawn to him

like a lodestone. Fascinated, she watched as Clint drew nearer. During his approach, he peeled his shirt off over his head then stopped in front of her, blocking her from the others. They took the hint and gave her their backs.

Julie stared at that broad, dark, hairy chest. He was more man than any man she'd ever seen, and the dizziness assailed her again.

With a surprisingly gentle touch, Clint went to one knee and laid the shirt over her chest. It was warm and damp from his body. His voice was low, a little rough when he spoke. "I'm going to cut your hands free. Just hold still a second, okay?"

Julie didn't answer. She *couldn't* answer. She'd been scared for so long now, what seemed like weeks but had only been a little more than a day. And now she was rescued.

She was safe.

A large lethal blade appeared in Clint's capable hands, but Julie felt no fear. Not now. Not with him so close.

He didn't go behind her to free her hands, but rather reached around her while looking over her shoulder and blocked her body with his own. Absurdly, she became aware of his hot scent, rich with the odor of sweat and anger and man. After smelling her own fear for hours on end, it was a delicious treat for her senses. She closed her eyes and concentrated on the smell of him, on his warmth and obvious strength and stunning ability.

He enveloped her with his size, and with the promise of safety.

She felt a small tug and the ropes fell away. But as Julie tried to move, red-hot fire rushed through her arms, into her shoulders and wrists, forcing a groan of pure agony from her tight lips.

"Shhhh, easy now." As if he'd known exactly what she'd feel, Clint sat in front of her. His long legs opened around her, and he braced her against his bare upper body. His flesh was hot, smooth beneath her cheek.

Slowly, carefully, he brought her arms around, and allowed

her to muffle her moans against his shoulder. He massaged her, kneading and rubbing from her upper back, her shoulders to her elbows, to her wrists and still crooning to her in that low gravely voice. His hard fingers dug deep into her soft flesh, working out the cramps with merciless determination and loosening her stiff joints that seemed frozen in place.

As the pain eased, tiredness sank in, and Julie slumped against him. She'd been living off adrenaline for hours and now being safe left her utterly drained, unable to stay upright.

It was like propping herself against a warm, vibrant brick wall. There was no give to Clint's hard shoulder, and Julie was comforted.

One thought kept reverberating through her weary brain: *He'd really saved her.*

Please turn the page for an exciting

preview of Erin McCarthy's

HOUSTON, WE HAVE A PROBLEM.

Available right now from Brava.

Josie Adkins had to stop waving her hot little ass in Houston's face, or he was going to have to slide his hands across it and squeeze.

Which would fall squarely under the heading of sexual harassment. He could see the headline: *State of Florida vs Dr. Houston Hayes. Surgeon fondles resident and loses license.*

Sweet little Josie had no idea he was plotting ways to lick her like a cat does cream. She wasn't tempting him with her curvy behind on purpose, so he couldn't really blame her for the detour his thoughts had been taking on a regular basis.

But just how in the hell an orthopedic surgeon could be so damn clumsy was beyond him. And Jesus, was Josie clumsy.

So clumsy that at least six times a day he was subjected to the sight of her, bent full over at the waist, retrieving something from the floor she had dropped. Today was even worse.

They were alone in a semidark alcove, for the purpose of looking at a patient's X ray, only Josie had done her usual butterfinger bit.

The film Josie had been holding had slipped out of her hand, hit the floor, and disappeared under the desk next to her. She was now on her hands and knees, wiggling around searching for it.

God help him.

No one with a body that lush and womanly should be wiggling on her hands and knees unless she was naked and it was part of foreplay.

"Whoops. It just jumped right out of my hand, Dr. Hayes," she said in a cheerful voice.

Houston counted from one to ten and back again until he was in control of himself and his bodily urges. He didn't know what it was about her that had him hiding hard-ons left and right and sweating through three pairs of surgical scrubs a day.

She wasn't his type at all. She was on the short side, with an odd haircut that made her light brown hair flip around at gravity-defying angles. When she smiled, twin dimples appeared and she looked about twenty years old. She talked constantly. He had heard other staff members affectionately refer to her as a dingbat.

Yet here he was, unable to look away, all too aware that her scrubs were worn thin in strategic places.

"It has to be here somewhere." She chattered on, her head half under the desk.

"What the . . . ?"

As she pulled her hand back, Houston saw she was holding a crust of moldy bread.

"Gross." She flung it down.

Time to leave a note for housekeeping.

Josie disappeared back under the desk—at least the front half.

The back half was still in full view.

He could see her underwear.

The thin scrubs hid nothing, and the position she was in on her knees pulled them taut, giving him a clear view of her panties. They were riding up just a little, sliding into the crevice between her cheeks, fitting close and tight. There was a little red lip print stamped on each side of her panties, and he wondered what she would do if he leaned forward and placed his own mouth right on one of those lip prints.

And bit her.

He was fascinated by the full curviness of her behind, and ached all over from the desire to taste her, to cup his hand between her legs and feel her heat pulsing through his fingers.

He wanted to know if there was a matching lip print on the front of her panties. So that if he kissed it he would feel her soft dewy mound give a little beneath his mouth.

It seriously annoyed him, this edgy uncontrollable desire.

Houston had never had a problem maintaining his professional distance with both patients and co-workers. If anything, he had been accused of being too reserved. Now this one woman, this tiny tornado of smiles and klutziness, had successfully breached his aloofness.

Impatient with his thoughts, he glanced at his watch. How long had she been on the floor? It felt like hours.

"Do I need to come back, Dr. Adkins, when you can make your X-ray films behave?" Visions of making her behave with his hand on her soft bottom flitted through his mind, playing like a porno video. He had meant it to sound like a cool rebuke, but it came out sounding suggestive.

Either of which seemed too subtle for Josie. She laughed from under the desk, like he was simply teasing her, than gave a little cough.

"Yuck. I think I inhaled a dust bunny."

Her head reemerged long enough to smile at him in reassurance. "Just give me a sec. I'll get it."

"Really, we can do this later." Since he had learned just about nothing could hurry her up.

Of course he could brush her aside and get the damn thing himself. But he didn't want to hurt her feelings. Josie always tried so hard to gloss over her gaffes. Plus he was a total masochist who didn't want to deny himself the glorious view

304 /   Erin McCarthy

of her backside, even though he knew he couldn't, shouldn't—
wouldn't act on his lust.

So Houston resented the distraction and cursed himself,
but still couldn't tear his eyes away from her, not even long
enough to pick up the X ray himself.

"Almost got it." She gave him another blinding smile,
head cocked to the right as she stretched her hand a little further.

He put his hands on his hips and reminded himself, again,
that getting involved with a resident would be a complete
nightmare, no matter how freaking adorable she was.

"I need one of those rubber arms, like Stretch Armstrong,
that really weird doll my cousin had when we were kids.
Remember that?" she asked him.

He shook his head. Rubber dolls were the least of his problems right now.

"Well, it was kind of cool, in a bizarre sort of way, kind of
like molded Silly Putty. What did you play with?"

Houston fought the urge to moan. Josie managed to mix
innocence with that lush body, all tossed alongside her brains
and her quirky personality. It was an unusual combination
he was finding damn hard to resist.

Especially in this room that wasn't really a room, but a
very small, very crowded alcove cut out of a corner in the
hallway. Where Josie was just inches away from him.

"When you were a kid, I mean, what did you play with?"
She kept feeling around on the floor. "Risk? World domina-
tion seems like your thing."

Should he be offended? "No."

"So what then? Nerf football? Twister? Chess club?"

He folded his arms and rubbed his chin. He'd forgotten to
shave that morning and the stubble was irritating and itchy.
He was well aware that if another co-worker had engaged in
this ridiculous conversation with him he would have walked
away.

"I played doctor." Let her figure out what exactly he meant by that. Except that Josie seemed immune to sexual innuendos.

"Here it is!" She pulled the film out and handed it to him.

Josie sat back on her heels and blew her hair out of her eyes. "Oh, well, that makes sense. Like Operation? That game that buzzed at you if you dropped the body part?"

Houston just stared at her as she brushed her knees off. He had read Josie's personnel file. On paper, she was only a few IQ points short of a genius. In person, she was a chatty, clumsy, sex nymph. Who had his nuts in a knot without even trying.

"Thank you, Dr. Adkins." He took the X ray, shaking a dust ball off of it, and wondered just when her residency was over.

With a little luck she would leave Acadia Inlet Hospital for another resident rotation at least fifty miles away, taking her sweet ass with her. Of course, she had just started her second year of residency so it could be a year or more before she left.

Until then, he was going to have to work overtime at pretending she didn't make him go hard just by entering the room. He'd had two rules since he had broken things off with his last semiserious girlfriend four years earlier. No long-term relationships. No anything with another hospital employee.

It had worked so far. He dated casually, and when it was mutually agreed upon, had some no-strings-attached sex. Neither of which were done with someone he had to see every day in a professional capacity.

But when he had joined the staff at Acadia Inlet three months ago, he had met Josie. And suddenly his hormones seemed to think rules were meant to be broken.

Taking this position had seemed like a good career move, allowing him to focus on reconstructive orthopedics, and he liked the other doctors in the orthopedic group. It was an intelligent decision and he wasn't going to let one sexy little resident interfere with that.

Please turn the page for an exciting

preview of Lucy Monroe's

THE REAL DEAL.

Also available right now from Brava.

Driving down the same road for the third time in twenty minutes, she was having difficulty applying the try-till-you-die approach. Where the heck was the turnoff? She'd missed it twice and was now driving slower than she could be walking in the attempt not to miss it a third time. Wait. Was that an opening in the trees? It was. Carefully camouflaged, the opening to Simon's drive could have easily been taken for a natural break in the flora and fauna alongside the road.

Eric had said Simon was a privacy nut, but this was ridiculous. One of them could have mentioned that the entrance to his property was as well hidden as your average state secret. Not that Simon had mentioned anything. He'd told Eric to give her directions and then dismissed the whole situation by leaving.

It was a good thing he was just a business associate and not her boyfriend. That kind of behavior would be really hard to take in a lover.

Fortunately, she reached the gate before her wayward thoughts had a chance to go any further afield.

She stopped the rented Taurus and pressed its automatic window button. It whirred softly as the glass disappeared between her and the small black box she was supposed to talk into. She reached through the window, inhaling a big breath of fresh, forest-scented air, and pressed the red button below the box.

"Yeah?" There was no mistaking that crotchety voice. She'd only heard it once, but Simon's housekeeper was unforgettable.

"It's Amanda Zachary."

"Expected you here a good twenty minutes ago, missy. It don't pay to be late if you expect to catch the boss out of his lab."

She glared at the box and reminded herself that this was business. For business, she could put up with a cranky old man.

"I'm sorry. I missed the turn."

"Guess you missed it more than once if it took you an extra twenty minutes."

What was this guy, the timeliness cop? "Perhaps, since I am already late, you would be kind enough to buzz the gates open so that I won't keep your employer waiting any longer."

"He ain't come out of the lab yet."

She ignored that bit of additional provocation and simply said, "The gate?"

"Can't."

"You can't open the gate?" She stared stupidly at the black box, at a complete loss.

"Right."

"Is it broken?"

"Nope."

Anger overcame confusion and good sense. *"Then what exactly is stopping you from opening he darn thing?"*

"You got to get out of the car. I need to make a visual I.D. before I can open the gate."

"Since you've never seen me before, what exactly are you trying to identify?"

"No need to get snippy. I done my job. I got a picture of

you. No use you asking how. I don't share my trade secrets with just anybody."

For Heaven's sake.

She got out of the car and stood so her head and shoulders were clearly visible above the car door.

"You'll have to step around the door, if you don't mind."

Now he decided to be polite, while asking her to do something totally ludicrous.

"What difference does it make?" She glared with unconcealed belligerence at the camera at the top of the gate.

"You got something to hide, missy?"

"Not if you discount a body that wasn't femme fatale material," she muttered to herself as she stepped around the silver car's door.

Thoroughly out of sorts, she threw her arms wide. "Look, no automatic weapons, no hidden cameras, no nerve gas. Are you satisfied?"

"I think I could be."

No! No. No. Darn it. No. This had not been the housekeeper's voice, but another, unforgettable one—that of Simon Brant. In a reflex move, she crossed her arms over her chest as she felt heat crawl from the back of her ankles right up her body and into her cheeks. She was going to kill that housekeeper when she got her hands on him.

She was going to pick him up by his toes and hang him above a tar pit. And then she was going to let go.

"Hello, Mr. Brant. I've been informed that I'm late."

He didn't answer, but the gate swung inward.

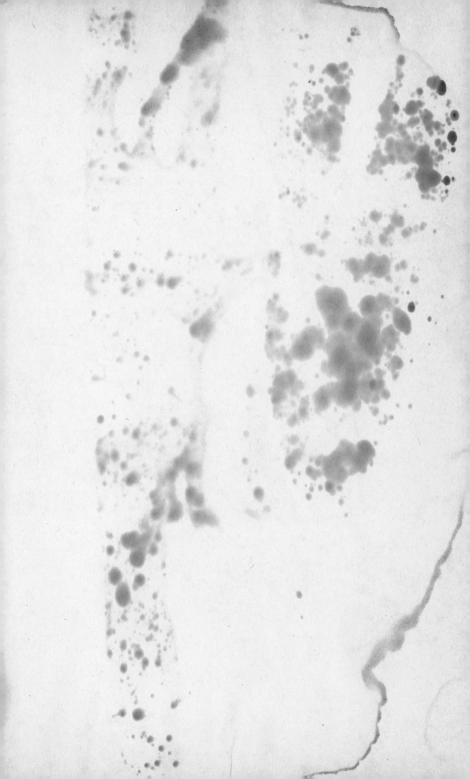